THE LONG ROAD

THE LONG ROAD

Mary Minton

PAN BOOKS

This edition published 1999 by Pan Books
an imprint of Macmillan Publishers Ltd
25 Eccleston Place, London SW1W 9NF
Basingstoke and Oxford
Associated companies throughout the world
www.macmillan.co.uk

This first world edition published in Great Britain 1993 by
SEVERN HOUSE PUBLISHERS LTD of
9-15 High Street, Sutton, Surrey SM1 1DF
First published in the USA 1994 by
SEVERN HOUSE PUBLISHERS INC of
475 Fifth Avenue, New York, NY 10017

British Library Cataloguing in Publication Data
Minton, Mary
   Long Road
   I. Title
   823.914 [F]

   ISBN 0 330 39654 4

Typeset by Hewer Text Composition Services, Edinburgh
Printed and bound in Great Britain by
Mackays of Chatham plc, Chatham, Kent

Chapter One
1928

When the Lingard family had been evicted from their
home outside Middlesborough early that morning a
few snowflakes had been drifting around. At midday
the ground had a light covering of white but by late
afternoon they found themselves in the middle of a
blizzard and seventeen-year-old Lucy, who was sure
she would remember the way to her relative's house
near Whitby on the Yorkshire moors, was beginning
to accept she was lost.

Only one part of her body seemed to have life
and that was her face which ached unbearably from
the constant bombardment of icy particles. The wind
would be shrieking one minute and moaning the next.
At last, gasping for breath, she turned her back on the
driving storm and stood listening for the crunching of
the handcart wheels on the snow.

The cart and an old feather bed, were the only
possessions which her two elder brothers, David and
William, had managed to hide from the beady eyes
of the bailiff's men that morning. Under a piece
of tarpaulin on the cart were the two youngest
children, three-year-old twins, Tom and Sarah, who
had mercifully slept for most of the way.

In a sudden lull, Lucy thought what a terrible time

it was. After the end of the Great War unemployment was high. Then by the mid-twenties came the Miners' Strike and the General Strike and the situation worsened.

Her father, who had been a drunkard and a gambler, had been drowned in the river in a drunken stupor. It had been difficult for the family, large as they were. The two boys had lost their jobs and the three elder girls had started doing menial work for a pittance. Her mother had done charring but had had to give it up when she became ill. They got behind with the rent, hence the bailiffs turning them out.

Lucy, as though in a trance, suddenly became aware of someone shouting.

"Lucy, Lucy, where are you? Shout back."

"Oh . . . I'm here, just ahead of you."

She could hear both of her brothers now, both were panting. The handcart stopped and William came up to her. "We're lost, aren't we?"

"Yes, the road just seemed to peter out."

Her mother, her arms huddled around Deborah and Beth, the two middle sisters, who were shaking with cold, came up saying, "It's unwise to stand about." There was a sudden lull in the storm and she looked about her. "We must find shelter of some kind."

David who had walked ahead suddenly called, "There's a barn down here in a hollow." He came up blowing on his hands. "It's not much of a place, there's some holes in one part of the roof, but it will at least give us some protection."

The wind had risen again and they battled their way to the barn. No one could have said there was any warmth in it but at least it sheltered them from the blizzard that was raging again and there was enough room to keep the handcart under cover. The twins were still sleeping.

Helen had Deborah and Beth crossing their arms and slapping their palms against their backs, but the pain of the blood circulating had them shouting out. William who was stamping his feet said, "At this minute I would give my right arm for a piece of bread and cheese. They hadn't eaten since six o'clock that morning when they had shared half a loaf of bread given to them by an elderly neighbour who had said, "It's all I have, Mrs Lingard, me love. I hope you'll soon find your cousin."

Helen had prayed so, but was now losing hope. It was years since she had seen her cousin Anne but her words at their parting had been, "If you're ever in need, come to me."

William who had been peering through a small, dirty pane of glass in the barn shouted, "Someone's coming." The ripple of excitement that ran through them was almost tangible. David pulled the door open and, disregarding the rush of icy snow, yelled, "Hello there!" A woman's voice replied, "Well, bugger me, who's out in this blizzard?"

Angelina Trippet entered their lives; a small straight-backed woman, a shawl wrapped round her and tied at the back and a scarf tied round a woollen hat.

When she heard their story she said, "God Almighty, what sort of people would turn a family out of their home in this weather? Look, I've lost my dog. If your lads can find her I'll see you have shelter for the time being. Rags doesn't go far. I would go after her but my back is playing me up."

The boys were willing to look but their mother

pointed out they didn't know the moors and could get hopelessly lost.

David said, "If the dog hasn't gone far I'll have her back in seconds." He opened the barn door, letting in again a blasting of snow and gave a strange whistle. An immediate barking had Mrs Trippet peering ahead.

"Well, glory be. Who would have believed it? Never heard a whistle like that. Here, Rags girl, here."

The dog, barking, came up, struggling through the deep snow. David went out and picked her up and she licked all over his face. They went back into the barn. The dog, a white fox terrier, had a clownish look with a ring of black around one eye and the other one crossed. Deborah and Beth forgot their misery and started crooning over and patting the dog. Tom and Sarah, who were suddenly wide awake, knelt up, a look of wonder in their eyes as though they had never seen a dog before.

Mrs Trippet said, "Come on, let's go, it's getting darker every minute." She tied a piece of rope to the dog's collar then fastened the rope to the handle of the cart. "The house isn't far. Don't expect Buckingham Palace."

David said cheerfully, "A barn with a whole roof would be a palace to me at this moment."

The driving icy snow in their faces was a torment but it was not long before a house loomed up. It was a big house and looked bleak. Lucy tried to stifle her disappointment. She had at least expected to see the cheeriness of a fire burning in one of the rooms but the windows were all dark and unwelcoming.

Mrs Trippet flung open the big front door. "Inside, all of you, I'll soon get a fire going. We'll go into the

4

kitchen." She went ahead and opened a door to the left of the staircase. "It's warmer in here."

Warmer? Lucy's stomach contracted. The place was freezing.

While Mrs Trippet laid the fire she asked them where they'd come from. Their mother said from the outskirts of Middlesborough. Mrs Trippet looked around at the children and said, surprise in her voice, "You walked all that way?"

"No, we were lucky enough to get a lift from a man with a big lorry," Helen said. "He put the handcart in as well. He brought us over half the way, then he branched off. We were so grateful; I don't think we would have made it if we'd had to walk so far."

"Well," said Mrs Trippet, "there's always some kind soul ready to help." She put a light to the kindling and to an oil lamp, adding, "There's plenty of logs. Pile 'em on."

There was a big iron grate in the centre of a huge stone fireplace with an oven on one side and a boiler on the other.

Mrs Trippet had William and David and the two older girls working. They were to come upstairs and help her to bring down mattresses and blankets, informing Helen at the same time that it would be best if they all slept in the kitchen for the one night. The bedrooms would have to be warmed up.

Warmed up? Lucy doubted if this barn of a place would ever get warmed up, then immediately chided herself for her thoughts. She should be grateful that they at least had a roof over their heads.

The kindling lit at once and soon flames were sprouting among the twigs. She found some smaller logs and they too must have been dry to catch so quickly. Soon red and orange flames were dancing

5

along bigger logs and Lucy was lapping up the heat, as she listened to feet crossing bare boards upstairs then come clumping down the uncarpeted stairs.

When they came back to the kitchen with the mattresses and blankets Beth dropped her bundle and rushed to the fireplace. "A fire! What bliss." She held out her hands to the blaze.

Helen, who had seated the twins on the feather bed while she helped with the bedding, said softly, "Aren't we lucky?"

Mrs Trippet called, "Come on all you shirkers. Get these mattresses propped up at the sides of the fireplace, and the blankets want throwing over the driers to air."

When the overhead driers, heavy with blankets, were winched up, Mrs Trippet said she would go home and find them something to eat.

There was a sudden silence and they all stared at her. Lucy said, "I thought you lived here?"

"In this barn of a place? Not on your life. I'll sell it when I get a buyer. William, David, you'd better come with me to carry the food over."

When they had gone Beth said, "Food. I'd forgotten what it tasted like."

Her mother warned her not to expect much. "It's kind of Mrs Trippet to try and find us something to eat." To Lucy she said, "I only hope she'll let us stay here for a few days, then we can have a chance of finding cousin Anne."

"I hope so."

"Mind you, I don't like her swearing."

"Oh, Mother, for heaven's sake. Does it matter? One swear word and you put such importance on it. We have a roof over our heads, a fire and we're

6

going to get food. Isn't it more important that we have shelter?"

"I just don't want the boys to pick up these words."

"They must hear them every day," Lucy said under her breath. The door opened and the boys came in laughing, followed by Mrs Trippet. David held up an iron pot. "Guess what we've got. Broth!"

William, grinning broadly, offered a bag. "Guess what else we've got. Bread . . . *and* buttered scones. A feast for the Gods."

"Buttered?" Excitement rippled among the children and the dog, who had been untied, ran from one to the other, sharing it.

The pot of broth was hung on a ring above the fire and when Mrs Trippet said she was sorry it wasn't something more substantial, William, looking blissful, closed his eyes and murmured, "It'll be nectar to us, ma'am, we are indeed blest."

Lucy had not heard such jollity from her family for years.

Mrs Trippet had them all seated on the long wooden forms at each side of the white scrubbed table and the girls filled earthenware bowls with a long-handled spoon. Heads were bowed as their mother said grace.

"We thank thee Lord for leading us to this most blessed of houses. Amen."

There was a strong chorus of amens but Lucy noticed that her mother's eyes were filled with tears and she felt ashamed for having made her tongue go earlier. Her mother had always loved them all and done her best for them

She marvelled at her. When she was younger she had been beautiful and there were still traces of it in the finely chiselled features. She was the daughter of a vicar who had died just after she married. Lucy wondered how her mother had managed to bring them up, with her father drinking and gambling the way he had done.

The twins sat between their mother and Lucy. They were both wide-eyed and were so absorbed in the scene they had to be coaxed at times to eat. Nectar was the right word for the broth and hardly a word was spoken as they cleared their bowls. But when the scones were handed around and Mrs Trippet smilingly slid a jar of raspberry jam on to the table, all the young ones began to laugh and talk.

The dog had been given a meal then told by its mistress to sit. It did for a while, then gradually edged its way, paw by paw to where David was seated and sat behind him, every now and then raising a paw and touching him tentatively.

When David eventually became aware of its presence he said, "Hello there, Rags." The dog sat up alert and its tail began a thumping tattoo on the bare floorboards.

When they had finished the meal Mrs Trippet suggested they stack the bowls in the sink until later when the water had heated in the boiler. She told the boys to bring the wooden benches around the fire, then they could tell her their plans.

"But first," she said, "let's have the bloody curtains drawn and shut out the night."

Lucy, seeing her mother wince at the swearing said quickly to Mrs Trippet, "What a lovely smell comes from the logs."

"Yes, it's applewood. Do you know the old saying;

8

> Pear logs and apple logs,
> They will scent your room,
> Cherry logs across the dogs
> Smell like flowers in bloom.
>
> But ash logs, all smooth and grey,
> Burn them green or old,
> Buy up all that come your way
> They're worth their weight in gold.

There's more," said Mrs Trippet, "but I've forgotten the rest."

Helen Lingard smiled. "I remember another verse.

> Holly logs will burn like wax –
> You should burn them green,
> Elm logs like smouldering flax,
> No flame is ever seen.

And then there's a verse about chestnut logs. Mmm, I can only remember that chestnut logs are good to last if cut in the fall." Helen paused then said, "Mrs Trippet, I hope you don't mind my mentioning this but I don't like to hear swearing. The children . . ."

"Was I swearing?"

"You said bloody," William supplied with a gleeful expression.

Helen raised her shoulders. "You see what I mean, Mrs Trippet?"

"It's like this, Mrs Lingard. My father was a racing man and as my mother died when I was quite young I spent a good part of my life in stables where conversation among the men was, let's say, choice. I had a nanny who thumped me when she heard me swearing but she was a lazy woman and when my father found out she was not doing the job she was

9

paid for he sacked her. By then, the damage was done. I'll try to remember not to swear while you're all here."

The last sentence sent a little shiver down Lucy's spine. She was just beginning to have a settled feeling of belonging here. Now it brought her to the fact that they would probably be on the move again the next morning. Mrs Trippet's next words confirmed this.

"Now then, about this cousin of yours, Mrs Lingard. What's her name and where did she live when you were last in touch with her? We can perhaps find her."

"Her name is Anne Flloyd. She never married. She lived about a mile this side of Whitby. Lucy stayed with her about three years ago and she thought she would remember the cottage, but we got lost."

"I know Anne Flloyd," declared Mrs Trippet, "she lived about a mile from Whitby. But Anne married last year and went to live in Liverpool."

"Married?" Helen queried. "She told us she would never marry."

"Oh, but she did," Mrs Trippet replied grimly. "And it was just about the worst thing she could have done. A nasty man was Ted Feathers. Turned out to be brutal to her."

"Oh, dear." Helen was distressed. "Anne was such a gentle soul."

"She was that, wouldn't hurt a fly. But I did hear a short time ago that she had upped and left her husband."

"I hope so," Helen said. "My husband was a gambling man and he drank heavily, but he never once raised a hand to me or any of the children." She paused. "He died a year ago."

Lucy looked up in surprise, as did her brothers and

sisters, their mother never having ever mentioned their father's drinking habits to anyone.

Mrs Trippet nodded slowly. "So that's why you've been turned out of your home. My sympathies are with you."

William asked boldly if that meant they might be able to stay for a while and his mother rebuked him.

"I've only done what any other person with feelings would have done," said Mrs Trippet. She slapped her knees and got up. "I'll have to go. My stepbrother and sister-in-law are living with me for the time being and although this house belongs to me my stepbrother seems to think he's my lawyer or something, telling me what I must and must not do."

Mrs Trippet grinned and gave a wink. "He hasn't realised yet who he's dealing with. I'll tell you the story sometime. I'll look in again later to see if there's anything else you want. I'll bring some cocoa with me so you can have a hot drink before going to bed."

David got up saying he would walk home with her and she said, "It's not often I have a young escort. Come on, Rags." The dog, who had been snoozing, was on her feet in seconds, tail wagging madly and looking up at David who was on his feet too.

Mrs Trippet chuckled. "You've won yourself a friend for life."

When they had gone there was silence for a moment then William, Beth and Deborah were all asking questions, all wanting to know if their mother thought that Mrs Trippet might allow them to go on living in the house. Beth suggested that she, Deborah and Lucy might find work in a big house.

Helen held up a hand. "The best we can hope for is some guidance from Mrs Trippet. She wants to sell

11

the house, but might allow us to stay here for a few days. If she does we shall be very lucky indeed. We shall let things take their course. Now, may I suggest that the washing up is done and the beds made up for the night."

They had moved the table and wooden forms and laid out the mattresses beside the feather bed, where the twins were already asleep when Mrs Trippet and David returned, David carrying a bucket of coal. Mrs Trippet said they would need to keep the fire on low all night and it needed coal to keep it going. "I think there's some more coal in the cellar."

Jobs for the young ones must have been on her mind because she broached it almost at once. She had been thinking for some time, she said, of starting a farm. She looked at the boys. "You've got two willing young men there. I might be able to take them on."

William said, "We've worked on farms, but – "

"You have? Well, that's a help, but remember that nothing is settled yet. In the meantime I can find you both some jobs to do."

Beth, ever the bold one, said, "Are there any jobs we girls can do, Mrs Trippet?"

Her mother started to scold her but Mrs Trippet said, "Stop worrying, Mrs Lingard. Beth wants to work, that's more than I can say for some young lasses. Actually, there's a job all the girls can do here. The attic wants clearing. It's stacked with all sorts of stuff. It'll be cold up there so wrap up well. And now I'm going. I'll see you in the morning. I hope you sleep all right."

The moment she had gone William was slapping David on the back. "What about that then, boyo, as the Irishman used to say. Work means money, so we can eat again."

12

Their mother suggested they get the blankets on the beds and as the last blanket was laid on Mrs Trippet turned up again. She clucked her tongue. "I'd forget my head if it was loose, wouldn't I?" She put cocoa and milk and sugar on the table.

Helen smiled. "You must have known that the kettle was singing on the hob. Sit down and have a cup with us."

"I'll do just that. I've talked myself dry trying to explain to my stepbrother that I shall start a farm if I want to and that he has no say in it. I also had to deal with his bossy wife Bella who wants to rule over everyone." She paused a moment to tell the girls to get the enamel mugs out of the dresser then went on, "My sister-in-law is a terrible person, has to know everybody's business. Nobody likes her. If someone farts she has to know which way the wind blows it."

A yelp of laughter came from William and a gasp from his mother.

Mrs Trippet clapped a hand over her mouth. "Oh, dear, I'll have to wash my mouth with soap and water. But the word is in the dictionary. What word do you use when a person breaks wind?"

"Pump," said William and rolled along the edge of the table.

His mother said sternly, "Outside, William, until you're got over that stupid hysterical laughter."

The others were having a job not to laugh and Mrs Trippet said, "I'm sorry, Mrs Lingard, I really am. I promised to control my tongue and I've let you down. I had better go." She made to get up and Helen put a hand on her shoulder. "No. Stay. I must seem very straight-laced. But it was the way I was brought up."

"I'm at fault. I really will try very hard not to swear again. You had better tell William to come in, it's freezing outside."

"I'm in," said a subdued William, but no sooner had he said it than he turned away and stuffed a handkerchief into his mouth.

It was the girls saying that the mugs were out for the coffee to be poured that partly stifled the mirth. Then Mrs Trippet told them about the farmhouse she was interested in buying.

"It's not far from here. Mr Dalby says he's ready to give up. It's getting to be too much for him and I've always fancied having a farm. Not that anyone in my family has been farmers. At least, none that I know of. I like animals. Ephraim and bossy Bella, of course, think I'm mad to even contemplate such a thing and they think they've talked me out of it, but – " She winked. "They'll get to know in time that when I say something, I mean it." She got up. "I'm going." She grinned. "Don't expect to see me until the morning."

The farm was discussed with Helen saying that the girls, as well as the boys, might get jobs to do, then said, "But that won't be for some time. Right now we'll get to bed. It's been a long day."

The fire had been banked up with logs, coal and slack for the night and a rusty fireguard put in front of it.

"What's Mrs Trippet's house like?" Lucy asked.

"Well furnished, cosy, carpets and rugs and heavy velvet curtains. You could have roasted an ox in the fireplace."

"What was her stepbrother and his wife like?"

"He's a bombastic man, knows everything. His wife was a sort of hoity-toity dame; nose in the air. Neither

14

of them took any notice of me. I would be scum in their eyes."

There was a sudden patter of hailstones on the windowpanes and the wind howled under the eaves. William groaned. "I wouldn't be surprised if the house takes off during the night."

Their mother said wearily, "If it does, we can't do anything about it. Let's get some sleep."

Lucy doubted that they would get any rest with the storm still raging, but within minutes of getting under the blankets on the hard, horsehair mattress, she was asleep.

Chapter Two

Lucy aroused slowly from her slumbers, aware of movement and voices and for seconds was unable to place where she was. She opened one eye and became aware that a lamp was burning.

Remembrance came and she sat up.

David said, "I got up to put some logs on the fire so you would all get up to a warm kitchen, then I dropped a log."

"What time is it?"

"A clock somewhere has just struck eight. William and I have been out to clear the snow away, so Ma could go to the privy. It's a fine clear morning, freezing but the wind's died down, thank goodness."

There was the sound of stamping feet outside then the door opened and their mother came in, a shawl held tightly around her. "I think this is the coldest morning I can ever remember. I met Mrs Trippet. She says she's sending some sausages over for our breakfast. We'll never be out of her debt."

She came across the room and suggested that the blankets be folded and the mattresses taken back upstairs. They all shared the work while their mother saw to the twins.

Sarah and Tom were sitting on the folded feather bed, just looking from one to the other of their brothers and sisters. Helen knelt down and gave each

17

a hug, her heart aching at the way the life seemed to have been knocked out of her two youngest. Before they came to understand the meaning of hardship they had been lively little souls.

There was a knock on the door and David went to answer it. The next moment he came in with a small, scrawny girl who was carrying a basket. "This is Polly Beckett," he said. "She works for Mrs Trippet."

The girl looked towards Helen. "She's sent you some sausages and bread for your breakfasts and some milk and tea," she said shyly.

Helen took the basket from her and said warmly, "What a good soul she is. I don't know what we would have done without her."

"Nor me, ma'am. She took me from the orphanage. But there, I must go. The visitors'll be down for their breakfasts."

Polly's expression and her emphasis on the word "visitors" left no doubt in Helen's mind as to her opinion of Mrs Trippet's relatives.

"I'll be seeing you again, ma'am."

As the door closed behind her Deborah said, "Well . . . it doesn't look as if *she* gets much to eat, does it? You'll soon find out that the good Samaritan, Mrs Trippet, isn't what she's cracked up to be!"

Her mother said gently, "We don't know how long Polly has been working for her, do we? Why are you behaving so nastily? Is it because of the hardships we've had to endure lately?"

Deborah's head went up in a defiant way. "No, it's because Dad would have been alive today if you hadn't turned him out. I loved him even if you didn't."

David strode over and, pulling his sister away, slapped her across the face.

"Don't you ever say anything like that again to your mother. Dad was a gambler and a drunkard. He made Ma's life a misery."

"I loved him if no one else did," Deborah shouted.

"Because you made up to him and he gave you money for sweets, money he'd stolen from Ma that she earned scrubbing floors so that we could be fed."

Helen, who was trembling, said, "Stop this at once." She turned to Deborah. "I loved your father too. Never forget that. Now, I think we had better have some breakfast."

Lucy, noticing that her mother was still trembling, said, "Look, we'll see to the breakfast, you sit down." But her mother refused and tried to make a joke of it.

"The more hands at the oars the sooner we'll make shore. We want the frying pan out, bread cut, plates in the oven, forms brought to the table, cutlery out and mugs."

There was a general bustling about and some small talk but all Lucy could think of was the day her father had been found in the river. It was thought at first that he had committed suicide but it was brought in as accidental death when a colleague of her father said he had been very drunk when he had left him.

Her father had again found money her mother had hidden and when he came home, rolling drunk and maudlin, she had pushed him outside and told him not to return.

After the funeral her mother had been ill for a time and lost her job of charring. The boys had been sacked from their farming jobs because of shortage of money with their employers and what the girls earned from their menial tasks was not enough to pay the rent and food. Hence the eviction.

The tantalising aroma of sausages sizzling had Lucy suddenly feeling ravenous and prayed that their present good luck would hold. Mrs Trippet had sent a basin of beef dripping and with their bread dipped in this special treat they were wiping dripping from their chins with beatific smiles on their faces.

William said, "I'll come to this hotel again."

Lucy took a drink of tea then looked around the table at her family. They had all lost weight lately, but William and David were big boned; otherwise they did not resemble one another in any other way. William, fair with blue eyes was ever lively. David, dark and brown eyed, was much more serious, but would join in any moments of fun.

Beth, also fair and blue eyed, was also lively, while Deborah, with brown, curly hair and green eyes was an enigma. She could be gentle in some ways but quite hard and determined in others. She was the prettiest and had been her father's favourite.

The twins were very much alike, both fair with blue eyes like Beth.

Lucy remembered when she was young how people had likened her to her mother. Now her hair was much darker and her eyes were a very dark blue. Her skin had never been creamy, nor did she have the delicacy of features of her mother but she had a well-shaped mouth (made for kissing, a lovesick boy had told her once) and she did have a finely shaped nose.

She had thought once, if she could have decent clothes she would pass as being fairly attractive. Lucy was smiling at her thoughts when William said, "Penny for them, Lucy."

She shrugged. "I was just wondering how long it would take to walk to Whitby."

"You're not walking anywhere," her mother said firmly. "The snow in places is in deep drifts. If you want something to do, you and the girls could help Mrs Trippet by starting to clear up the attic."

"It'll be like the Arctic up there," Deborah protested.

Beth said she thought it might be fun and Lucy was inclined to agree. They could always put on their coats and scarves.

Lucy got up and, going to the twins, said, "It'll be too cold for you both to be up there but there might be some old toys. If we find any we'll bring them down for you and you can play with them beside the nice warm fire."

The family had been evicted so suddenly that Sarah's precious rag doll, Betsy, and Tom's equally precious toy soldier had been left behind and when David had gone back for them the bailiff's men would not allow him to have them. They had even threatened him with cudgels and when a neighbour began to complain at such treatment, David had just managed to drag the old man aside to avoid a blow.

Helen had told the children that the soldier had had to go to war and that Betsy had gone to wave him off. The children had accepted this. It was Helen who suffered the most and begged the Good Lord that he would forgive her for the lie.

William clapped his hands. "Let's get started."

Deborah started to grumble that they would all catch colds but David spoke sharply to her. "We could catch a chill doing nothing. Clearing an attic will warm you up. Get your coat and scarf." The only attic Lucy had seen in the past had been

21

small and full of rubbish, pieces of threadbare matting, bundles of newspapers, books, moth-eaten curtains. This one was large with various pieces of decent furniture, pictures, watercolours, oil paintings and many ornaments. Then there were bundles of blankets, curtains, bedlinen, table linen and chests and boxes to be looked into.

Beth said, "Surely Mrs Trippet won't want all this thrown out."

David who had been downstairs and had just come up gave them the information that it had all to be taken to a big bedroom on the floor below and sorted into categories.

They all shivered in the icy attic at first but at the end of half an hour they were sweating as the bedroom below began to fill up. The furniture, all mahogany and in good condition, which consisted of two armchairs, two sofas, a sideboard, a dining table, chairs and a sideboard, were put to the right of the room. All the pictures were stacked against the walls and in front of them ornaments were arranged in rows.

Chests and boxes were put to the left of the room. Most of them were heavy and David having looked into one or two said the wooden boxes contained porcelain, dinner and tea sets.

Lucy said, "Pray we find some boxes of toys."

"Could be ten boxes of them," William said cheerfully, coming in with an oak cradle. "There have been children in this house and we're not even half way through the stuff yet."

It must have been ten minutes later when David held up a box containing children's books. His face was one big smile. "What about these? The twins will love them. Picture books and storybooks."

22

David held out a rag book. "This seems to have been handmade and hand painted. We could make some of these ourselves if we had the materials."

Beth grinned. "We could pinch a linen sheet. There are bundles of them. I don't think Mrs Trippet would miss one."

William teased her. "Now then, sister, don't let Ma hear you say that, and, who do you pinch the paints from?"

"There are some paints in another box. These books are about animals but they're all miserable-looking creatures. You could do better than that, our William. Look."

There was an unhappy looking cat with the caption underneath, "The cat sat on the mat." On the next page was a dog and the picture had the caption, "The dog has a bone."

"The poor thing certainly doesn't look very pleased with his bone and I don't wonder, it looks like a piece of stone."

David said briskly, "Come along, there's work to be done."

Lucy called him a slave-driver and he said, "It's the slave-drivers who get things done. If you started sorting through those big chests and boxes we would never get this lot cleared."

"Why, what's in them?"

"You'll find out later. Being kept in suspense will make you more keen to know and you'll get more pleasure when you do find out."

"Right, I'll take your word for it."

Although William had always been the fun-loving one, Lucy knew that David, more often than not, had been the one to lift them out of their dreary lives.

They carried down several large cotton bags that

were soft and smelled of lavender, but although they were pulled together by drawstrings Lucy was not even tempted to take a peep inside.

There were many big boxes carried down by the boys, the smaller ones by the girls, and they were so constantly on the move that it was some time before Lucy realised that Deborah was staying in the attic and moving things around half-heartedly.

When Lucy demanded to know why she wasn't taking anything down to the bedroom, Deborah pushed the hair away from her face and said, "Because I didn't feel like it, that's why and there's nothing you can do about it."

"Oh, isn't there?" Lucy, incensed by the sneer in her voice, went on. "I've seen you admiring yourself in front of a mirror; well you wouldn't be so pleased with your reflection if you had two black eyes, would you?"

The threat did nothing to change Deborah's attitude.

"If you must know, I don't feel well."

"And neither do we," Lucy retorted. "We're sweating like pigs."

"You know what they say," Deborah taunted. "Behave like animals and you become one."

"Oh, you, you – " Lucy went forward, her fists clenched, but Beth stepped between them.

"Come on, the pair of you." She turned to Deborah. "You can sit down when this attic is cleared and if you don't move now, I'll help Lucy give you the black eyes."

The girls had quarrelled in the past but never at any time had there been any hint of violence between them. For a moment, Deborah, her head up, looked as if she would defy them, then as the boys could be heard coming up the stairs chatting, she turned to the diminishing pile on the floor and said quietly, "I need help to move a brass fender and companion set. They seem to have got jammed."

Without a word Lucy and Beth went to help her.

When the boys came in David said, "I don't think it'll take long to move this lot." The girls were struggling to move the fender and he went to help them.

It turned out that a heavy piece of chain was looped through the end of the fender and was caught on the rope handle of a wooden chest. "Another treasure chest," David said cheerfully as he managed to release the chain.

When the fender was lifted away there were excited squeals from the girls as a box of toys was revealed and animosity was forgotten as each one mentioned an item. Beth yelled, "A steam engine for Tom!" Deborah pointed to a doll's cradle with rockers. "Oh, can you see Sarah's face?"

But Lucy, who had shouted when they had first seen the toys whispered, "Soldiers and a rag doll. Oh, thank you, Lord."

In spite of the fact that David and William had been moved by their find David refused to let the girls sort through the box. "Not until we've cleared this lot." And when Beth and Deborah called him a spoilsport he handed the box to William to take downstairs, saying, "You'll all have your fun later. That is final. And I'll tell you now, you won't regret it."

David was proved right.

Opening chests and boxes was the most exciting thing the girls had experienced in their lives, even though everything belonged to Mrs Trippet.

Beth said, "Well, I'm going to see that Tom has this steam engine and Sarah the cradle."

"You're wrong." Lucy spoke quietly. "What Tom has been deprived of are his precious soldiers and Sarah her rag doll."

"But nothing will be *taken* without permission," David said firmly. "We shall ask Mrs Trippet if we can have them."

"And what if she says no?" demanded Deborah.

"I don't think she will. I feel she's a fair woman."

"And I think you're in for a big surprise," Deborah retorted.

David, ignoring this, raised the lid of a second chest. "There you are, you girls, feast your eyes on these."

This chest was full of bedding, silken sheets and pillowcases, with several rolls of material. William said they obviously had been owned by wealthy people, but why were they in the attic? David waved a hand, encompassing the room. "Why are a lot of things here; good furniture, pictures, ornaments, beautiful porcelain, dinner services, tea sets?"

Deborah made to lift the lid of a cardboard box and David stayed her hand. "We'll see inside this later."

"If I want to look inside I'll look and you won't stop me," Deborah said in a defiant way.

"You attempt to open it and you'll regret it." David spoke quietly, but Lucy knew he was really angry.

Their mother came in and said, "There'll be no threats of violence."

"She takes no notice of kind words."

"We still have a hard road ahead of us and quarrelling isn't going to help. Deborah takes things harder because she was indulged when she was younger. I was partly to blame for that. Now we must all pull together."

Lucy snapped, "I wish that, just for *once*, Mother,

you would lose your temper and shout at us. You are always so gentle."

"At this moment, Lucy, I am seething with anger. I could scream at you all for this behaviour, but what do you think would happen if I started to threaten violence? Is that what you really want?"

There was a silence in which even Deborah looked ashamed.

She said she was to blame and she apologised to David. He apologised too and the incident was over.

"Right," Helen said. "Now can we get on with the clearing?"

When everything had been cleared there was the pleasure of opening chests and boxes, also the big calico bags. The next moment Lucy gave a cry of pleasure. "Oh, just look at these." She took out a cushion cover made of hexagons of coloured silks, done in an exquisite pattern. The hexagons were in all shades, some plain silk and others patterned. "How absolutely lovely. There's heaps of pieces to be made up."

Beth who had been exploring, opened another calico bag and found that this held velvet pieces and also had a completed cushion cover.

It was then that Lucy's mind began to explode with ideas. They could make rag books, cushion covers, embroider samplers. They could all be employed. Perhaps they could rent a shop!

"So," David said, "let us have a look in the other boxes and chests."

There was a big box of samplers. One which had been completed said, "Jesus Loves Us". Some of them were partially completed. There were masses of embroidered silks.

27

Lucy said eagerly, "I'm more interested in making silk and velvet patchwork cushion covers and rag storybooks. William is good at painting and David at printing. The girls can help me make the covers and the books."

Her mother came in and Lucy said, "What's wrong?"

"I asked her who had lived in the house. She told me and I wished I hadn't asked. It's a very sad story."

When Helen had her emotions under control she told the story. "Apparently Mrs Trippet had had a son and twin girls. When the girls were eighteen they met and fell in love with two brothers. When they were engaged the four of them decided they would like to share a house when they married."

Helen paused. "Mrs Trippet and her husband decided to buy a house for them and bought the one that Mrs Trippet lives in now. But the two couples decided they preferred the older house, as they all had hobbies and there was a lovely big attic where they could keep all their paraphernalia. Mr and Mrs Trippet, preferring the new house, agreed. And so they all settled down."

"Did the daughters and their husbands have children?" Lucy asked.

"Yes, they did. One couple had a boy and the other a girl and the children were inseparable. Then one day – " Helen paused. "The two couples and their children went for a picnic. After lunch the men decided to go for a walk but their wives said they would clear away and wash up. They got to talking and suddenly realised the children were missing. They were looking for them when they heard screams. The children had fallen in the water. The river was in spate after heavy rain and . . ." Helen's lips trembled. "The mothers jumped into the water and the men who had heard the screams came rushing back. They too jumped into the water . . . The two families drowned."

"Oh, God," murmured David.

There was a silence and it was broken by his mother who whispered, "Mrs Trippet also lost her husband a few months ago . . . and I felt I wanted to die yesterday when we were turned out of our home."

They discussed the dreadful tragedy and it was not until later that they got round to giving the twins their toys.

Tom accepted the soldier and swallowed hard as he saw an arm was missing. David said very gently, "He was a hero, Tom. You should be very proud of him."

Although the doll wore a darker coloured blue dress and the hair was lighter, Sarah hugged it with a mother love which brought a lump to Lucy's throat.

Half an hour later Mrs Trippet called. "I just wanted to thank you for all you've done. You see, I thought if I saw everything laid out it would clear the ghosts away, but it didn't work that way. I don't want to see what there is."

She turned to Helen. "I want to get rid of it, Mrs Lingard. Keep any of the things you want, the rest can be thrown away. I do want to sell the house eventually but you and your family can stay here until you find somewhere more suitable."

A bleak look came into her eyes. "The ghosts are pestering me. I'll call in the morning."

They were all silent as they watched the small, straight-backed woman walk away.

Chapter Three

Although the family were sensitive enough to know how Mrs Trippet must have suffered at the tragedy of her family, they could not help but feel pleasure in knowing they would be able to stay in the house until they found something more suitable.

It was later in the day before Mrs Trippet came back, but she had sent eggs for their breakfast and some bread.

With the family grateful for a good breakfast Lucy turned out the oil lamp and drew the curtains. The storm had died down and everywhere was still. She said, "There's not a soul anywhere. Not even a bird."

Her mother came and they stood in silence together, then Lucy said, in a musing way, "It's the whiteness that astonishes me. Not like in a town when the snow is dirty within minutes."

"Only on the ground," her mother said quietly. "There's a beauty in seeing snow on roofs and on the branches of the trees."

Lucy found herself wondering what scene her mother had in mind. There had been many moves over the years but they had never had a garden or trees anywhere near them, just factories. When the boys had worked on a farm they had had five miles to walk to their work.

When Mrs Trippet arrived there was a sombre air about her and Lucy wondered if there had been a change about the house.

"Well," she said, "I had better explain why I wanted the things taken out of the attic yesterday and laid out so I could see what there was." She sighed. "My stepbrother and his wife came with vans and took away carpets, silver, the good furniture, but didn't bother to look in the attic. I thought that the only things in the attic would be the various materials my daughters and their husbands worked with for their hobbies. But then Polly told me there was furniture, china and bedding."

"There's a lot more than that," Deborah said eagerly, but her mother shushed her.

Mrs Trippet continued. "I put up the house for sale, thinking I could move the stuff out of the attic if anyone came to buy. But no one came. I suppose people thought there was a curse on the house with six people dying suddenly. Then you all arrived and not only did I think it would give you something to do but at that moment felt I couldn't bear to see any of the materials that my family had worked with."

She sighed again. "How wrong I've been. I realised last night in bed that ghosts won't be laid because of removing a few personal things. It's people who will do it, people who can laugh and tease in spite of adversity. People who are willing to work. I stood at the bottom of the stairs yesterday for a time, listening to the laughter of you young ones, listening to all the movement from the attic to the bedroom and back again and I said to myself, Angelina Trippet, you are a fool, and that was when I decided to let you stay in the house rent-free, until you find something you really want."

32

For a moment they all stared at one another as though unable to take it all in then Helen protested that they could only accept the offer on condition that they would pay the rent in full when the boys and the girls had found work.

David said, "I think we'll all have jobs to do, Mrs Trippet, if I can put a suggestion to you."

Seeing his mother shaking her head he hesitated but Mrs Trippet gave him a nod to go on and he plunged in about making the rag books and about the other things the girls could tackle.

Deborah brought up the question of the box of toys but Mrs Trippet wasn't listening. She encouraged the girls with their plans but suggested that the boys make the rag books a hobby. "If I get the farm, and I think that the old man is weakening, you can work there. You need a steady weekly wage. Rag books will take time to make and you don't know what demand there will be for them."

William spoke up. "I think there would be a good sale, especially in the summer with holiday-makers at places like Whitby and all the other resorts along the coast, Sandscar, Runswick, Staithes. And there's Scarborough where hundreds of people go. We can perhaps open a shop somewhere and sell other books, comics, newspapers, and women's magazines."

Lucy mentioned the silk sheets and pillowcases and Mrs Trippet said, "I'd forgotten those. The girls sold them to the wealthy and to hotels for honeymoon suites. The girls sometimes spent a night at some of the hotels."

"Oh, I would love a life doing that," said Deborah, her eyes alight with excitement.

Lucy said, "I suggest that some of these items be made before we fly into any realms of fantasy."

Mrs Trippet nodded and then added to Helen, "I told you that everything belongs to you and I meant it."

Helen said quietly, "I can't, Mrs Trippet. There's some really beautiful china, tea sets and dinner services. Take time to think about it. Look over everything again."

"Mrs Lingard, at one time I would have wanted to keep them to grieve over, but not any more. I've come to my senses." She got up. "Think of your loved ones that have gone, but don't let their ghosts destroy your lives. Polly will be over later with some boiled mutton stew for your dinner."

Helen tried to make a protest but Mrs Trippet was away and once out of the house there were shouts of glee and dancing around with William shouting, "We're in business, we're on our way!" The twins who had been asleep on the folded feather bed while Mrs Trippet was there, awoke and looked around them, bewildered.

Sarah, scared by all the noise, began to whimper and Helen took the child from her, calling, "Calm down all of you. You're frightening the children. And *sit* down. There's a great deal to discuss."

They brought the forms up around the fire and Lucy could see they were all keyed up with excitement. David had Tom on his lap and Helen held Sarah, who sucked her thumb as she cuddled into her.

"Now then," Helen began. "This is a wonderful thing that has happened to us, but we musn't let it go to our heads."

"Why not?" Deborah demanded. "Surely we should be allowed to celebrate after all the misery we've suffered?"

"You are right to a certain extent, Deborah, but

there are so many things that will have to be done before we can earn even one penny. It's all right to say we are in business, easy to say a shop can be opened and we'll sell rag books, et cetera. There's a chest of material for silken sheets and pillowcases. But how do we get them to hotels in London? We have no money at present to buy food, we're dependent on Mrs Trippet to feed us. This to me is terrible. Until recently, we've always been independent, even though we've been near to starving." There was a break in her voice and David said softly, "May I say something, Ma?"

She nodded and he looked from side to side of him. "What Ma says makes sense, but I have some suggestions to make. Mrs Trippet very generously made Ma a present of the contents of the attic. I suggest that there are items that can be sold, so we can hold our own as far as food is concerned."

There was a chorus of "Hear, hear!"

"Ready-made samplers can be sold, and the cushions. We have the handcart, we can take them round the big houses and also try and sell them in Whitby. William and I can take them."

"Not in this weather," their mother said firmly.

"Yes, in this weather, Ma. We walked miles, part of the time in a blizzard to find somewhere to sleep. We can walk two miles to get money for food."

"And if you don't sell anything, what then?" Beth asked.

"Then we beg. I promise you that we are not going to starve."

Various items were suggested for sale. "What about the dinner services and tea services? We won't need them," said William.

Helen shook her head. "They're beautiful. Mrs

Trippet might regret parting with them later. I insist they are kept."

"All right, what about the furniture? We can live without it."

"And who are you going to sell it to?" Lucy asked. "Are you going to make several journeys to Whitby carrying it piece by piece on the cart in the hope of selling something? No, Mrs Trippet was right. Start small and try and build. We might think of other things to make and sell, but start with what we already have."

Their mother talked a lot more and they all came to realise that what she said made sense. She suggested they write down all the different items they had carried into the bedroom and see if there was anything they could sell and came up with only one thing. Not to sell, but to use. How had they managed to miss it?

There was a small handmade theatre with tiny wooden puppets. They were all excited about them, remembering their Uncle Dick bringing a similar theatre and puppets one time.

Lucy said, "Don't you remember, Mother, Uncle Dick teaching us to work the puppets and to do the voices of them? We could give a show, I'm sure."

Their mother said, "I certainly do remember, but I think you have a lot of things on your minds at the moment. Also, if you ever wanted to give a show and charge a fee you would need a larger theatre and larger puppets.'

'We could make a larger one, there's plenty of big cardboard boxes. And I know that David and William could make them and the puppets."

"I suggest we calm down," David said. "It's something that will be used later, but right now I feel we should deal with what we have that's already usable. Agreed?"

William said, with a grin, "Do you know what? We're a very clever family who are wasting our talents."

Polly Beckett came with some mutton stew. Her face was flushed and she looked near to tears. When Lucy asked her what was wrong she said, "It's that 'orrible stepbrother of the mistress and 'is 'orribler wife. 'E punched me in the back and called me a slattern, an' she punched me on the arm and said I should go back to the gutter."

Helen came over. "That's terrible. Does Mrs Trippet know?"

"No, and I don't want 'er to know. She 'as enough worries." Polly picked up the corner of her apron and wiped her eyes. "All I did was spill a bit of milk on t'cloth when I was clearing table. T'were bad enough at the orphanage, but it's getting as bad with them both thumping me."

Helen looked distressed and said that someone should know about this. When she asked if there was a cook Polly nodded, "Yes, but she's scared to death of 'em. They found her 'aving a nip o' gin once and told her if she did it again she would be out. An' poor cook 'as no family and nowhere to go."

Polly said suddenly she must get back and begged Helen not to say anything to Mrs Trippet, adding that apart from the poor woman having enough to worry about, her stepbrother and his wife were, after all, kin. Helen promised, but Lucy didn't and decided that Mrs Trippet would be told what was going on.

An opportunity came that afternoon when, seeing Mrs Trippet coming towards the house, she snatched a shawl, threw it around her shoulders and went out to meet her. She told her quickly about Polly and explained the difficulty as her mother had promised not to mention Polly's treatment. Mrs Trippet, who was furious, said grimly, "Don't worry about that. I saw Polly one morning without her dress and remarked about the bruises on her arms. She made the excuse she had had a fall. I'll certainly make my tongue go. How dare they treat my staff in that way?"

They walked to the house together, with Mrs Trippet talking about how her stepbrother and his wife had gone to live in India and how, when they decided to return to England, she had offered them a temporary home.

"Temporary!" she exclaimed. "I can't get rid of them! They've been here months. I came to the conclusion the other day that they want me to move back to this house and they want mine . . . no doubt for a song. Well, they've got another think coming."

Lucy took off her shawl when they went in and called, "Mrs Trippet's here."

Her mother came out of the kitchen smiling. "How nice to see you, Mrs Trippet. Did you hear the sawing? It's the boys. An elderly man told them that the spinney belonged to him and said if they would cut some logs and bring them to the farm up the road he would pay them for their work."

"Oh, he did, did he?" Mrs Trippet looked grim. "The spinney belongs to me but I let him cut an odd tree down. It's his farm I want to buy. He's a mean man and doesn't pay anyone if he can get away with it."

They went back to the fire and Lucy made some tea. Mrs Trippet went on with her story. "A proper old Scrooge he is, *and* he has money. If he doesn't pay David and William for their work – "

"Don't worry, Mrs Trippet," Lucy said. "The boys will help anyone poor but won't be put upon by anyone who can afford to pay. And as soon as we can get organised to make some money we'll pay you back for your kindness."

"You'll do no such thing. I'll be happy if I see you all getting on your feet again." In the next breath she said, "When I've had my cup of tea I'll have a walk to the farm and have a word with old Dalby. Do you want to come with me, Mrs Lingard?"

"Forgive me if I don't, Mrs Trippet. I'm a coward. I hate to be embroiled in anything unpleasant."

"One has to fight for rights," Mrs Trippet declared.

Lucy spoke up. "Mother has done nothing but fight all her married life to keep us fed. I think she's done more than her share. I'll come with you."

"Good." Mrs Trippet gave a lopsided smile. "I've done a lot of fighting too, but I can't stop." Her expression softened. "The difference between us is, Mrs Lingard, that you are a gentle soul and I'm as tough as a pair of old boots. But then, it would be a dull old world if we were all alike, wouldn't it?"

"Lucy is a fighter. I used to wish she wasn't, but I realise there have to be fighters or the weak would be trodden on."

Mrs Trippet chuckled. "A wily old bird would be a better description." She drank the rest of her tea and got up. "Well, Lucy, shall we go and visit him in his eyrie?"

With the clearing of the attic having taken so much time there had been no opportunity for Lucy to explore the area. They walked towards a small spinney ahead, where beyond, in the still air, smoke rose lazily from tall, twisted chimneypots.

Footsteps had made a pathway from the old house which continued through the spinney and beyond to a brick-built house. Mrs Trippet had not spoken a word until they neared it then said, "Well, that's it. My second abode." She had given it a quick glance and spoken as though it belonged to someone else.

The house, with a carved stone arch above the tall front door had a well cared for look, the third storey windows having an extra brightness from the sun sparkling on the snow.

Lucy took a deep breath. "What a lovely morning. It's so wonderfully fresh."

"It won't be when we reach the Dalby place," she said drily. "It's in a hollow at the end of the ridge. You need to nip your nose in the summer."

Lucy had not realised they were going up a slope until they reached the ridge and she was out of breath. They stopped as she saw a farmstead on the side of the hollow with several sheds nearby. This area had a few fields divided by dry-stone walls, where in one, sheep grazed.

A road ahead that led out of the hollow had been cleared of snow and two men with carts were standing talking.

Suddenly the stillness was broken by the sound of sawing starting up again, this sound mingling with the baaing of sheep as a flock, seemingly appearing from nowhere, came into view and moved along the road where the man with the carts were. The drover hailed them and the men moved the carts to let them pass. Then the three men started talking and Mrs Trippet said, "Well, let's get going and meet the redoubtable Farmer Dalby."

As they neared the farm Lucy could hear the grunting of pigs and the cackling of hens. The pigs were in pens and the birds in a hen-house in the backyard, where there were piles of rubbish. She knew then what Mrs Trippet had meant when she said she would need to hold her nose in the summer.

When Mrs Trippet called out at the open door, "Are you in, Mr Dalby?" a man's voice replied, "Come in. Why stand there?"

They went along a short passage into a kitchen where a white-haired man was putting a small log on a very small fire.

Mrs Trippet introduced Lucy to him. He gave Lucy a nod then protested as Mrs Trippet bent down and, taking some small logs from a battered tin dish, began to place them on the log he had just put on the hearth.

"How'd on there, missus, everyone ain't got a fortune like you."

"A fortune? No, I do have some money put by for a rainy day but you must be the richest farmer in these parts. You never spend money on repairs, you get folks to saw logs for you, other people bring you food and – "

"And you come and cheer me up." The old man grinned.

"I come to try and knock some sense into you," she retorted. "It's freezing. If you don't keep the place warm you'll end up under the soil before you have a chance to retire."

"Now then, Mrs Trippety-Trippet," he teased. "Stop coddling me."

"Coddling you?" She flung out her hands with a despairing gesture.

"I'm lost for words."

"Never, not you."

"You won't pay for help," she went on. "The kitchen's filthy, the ashes in the grate are piled up and I don't think the table has been washed since I gave it a scrub a week ago. You have Lucy's two brothers sawing up logs, but don't think that they're going to work for you for nothing because they're not."

"Nice young fellas," he said amiably. "Very willing."

"The longest you'll have them will be about a week and then they go to proper jobs."

Lucy was beginning to think that Mrs Trippet was being a bit hard on the old man but suddenly she saw a crafty look in his eyes.

"What d'ye mean by a proper job?"

"It's none of your business."

"It is my business, I get along fine wi' em. You keep your nose out of it. An' don't think I'll sell the farm to you if I retire."

Mrs Trippet sniffed. "I don't want it. Andy Biggs is thinking of putting his place up for sale and he's giving me the first chance of it. It's a damned sight better deal than this dump. I'll wash your dirty dishes then we're going."

"You needn't bother," he shouted.

"Oh, stop niggling. No one else will touch that sinkful. Lucy'll give me a hand."

Lucy had been so interested in the conversation taking place that she had not realised until then just how dirty and untidy the kitchen was and how shabby the old man looked.

Mrs Trippet, after filling the sink with hot water from the range boiler, put in a handful of soda and swished it around. The dishes were washed noisily, enamel plates and mugs being banged down on the bench to drain, obviously to relieve her temper.

The farmer had looked a little frail when he was seated but after saying he wasn't going to be bossed around by anyone he got up with some alacrity and stormed out.

Looking over her shoulder, Mrs Trippet said, "I can't stand folks who play on the kindness of other people." The rest of the dishes came in for a more gentle treatment.

After the dishes had been stacked away, the kitchen table scrubbed, the ashes taken out and the kitchen tidied, with Lucy's help, Mrs Trippet said, "Well, that's our good deed for the day." She took a pie from her bag and put it on the table saying, wryly, "I hope he has the strength to put it into the oven to warm." She handed Lucy her coat and Mrs Trippet was shrugging herself into her own coat when Mr Dalby came in. He was smiling.

"I've just been down to the spinney to see the lads. They say they're willing to do a bit more work for me. I'll pay them each day."

"Well, I hope you do. I've left a steak pie for you. See that the fire's built up to warm the oven. I'll call again sometime."

When they left the house Mrs Trippet gave a deep sigh.

"Why is that I come to the farm? I don't like the man, can't stand his mean ways, yet I wash his dishes, tidy his kitchen and bring him a pie for his dinner, which he never even thanked me for."

"You must like him for something. He's been a good-looking man. Still is, although he's elderly. He has quite a bearing when he walks. His clothes looked shabby, but he wasn't unshaven."

"Ah, that was because we arrived on the day he must have decided to shave. I haven't seen him without stubble for months. No, as far as I'm concerned there's nothing to like about him and we'll see the boys in the spinney and warn them not to work for the wretched Dalby without pay."

The sound of sawing was continuous and when they reached the boys in the spinney both were sweating. When Mrs Trippet admonished them for working so hard for a man who had no intention of paying them for their work, David removed his cap, rubbed his brow with a piece of rag and grinned.

"In the first place, we'll have a goodly pile for home burning. Secondly, I promise we shall be paid in kind, if not in cash."

"How?"

"Leave it with us. See you later." Both boys started sawing again and Mrs Trippet and Lucy moved away, with Mrs Trippet saying grimly, "They're fooling themselves. They'll never get the best of our *dear* Mr Dalby."

To which Lucy replied cheerfully, "You don't know my brothers. Wait and see."

Chapter Four

The boys came back from the farm that evening with a brace of rabbits and his mother asked if Mr Dalby had given them to him.

He dropped them to the floor. "No, I took them. Dalby didn't want to pay for our day's work, so I lifted the rabbits off a hook and told him we would have them in lieu, and walked out."

"Oh, it was great," William said, looking gleeful. "He shouted to us that we needn't come back again."

"It's all right, Ma." David spoke quietly. "We did a hard day's work and he had the cheek to tell us that we would be paid in kind tomorrow. Why not today?"

"It's wrong," Helen said. "You were employed by Mr Dalby."

"Ma, we were not employed by him. We were asked if we would do one or two jobs. We sawed up logs, put up a small hut to hold his potatoes then he asked us to take parcels of meat to people on the moors. *And* told us we were not to leave it until we were paid for it. That meat was heavy and snow at times went over the top of our wellingtons. The people told us that Dalby wouldn't pay us anything so we started to tell every house and cottage that we would be willing to do home repairs at a reasonable cost."

"We have a list," William said. "He had the money for the meat and had the cheek to tell us it would take it all to pay for it. That was when I took the rabbits and I have no regrets."

Mrs Trippet arrived then and she was indignant when she knew what had happened. "I knew he wouldn't pay you. But you can rest assured he'll be after you to come again."

"We've decided to do things to sell," said William. "We'll make rag books and the girls can make cushions and samplers."

"So what about all these little jobs you were going to do for the people on the moor?" Lucy demanded. "You can't just drop them."

William said, "They're just little things, we'll do them sometime. There's just a broken spring in an armchair to be mended, a kettle that leaks, putting a small pane of glass in a window and – "

"Important things to the people you said you'd help," Lucy declared.

"Lucy's right," their mother said. "You gave your word." David sighed. "All right, we'll do them."

"You know I can't help but feel sorry for the old man."

"Ma, he cheated us."

"We're not responsible for our faults."

"Oh, no." Mrs Trippet came into the discussion. "I won't accept that. Circumstances can make us cheat or steal, but if we continue to do so when our circumstances have changed then that's greed."

"No, you've got it all wrong," said Helen earnestly. "I think we've all been born with good and bad in us, but we have the power to control the bad if helped gently along."

"Look, take a man who is brutal to people. He'll

go on being brutal if no one protests. But if that man was beaten up every time he knocked other folk about he would soon use some sense."

"Oh, no, Mrs Trippet. Kindness and understanding can help people like that."

"Let me put it this way, Mrs Lingard. If you were shipwrecked on a desert island with five men, one of them brutal, which would you prefer the other four to be? Kind and gentle or aggressive?"

Helen thought about it for a moment then said, "I would choose the kind, gentle ones because there would be a chance that they might convert the brutal man."

"But if they couldn't, what then?"

"Then there would be one brutal man and four men injured and heaven help me." There was an impish look in Helen's eyes that Lucy had not seen for a long time. The boys were smiling and so was Mrs Trippet but she still persisted with her reasoning.

"Let me give you another example. Suppose you were out with the twins and a man attempted to attack them with a knife and there was a heavy stick nearby. What would you do?"

"Hit him with the stick," Helen replied promptly.

"There you are!" Mrs Trippet announced triumphantly. "It's right that brutal people should have a taste of their own medicine."

"But this man you mentioned would be mental to want to attack children. I was forced to attack him. That is a different matter."

Mrs Trippet threw up her hands. "I give up. I can see now what a problem Solomon must have had." She turned to David and William. "If you need to fight for your wages take your mother with you. She would blind them with science."

They all laughed then David said, "We'll do some of the repairs this morning. This evening we'll do the rag books and perhaps start some theatre settings."

The girls brought bags down with the silk and the velvet pieces for the cushions, which Lucy was keen on sewing and then went back up for the samplers and embroidery silks.

Lucy spent a long time laying out the designs she would do for the cushions. Deborah and Beth started sorting out the samplers which were partially started, with Deborah saying, "The more we embroider, the quicker we'll sell them."

Lucy was surprised at how many velvet pieces she stitched that day. She had a good design, plain pieces of velvet intermingling with the lovely patterned pieces.

David sniffed at the appetising smell of rabbits roasting. "I feel I could eat them both. We'll get quicker as we go along with the jobs. We'll sort out the rag books tonight and the theatres."

The rabbits were delicious and none of them felt like starting work, but Lucy, as usual, urged them on, and not only brought down a sheet to cut up for the books but also carted down cardboard boxes to make the theatres.

Once they had started there was an underlying feeling of excitement. They had found pinking shears to cut the pages of the books and Lucy, after routing around upstairs, found paints to do the words and the story. David printed excellently and William shone at the paintings.

The story they mapped out among them was of a little girl who was always running away, the story starting on the first page with "ANN RAN AWAY AGAIN" and a painting of a chubby child running down the path from her house, her face alight with pleasure.

The boys mapped out the next pages: Ann going to a field where there was a pony and to a barn where she found a kitten. From there she went into a wood and got lost. It grew dark and she was frightened. The farmer found her and took her home and Ann said she would never run away again.

The first three pages were completed and they left it there, wanting to get on with the theatres and the puppets, David saying that the girls could dress the puppets, gluing on a dress and hat. Also jackets, trousers and hats for the men.

David and William had worked out the plays they wanted and were vetted by the girls.

They started the theatres and cut puppets from plywood. They worked in the kitchen the first night but decided they would put a fire in the sitting room the following night as they needed more space.

The girls went on with their work and once the twins were in bed and asleep Helen helped them with their sewing.

On the fourth night David called them in. He hadn't allowed them to see what he and William had done before then.

The theatre was put together and there was a rare excitement. The theatre was larger than they had expected, thirty inches by fourteen. The backdrop had been painted a woodland scene and at the sides, also painted, were tiers of boxes with people sitting in them.

How lovely . . . How beautiful . . . How had they made it so real? Mrs Trippet arrived and was as enthusiastic as the rest.

They must put on a theatre show and she knew the

very one who would do it. Her friend, Mrs Merryfield, who lived at Whitby. She had a big house with an attic. They could charge twopence each. Very young children could sit on their parents' knees. A Saturday afternoon would be ideal.

The next morning she informed them that Mrs Merryfield was delighted to have the show and what about this Saturday?

David said it would be pushing it, he still had the orchestra to do, which was a strip that fitted on the front where only the heads of the men would be seen. But with luck . . .

He described how there would be a black strip of material along the back and he and William would be behind it working the puppets and mimicking them. Lucy would do the lady part. She used to be good at it when they were younger.

It was all talk after that and it was late before David said to the girls that they would have the opportunity of going to a shop in Whitby on Saturday and seeing the owner about selling the samplers.

"And the cushions," Deborah said happily.

Lucy spoke sharply. "I only have one completed and I thought of those for the big houses."

Beth agreed with this. "It's just so beautiful, it needs women who have money to buy them."

David raised his shoulders. "I shall leave that to you ladies. Any questions?"

Deborah's hand shot up. "This theatre is quite large. Will you make some smaller ones to sell?"

"Yes, they'll be about half this size." He nodded to William who brought one from a cupboard.

"Oh, yes, perfect. This is nearly finished."

"We hope to have a few more to take with us. They all fold."

Everything was ready by the Saturday morning and the party set out for Whitby with the boys pushing the handcart containing the equipment ready for the Saturday show and the twins, Tom with his "wounded" soldier and Sarah with her rag doll clutched to her. The snow had all but cleared. It lay on the higher peaks but only patches of it were on the ground.

They passed huddles of cottages, small villages and eventually came into Whitby by the moorland road and saw the sea and the ruins of St Mary's Church and those of St Hilda's Abbey.

"Why did they build them up here in this cold place?" Beth asked.

"They needed space," said David.

Lucy drew in a quick breath. "Oh that lovely smell of the sea. I remember it."

"Come along," he said, "we'll go down by the steps."

"A hundred and ninety-nine of them," Beth said cheerfully.

The steps ran in a curve around the green. "I shall go in front and hold the cart. The top ones are a bit narrower than those further down which are quite wide. You all right, Ma?"

"Yes, I'm wondering if we should carry the twins."

"No, they'll be fine." This from David who was holding the end of the cart while William had the handles.

As they went down carefully Lucy noticed the terra-cotta tiles of the houses with their whitewashed walls. She had always liked this part.

When they at last reached the bottom of the steps they turned left and walked along by the shops towards the market. There was a tempting aroma

51

of fish and chips being cooked in one of the shops. It brought a rumbling to her stomach.

There was a river, on one side of which were fishing boats. The party made for the bridge that rose over the flowing water and stopped for a moment in the centre. Ahead were two piers, one on either side of the river. They stood for a moment and looked at the big hotels and four-storeyed Georgian houses, most of which were boarding houses, as well as the other houses on the riverbank.

They walked on with Helen worrying about there being too many of them for Mrs Merryfield, but Mrs Trippet assured her cheerfully that there was plenty of room.

When a small, plump woman opened the door to them she looked as if she wanted to embrace them all. "Welcome," she cried. "Come into the kitchen and I'll make you all a cup of tea. In here." Mrs Merryfield ushered them into the big kitchen. A lovely fire blazed. They all drifted towards it. Mugs were laid out on the table, which was covered with a green plush tablecloth. There were plates of scones and iced buns. "Sit down now and I'll make the tea. Isn't it lovely having a theatre session? The attic is all laid out ready, plenty of seats. Do you know, we've sold forty-two tickets."

"Forty-two?" David said, astonished. "Why, that's wonderful."

"I advertised it in some shops. More should come and pay at the door. It's a very big attic and we've plenty of seats. Chairs and forms and stools." She laughed. "They'll have a lovely time, you'll see. I put a fire on, thought it might smoke, but it hasn't. It'll be warm when everyone is in the attic."

She made the tea then said, "Help yourself to scones and buns."

Lucy and Mrs Trippet handed them around. David and Mrs Merryfield talked about the theatre for a few minutes then she turned to the twins. "And how are you two lovely little souls? Bless you both. Have you got a bun, my loves?"

They didn't say a word until they had finished them then Tom held out his soldier. "He lost an arm in the war."

Then the rag doll was thrust out by Sarah but when Mrs Merryfield made to take it she drew it back. Sarah had nothing to say.

Mrs Merryfield kept asking questions and getting no answers and David kept looking at the clock on the wall, and in the end Mrs Trippet said, "Well, I suppose we'll have to get on with the work to be done." The boys jumped up, then the rest followed suit.

The attic was at the top of four flights of stairs. Mrs Merryfield led the way, saying she always had over twenty guests in the summer, but then this was winter. She opened the door. "There, I think the table will be big enough for the theatre."

"Just right," David said cheerfully. "Splendid."

They placed a dark plum velvet cloth on the table and the toy theatre fitted perfectly. The stage looked quite large. David said, "Now you girls can find me the dark curtain to go right across the back." It was found and nails were knocked in the walls to take it.

Smaller curtains went across the stage and the last job was to check that all the curtains moved easily.

People were beginning to arrive and neighbour greeted neighbour. They were a mixed audience, some of them well dressed, others not so well dressed, but they all socialised. There was plenty of talk and it was a job to get them quietened.

The two boys and Lucy went behind the curtain, Lucy to do the lady puppet's voice. The theatre curtains were drawn and the show began. There had been plenty of rehearsals.

The small figure of a young lady, wearing a full-skirted dress and bonnet, came on the stage and went prancing this way and that. The young lady tripped and fell and William's voice said, "Oh, Lord, hang on a minute."

There was a gale of laughter from the audience. David came from behind the curtains. He was grinning. "The lady got entangled with the strings. Forgive us. We shall try again."

The lady was up and looking about her. "Oh, fie," she said, "I have lost my way." Some of the audience were still laughing.

A puppet in a dark suit and top hat appeared. He gave her a bow and asked, in David's voice, if he could help her.

Then the hero appeared, on a horse. The young lady dropped a curtsy and apologised for having lost her way but – the hero refused to believe her. She had obviously come to meet the other man.

No matter how much she pleaded for him to understand the hero refused to listen. The other man added his pleas to hers but it made no difference.

The laughter had died now. So far it was going very well.

The next event was the hero drew a sword and tried to strike the other man. The top-hatted puppet's walking stick transformed into a sword and they began to fight, the top-hatted man dodging his opponent

54

quite cleverly. The fight went on then suddenly the nice man pulled the other man from his horse and stood over him, his sword to the horse-rider's chest.

A small boy in the audience shouted, "Kill him!"

Our hero pleaded for his life and the other man gave in. He was walking away when the hero tried to stab him in the back.

Some more children cried, "Kill him!" and now no one was laughing.

The hero then slunk away and the other man held out his hand to the young lady and they began to walk in the opposite direction.

The curtain came down to wild applause.

David, William and Lucy came from behind the curtains and bowed. They were congratulated but their mother said, in her gentle way, that she thought they ought to have put the children's plays on first.

Deborah said, "You should have seen the faces of all the children. They loved the fight. They wanted right to win. Look at Sarah and Tom, their faces are alight with excitement."

No one refuted this.

The first of the two plays to follow was based on a Cinderella story and the second was about a little lost boy who was saved by a giraffe who could see over all the hedges.

These were just as enthusiastically received and Lucy thought it was lovely of people to come and say how much they had enjoyed them, and thank them for a truly wonderful afternoon.

Lucy met a young man who said, "It must be interesting doing a show like this. I came with my landlady and her two small boys. They all enjoyed it and I did too."

The young man's eyes were a deep blue. His hair

was dark. "Do you live in Whitby?" he asked, in a rather shy way.

She told him no and explained where they lived and he said, smiling, "Well! We won't be far away. We'll be moving into the Dalby farm soon. My father went to buy it this morning."

"Oh." She looked at him with concern and he said, "What is it, what's wrong?"

"It's nothing. It was just that a friend of ours was after it and – I'm sorry, I must go and help to take the things apart."

"I'll look out for you," he called after her.

She raised a hand to acknowledge what he had said, but pushed her way through the crowd. What would Mrs Trippet have to say about the news? She would be upset. Bound to be. She had set her heart on having the farm. When Lucy found her she was beaming all over her face.

"You all did so well. They have had orders for two of the larger theatres and three or four of the smaller ones. By the way, you haven't taken the samplers to the drapery shop. Perhaps you'd better go now."

"Yes, I shall. Mrs Trippet, I wanted to tell you . . ."

Someone called to Mrs Trippet and Lucy, after waiting a moment for her, looked around for the girls. She saw them talking to two young men, saw they were enjoying themselves and left on her own.

The woman in the shop was pleasant, said she would display the testers and asked the price. Lucy told her that she would like a shilling each. This was accepted. She left, her legs feeling weak.

When she got back, most of the audience had gone. Mrs Merryfield had made a tea for her "lovely workers".

56

They talked and ate the ham and egg pies, the bilberry tarts, the rice cake and gingerbread and when they eventually said they would have to think about getting home, Mrs Merryfield replied that a friend of hers had offered them a lift. He was going in their direction and the boys could leave their handcart and collect it on another day.

The boys said, "Splendid!" and away they all went in a big van. The only ones who slept on the long journey were the twins. It was all so jolly, Lucy could not tell Mrs Trippet about Mr Dalby selling the farm.

It was the next morning that Mrs Trippet found out. She was furious. "How could he have done such a thing to me? The bastard! He knew I wanted it. I shall go and see him and tell him what I think of him." She stormed out.

She was away for a long time and when she returned she was crying.

"Mr Dalby is dead, Lucy. A horse kicked him in the stomach. He managed to tell me he sold the farm to spite me and that he had wanted me to have it."

There was to be more bad news for Mrs Trippet that day. A cable came from America to say that her son was dangerously ill and could she go over to see him.

In less than two hours she was ready to leave for Southampton and Lucy and the family did not see her before she departed. She sent a message with Polly, giving them her son's address and saying she would write to them.

The boys carried on working on the theatres and went to do the jobs at the houses they had promised to help; because of this they got further orders from other people. But they still did not have enough ready money and on the third day after Mrs Trippet's departure they took a chest of drawers from the attic and sold it in Whitby. They had to go on living, they had to eat.

Mrs Trippet had been away five days when a police constable came to the house and said he had come to arrest David and William Lingard for selling stolen property.

Lucy, her body feeling weak, said it was her mother's property they had sold. It was furniture, given to her by Mrs Trippet from the big house.

The policeman, looking uncomfortable, said he was only doing what he had been advised by Ephraim Brewster and his wife, Isabelle Brewster.

All Lucy's strength returned to her. She went in to tell her mother of this new event and, going out, she picked up a shawl, flung it around her and ran all the way to Mrs Trippet's big house and knocked on the door.

Poppy came to answer it. Her left eye was swollen. She was pushed aside by the pompous Brewster.

"And you," he said to Lucy, "can get off my premises. At once, do you hear?" He started to push her but Lucy pushed back.

"Get your dirty hands off me!" she shouted. "How dare you have my brothers accused of stealing?"

"Leave my door at once or – "

"Or what?"

He struck her across the face. The next moment his wife was there. "What the devil do you think you're playing at, you fool?" To Lucy she said, in disparaging tones, "And you, just leave, will you? We don't want any more trouble than we've already got."

Lucy, who was shivering with anger, said quietly, "You'll regret this, I promise," and, turning, walked back the way she had come.

She was crying, not because he had hit her, but because she knew there was nothing she could do against a bully like Brewster.

The police constable was coming out of the house as she approached it. He stopped and told her he had talked to her mother. He would do all he could to help. But first he would have to go and fetch the boys from the cottage they were working at, as he had been ordered. He got into a police van and drove away.

Lucy knew she had the constable's sympathy, but what good would that be? She went inside.

Her mother's face was void of colour. "Oh, Lucy," she said, "what are we to do? The minute the police know we were evicted, we'll be out of this house and into the workhouse."

Deborah was standing sobbing. Beth was as pale as her mother.

"No." Lucy's head came up. "No, I'll write to Mrs Trippet tonight. We're not going to be pushed aside any more. We had a right to do what we did."

Chapter Five

David and William had been taken to Whitby to be charged. The case would come up the following morning at ten o'clock.

The family spent a terrible day, not knowing what to do. Mrs Trippet had been their lifeline. The only ones in the house who had eaten were the twins who had had the last of the bread.

At four o'clock Lucy got up and said she was going to ask Mrs Taylor for some food.

Her mother looked up. "Who is Mrs Taylor?"

"She has a shop in her front parlour on the moors."

Helen looked at her aghast. "You can't go and ask a woman we don't know to give us food."

"David and William have done little jobs for her. She may not be willing to give tick, but if I don't ask I won't know the kind of person she is, will I?"

"You can't do that, Lucy. We've never had tick from anyone."

"Well, this will be the first time, won't it? If I can't get anything there, I'll try elsewhere."

"Lucy, you can't, you musn't do it."

But Lucy, who had put on her hat and coat, had gone.

She had gradually worked herself up into a temper. The boys would have money soon. Why should the

61

family be deprived of food because of that dreadful Ephraim Brewster? The path across the moors was turning to slush. Only the hills were still covered in snow, and where it had lain deep. It was bad walking, but she didn't care. If the woman wouldn't give her anything she had lost nothing. She found nothing beautiful about the day. She hated it. It was cold, her feet felt like lumps of ice and she wanted to cry. Not that it would help.

There was a group of houses, a few scattered around, a small school and away in the distance, a church. No one from the church had bothered to call and see if they needed help. Lucy kicked at a stone and sent it splashing into a clump of snow. What sort of life was this? Chasing across a moor to try to get some food. And what if she refused? Lucy would think no further.

Her footsteps slowed as she neared the shop. The window was lit with a small lamp. If there was a customer in would she ask? Her footsteps slowed and it was not until she drew close and there seemed to be no one in the shop that she stepped out again.

As she went into the small shop she was conscious of the strong smell of paraffin that mingled with that of onions. The onions made her conscious of her hunger. A woman came from a door at the back of the shop and smiled.

Lucy said, without preamble, "I have no money, Mrs Taylor, but I need food. I'm the sister of David and William Lingard. Can you let me have something?" She went on to tell the woman about her mother and the two small children and her two other sisters and herself who needed food.

"I've never asked such a thing before. My brothers

will be charged in the morning. I don't want to arrive in a weak state."

"Of course you don't. You can have something, Miss Lingard. We were all very sorry to hear what had happened." She had a rather gentle voice. "We all like the boys and we know they would never have stolen anything."

"The boys have money, they had sold all the rag books they made, they were making theatres. It might be a while before we get the money, but I promise you will get it."

"I know we shall. Now, what would you like?"

Lucy asked for flour and yeast to make bread, some split peas, a piece of bacon to boil and a few eggs. If that would be all right.

Mrs Taylor put them ready and after going into the back came out with an apple tart. "This is from me."

"Oh, Mrs Taylor." Lucy's eyes filled with tears. "I got all worked up coming and you've been so kind."

"If we can't help others what good are we? Tell the boys that everyone is on their side."

"I will and thank you again."

When she got back home her mother said, "I didn't expect you to get anything. I really didn't."

"We've always found kindness, even if it was just half a loaf of bread. I'll make some bread and some soup."

There were plenty of jobs that could have been done that day but it was impossible to settle down to anything. They were all in bed by nine o'clock and slept fitfully, Lucy having made up her mind that she would be up at six o'clock the following morning.

Beth had said the night before that she would go with her. Helen also got up, to make them a hot drink to warm them before they left. Neither of the girls wanted anything to eat. Helen tried to persuade them to have an egg but Lucy said they would have something to eat when they came back.

Deborah suddenly roused herself and wailed to go with them. Lucy said that Beth was coming and that was it. Nor would she be budged. She pointed out that Deborah had cried nearly the whole of the day before and added that the magistrate would not want any weepy women in court.

The morning was cold and dark and Helen came to the door with them and stressed that they keep to the main road. They promised, with Beth saying cheerfully, "Don't worry, we'll come back with some good news."

Once they were on the road they became quiet. The slush made it a trudge and once Lucy said, "It seems like twenty miles." They had walked for about half a mile when they heard a horse and cart coming. They stopped and turned eagerly. It was a farmer going to Whitby market. "Jump up," he said.

"So where are you two lasses going to at this time in the morning?" he asked, when they were seated beside him under the cart's cover.

"We're going to cour . . ." Beth began, and was given a dig in the ribs by Lucy.

"We want to try and sell some things we've been making," said Lucy. "We were told to come early."

"Ay, that's not a bad thing to be told. And what good things are you wanting to sell?" He flicked the whip gently on the back of the horse. "Come on, Hop, get up, gal. We got to get t'young ladies to the market to sell their wares."

"No, not the market." Lucy forced a laugh. "We make samplers, you know, little texts with good

64

words on them. such as, 'A stitch in time, saves nine.' Or – "

"Oh, you want the shops. Now then – "

"What do you sell?" Lucy interrupted.

Lucy learned quite a lot about the price of vegetables, what he wanted and what he got. Beth slept through it all. But Lucy was grateful for the lift. And more than grateful for the Brussels sprouts he gave her before they left him.

They had plenty of time to fill in before going to the court and they wandered around the town, exploring streets and alleyways where two or three houses put them in a little world of their own.

The woman in the shop said she had only sold two samplers. They were not things that sold every day.

Lucy told her they needed the money and the woman nodded, understanding.

Beth said, "What if the boys are kept in?"

"Don't let's think about it. We'd better find the court."

Lucy had imagined a large, impressive place. The room was quite small, and only a few people were in it when they arrived. Lucy's heart began a quick beating when she saw Ephraim Brewster arrive with an elderly man. They talked to each other, huddled together in close conversation.

Various people who worked in the court were in and out. Then David and William were brought in. They were in the charge of the constable who had arrested them. Lucy thought her brothers looked terrible. They caught sight of the girls and managed a smile. Lucy just raised a hand, acknowledging the greeting. Thank heaven her mother had made no attempt to see them. She would have made herself ill.

65

Then the magistrate appeared and everyone stood up. Lucy found she was shaking and was glad to sit down again.

The proceedings began with the magistrate asking Ephraim Brewster if enquiries had been made of Mrs Trippet to find out if it was true that she had given the young men the goods that had been sold.

Brewster stood up and said in his pompous way, "No, your worship, I had no need. The goods belonged to one of my stepsisters, and my stepmother would not have parted with any of them."

Lucy, knowing the truth, sat, her hands clenched.

She missed the magistrate's reply then saw that David was standing. He stood very straight, his head up, and she was proud of the way he replied. He explained that Mrs Trippet had given all the goods that were in the attic to his mother, to do with them as she wished.

Brewster jumped to his feet. "That's a lie! His family were evicted from their home for non-payment of rent and – "

"Sit down, Mr Brewster," declared the magistrate sternly. "I am handling the case. If I need any further questions, I shall approach you."

The magistrate turned to David. "Now, Mr Lingard. Would you please proceed to tell me how you came to be in charge of the chest of drawers you had sold."

David, quite quickly, explained why they needed the money and how he and his brother had made the toy theatre and given the show the previous afternoon and, as they needed various items to make more theatres, with his mother's permission, he had taken the chest of drawers to sell.

The magistrate asked if there was anyone in court

who would contact Mrs Trippet. Lucy stood up, said she was David and William's sister and that she had written to Mrs Trippet and was waiting for a reply.

"Good." He then said he would hold the boys at the courthouse in remand until a reply was forthcoming.

Ephraim Brewster stormed out. Lucy and Beth were able to talk to David and William for only a minute, then the boys were taken away with David calling, "Look after Ma, tell her we'll soon be home."

The girls were walking away from the court when they were approached by a tall, well-dressed man, who said, "Excuse me. May I have a word with you? I would like to help you."

They stopped and Lucy said, "Yes?"

"I thought if I had the address of Mrs Trippet I could cable her, tell her the trouble and get a reply back soon for you. My name is James Dexter."

Lucy, who had been warned about talking to strangers by her mother said, "I'm afraid I don't know you, Mr Dexter."

"This must seem strange to you, Miss Lingard, but I had a younger brother who died in prison. Not this one. He proclaimed his innocence but was ignored. After he died it was found he had been telling the truth. That is why I want to help, especially when I heard that odious Brewster trying to condemn your brothers."

Lucy was won over. She was trying to get Mrs Trippet's address from her handbag when he said, "Shall we all have a coffee? There's a place quite close."

The strong aroma of coffee made Lucy's stomach rumble.

A girl in the café led them to a corner table. James took off his hat and coat, hung them on a stand then sat down opposite them. Lucy had been taking stock of him. She guessed he would be in his early thirties. He had a strong, stern but attractive face. His dark hair was thick and his eyes were dark too.

The waitress came up to take the order. He gave her a brief smile, then asked the girls if they would like cakes with their coffee. His smile held a lot of charm and as Lucy saw the pleading look on her sister's face she said, "Yes, please."

While they waited for the coffee and cakes Dexter asked Lucy how they had reached this stage. She explained the reason why they had been evicted and how they had met Mrs Trippet and how they had done the show the day before at Mrs Merryfield's house.

"It was so awful for my brothers to be charged," Lucy said. "We didn't know what to expect. How did you know about it?"

His face was stern again. "I go to the court whenever I can to see if I can help anyone. Your brother's answers were so honest I could see his innocence and wanted to help."

The girl came with the coffee and cakes.

When the coffee had been poured Dexter asked how they would manage without the boys' help and she said, "Oh, we'll be all right. Everyone has been very kind." She told him about the farmer who had given them a lift that morning and how he had given them some Brussels sprouts.

He talked about Mrs Trippet, how he had met her twice and liked her. He spoke about his journeying abroad and while he talked Beth happily ate a piece of orange cake and a piece of fruit cake and offered nothing in the way of conversation.

Beth was about to reach for another piece of cake when Lucy kicked her foot then got up. "We must go, Mr Dexter. My mother will be waiting to know what has happened. She'll be so grateful for all you are doing for us. Beth and I thank you too."

"Oh, yes," Beth said, "they were lovely cakes."

He told them he would let them know as soon as he heard anything.

Helen was waiting at the door when the girls arrived home. They ran the last few yards and Lucy gave her a hug and said, "I think that everything will be all right." Then told her quickly of all that had happened, adding, "I feel sure we'll have David and William home in a few days' time."

"And we had some lovely cakes," Beth said.

Lucy shook her head at her and held up the paper bag. "And the farmer gave us some Brussels sprouts." She opened it to show them and saw a pound note. "Mr Dexter must have dropped it in the bag," she gasped. "He must have known I would have found it difficult to take."

"For heaven's sake let us use it," Deborah begged. "All we had yesterday was soup with some bits of bacon."

The three girls went shopping that afternoon. Lucy was glad she was able to pay the bill. There was a young man at the counter who both Deborah and Beth had their eye on. They talked and joked and Mrs Taylor came in and introduced the young man as her nephew, Fred, who was thinking of going into business in the town, when he got the hang of the business.

Mrs Taylor was having some time off herself, so Lucy left the money she owed Mrs Taylor and bought the new things she wanted.

When they were walking back and the girls were talking in an excited way about Fred, Lucy let her mind go back to James Dexter. Although she was never likely to become involved with him, it was nice to have a little daydream about him.

How wonderful to be with a person like that who would take you to dances, to the theatre, to dine. Lucy lived an evening like that in her mind, but came to earth with a bump when she realised that Deborah and Beth were arguing. She sighed. What was the use of trying to imagine living a different kind of life?

They turned a bend in the road and Lucy saw a glorious sight. The sun was going down in reds and golds and she felt choked. So much beauty in a cold, cold world.

That night they made samplers and Deborah worked as hard at them as her sisters did and Lucy found herself thinking, was it worth all the upset there had been? They had to work and go on working. Even if the boys were home they would have to do their share and it seemed to her then that they were in a groove and would never get out of it.

The next morning the boys came back. They arrived with Mr Dexter in a beautiful, chauffeur driven limousine. Lucy's hopes soared. There were cries of, "Here are the boys".

Mr Dexter got out of the car first. He wore a trilby hat, cocked slightly at an angle and had a fawn camel coat, draped around his shoulders. Then the boys stepped down. They both looked pale but came quickly to their mother and gave her a hug. "Hello, Ma," said David.

"Ma!" exclaimed William.

Helen drew away and said to Mr Dexter, her voice a little trembly, "I don't know what to say, to thank you for all you have done for the boys, Mr Dexter. Will you come in?"

"Unfortunately, I can't, Mrs Lingard. I'm off to London, on business. May I say, I hope to have the pleasure of getting to know you all in the future." His gaze was on Lucy. He then glanced at his watch. "I'm sorry, but I must leave." To the boys he said, "Think of my offer."

"We will, sir."

He raised his hat to them, got in the car and the next moment the limousine was away. They all stood until it was over the ridge then Helen said, "This moment will be in my mind for years. You must tell us all that happened."

Deborah said dreamily, "I do hope he does come back."

"He will," said David. "He promised and he's a man of his word."

They talked for ages. It had been a horrific time for both boys, not knowing what was going to happen. "That bombastic Brewster," said David. "He was responsible for all this. I feel I could kill him."

"Don't talk like that, David. Think instead of what Mr Dexter did for you both."

"Yes, I know. He offered William and I jobs. We had been talking about buildings and he asked if we could build a summerhouse at his house, Silver Acres. We said we thought we could but that we have the little jobs to do on the moors, and we do want to go on doing the rag books, the theatres – "

"If you feel you could build a summerhouse for Mr Dexter, I think you should take it. You'll have regular wages, which I was thinking last night is so important."

"Yes, I know. We have time to think about it. He's away for a week. We don't want to do gardening work forever."

Deborah wanted to know how they had got on with the police and William said, "They told us a lot of hair-raising tales. We were told one where – "

David interrupted. "They don't want to hear gruesome tales." He turned to his mother. "You look worried, Ma. You have no need to. All that is over. We'll keep on with the jobs we have."

Already Lucy found herself living in two worlds, one where in bed at night she would daydream about being dressed in a wonderful satin dress and in James Dexter's arms, dancing in a ballroom where an orchestra played softly. Other nights she would be achingly tired and crawl into bed, her fingers numb through pushing the needle through a sampler that would end up with the words, "Jesus Loves Us".

Two letters came from Mrs Trippet, the first one saying how annoyed she had been not to have remembered to have left their mother with a receipt for all the goods she had given her from the attic. The second was to say she would be home soon. Her son had made a good recovery, she just wanted to wait a little longer to make sure he was all right before she left. She would let them know when she would be sailing.

Mrs Trippet was not a good letter writer. It was the middle of February when Poppy came running over, all breathless, to say that her mistress was on her way home and that Ephraim and his wife had disappeared, taking all sorts of things from the house. "I wanted to tell t'police, but Cook won't 'ear of it. Said it's up to Mrs Trippet, so we'll just 'ave t'wait until she gets 'ome. I'll 'ave to go." She took a parcel from under her pinafore. "'Ere's a bit of cheese an' stuff. See you later." And away she went.

Lucy opened the packet and found not only cheese but pieces of ham, six kippers, some sausages and some bread, and hoped that Cook knew about them.

Her mother said the same. "I don't want Polly to get into trouble. She's been a good little soul to us. We haven't had taste of a kipper for months. We'll enjoy them."

Lucy said, "Do you think our lives will go on like this, Beth, sewing and selling a few things? I need something more."

"So do I. The boys have the best of it. They meet people. I want to meet people. But what can we do? Nothing, but sew and sew."

The one bright thing in their lives at that moment was in getting home and finding Mrs Trippet waiting to see them.

Chapter Six

There were hugs and cries of, "How are you? Don't you look well? When did you arrive back?"

Mrs Trippet flicked a tear from her eye. "My goodness, I've never had such a lovely welcome from anyone."

Even the twins were fussing around her, with an affection they had not shown to anyone else. Both were holding on to her skirt and smiling up at her. "You little loves," she said, "how good it is to be home again."

"Come along, sit down," said Helen. "I'll make us all a cup of tea and you can tell us all about it. It's so nice to have you back, and how good it is to know that your son recovered. What a worry it must have been for you having to go all that way."

"It was. When I first arrived I thought he would never get well. Joseph clung to me when he first saw me. He couldn't speak, not a word. His wife Stella is a capable girl but seemed lost. They haven't had any children. Then somehow, just gradually, he seemed to get better and better each day. Pneumonia, it was. The funny thing was, the better he got, the less he seemed to want me there. A strange lad. I never could quite understand him. A week ago he said quite boldly, 'Mother, when are you going home?'"

"He was probably worrying about you being away from home," said Helen.

"No, he didn't want me there any more. I think the two of them just wanted to be left on their own. I told them I would see about booking a cabin home but I stayed on because I still felt he wasn't quite right. Then one day I thought, he's back to normal. I'll get back home to my nice family and here I am!"

Her eyes were full of tears and Lucy said softly, "We all missed you terribly."

"Yes." She managed a smile. "Fancy leaving your only lad and complaining about the way he was. Now, tell me, about the boys. What a thing that was. I couldn't believe it when I had the cable. I sent one back straight away to James Dexter and one to the court. A nice man, James." Lucy hoped she was going to talk about him but she went on, "And when I got home about an hour ago I found that – that rotten stepbrother of mine and his wife had gone off with nearly all my china, cutlery, crystalware, paintings . . . oh, I couldn't tell you all they've stolen from me."

Lucy said, "You're not going to let them get away with it?"

"I am. I'm only too glad to be rid of the pair of them."

"But it's wrong, Mrs Trippet."

"I don't care. I hate them both and wonder now how I put up with them for so long. It's a relief to know they are out of my house."

"You're back in your own home," Helen said gently.

"And it's good to be back, I can tell you. There's Cook and little Polly Beckett. Yes, it's good to be back."

Deborah asked her if she had bought any American clothes.

"Not a thing. I enjoyed the crossings but never saw much of America. Joseph and Stella keep to themselves. I asked them if they would like to come home for a holiday but they said no. I think they're happy enough. I couldn't do more than ask them, could I?"

There was still a desolation in her voice and Beth said, "Just wait until the boys know you're back. Our David knew you would never let them down."

"Of course I wouldn't. I'm looking forward to seeing them." She paused then went on in a low voice, "Do you know who I grieved over while I was away? Mr Dalby. Have you been to the farm since the time I was there?"

Lucy told her no, but said, "Joel came to see us about the boys. I thought it was nice of him."

They talked and talked, then Mrs Trippet got up, saying she must go: Cook was going to do her some rump steak. She said she would call again and then she would bring them all a little present. They were just small gifts.

Helen said when she had gone, "It must have hurt, her son wanting to be rid of her. Men are so thoughtless."

"Not all are," Lucy said, thinking of James Dexter. How she wished she could see him again. He lived somewhere on the moorland but she had no idea where.

The boys were home late that evening and when they came in they said they had seen Polly who told them that Mrs Trippet had fallen asleep after her dinner and had just woken up a while ago. She had gone to bed.

"The best place," said David, stifling a yawn.

When Helen mentioned the kippers, both boys said they didn't want anything. They had had meals; it was everything else that had gone wrong that day. "Every little thing took three or four times what we thought it would," David said. "Then there was a tile to be put on a roof and when we got up there, we found part of the timbers were weakened in that part by the deathwatch beetle. The old couple couldn't afford a big job so we've patched it up." David sighed. "It took nearly three hours and we feel we have to try something else. William and I decided you were right, Ma, about having a steady wage coming in. We thought we would go and see Mr Dexter today."

Lucy sat up slowly, her heart increasing its beating.

William tipped coppers on the table with two sixpenny and three threepenny pieces. "That's the lot for both of us working a day."

"With your meals included."

"That's today. What about the other days when we're lucky to get a cup of weak cocoa? No, Ma, we'll try Mr Dexter. There might be a day when there won't be any jobs to be done. We have to eat. I won't go through those days again when we went a whole day without eating a thing." He swung a leg over the form. "I'm tired. I'm going to bed." He brought his other leg over. "I want to be paid for my work."

The two boys were sleeping in one of the bedrooms upstairs with only a bed in it. It was huge and would have slept six.

After they had gone Helen said, "I only hope they get a good night's sleep in it."

Lucy was a long time going to sleep that evening. She had been thinking about James Dexter when it

78

suddenly occurred to her that he might have a wife. Why had she not thought about it before? He was a very attractive man and had a lot of charm. Now she would have to wait until the boys went to Silver Acres to find out.

The fire had been banked up for the night, but now and then a flame would come through and put shadow patterns on the ceiling. She watched them for a long time and eventually drifted into sleep.

The boys had gone the next morning when Lucy roused. Her mother had seen the boys off and the fire was glowing. Another day of work, Lucy thought and what would be at the end of it? The only glow there was came from the fire. They were all quiet, apart from the twins who had taken on a new lease of life. They talked with animation about Mrs Trippet and Lucy realised how much must have gone on in their minds when they had sat sucking their thumbs, wondering about her having gone away on a boat; absorbing the little stories of the plays during the playing of the puppet-theatre. Caught up in the web of life. No one had bothered to tell them about Mrs Trippet, about the awfulness of the boys being whipped away by the police.

The boys were now back, Mrs Trippet was back and everything was going to be all right.

Sarah came over and put her arms around Lucy's legs and said, smiling up at her, "Mrs Trippet is back."

"Yes, she is." Lucy picked her up and held her close. The innocence of youth. All was right with the world because Mrs Trippet was back.

Sarah wriggled down to get her beloved Betsy.

* * *

It was a quiet morning, all of them sewing, without much being said.

Joel called about ten o'clock and Lucy was pleased to see him.

They had got to know each other whilst Mrs Trippet was away. When Lucy had mentioned her brothers' predicament he had confided in her that all was not well in the Morrison family either: his parents had not got on for a while but now they were fighting more than ever, and physically too.

"How are things going at the moment?" Lucy asked Joel when he came that morning.

"All right. Dad's giving Mum a wide berth and she's worrying herself silly, sure he's got another woman. Who would have him?"

"Some women like to be bashed about," Deborah said happily.

"Deborah, stop saying such things!" her mother scolded her.

"I think she could be right, Mrs Lingard." Joel's voice held a bitterness. "I think my mother feels she's not being the right kind of wife if my father isn't knocking her about."

Lucy said, "I know it's none of my business, but you're big, you're strong. Why don't you try and stop him?"

"Because my mother pleads with me not to interfere," he said, a bitter note in his voice. "There've been many times when I wanted to knock him down."

"I think you should."

"Lucy." Her mother spoke softly. "As you so rightly said, it's none of your business."

"I will tackle my father one of these days," Joel said grimly. "The trouble is, he hits her when I'm not around. I shall have to try and catch him at it."

80

On a sudden, brighter note he asked how they were getting on with their sewing. There was only Lucy and her mother there at the time and Lucy said, "Sometimes we're not in the mood, but it's something that has to be done."

Joel grinned. "I know that feeling." Then he added more soberly, "David and William were telling me that they were going to see Mr Dexter about working for him. I wish they were working for me, but then it's not my farm. Some day, I don't know when that will be, I'll have my own place. And now I must go. I'll see you again."

Ten minutes later Mrs Trippet arrived. She peeped around the door. "I told you I was coming back last night."

"Come in, Mrs Trippet," Helen called. "You are welcome at any time of the day or evening."

She had brought a bar of chocolate for each of them. "It's not much, just a little loving gesture."

It was a kind of chocolate they had never tasted before and said how much they appreciated it.

Mrs Trippet talked of all the things she had talked of before, but now with additions which showed the kind of people they all were, or had been – her son, her stepbrother and his wife and her daughters and their husbands – and Lucy found herself feeling sorry for this lively little woman who had suffered so much in her life. The only person who had seemed to be truly kind to her was her husband. And of those people who had died, she had grieved the most for Mr Dalby.

"I felt truly sorry for him. In a way, perhaps, I might have loved him. Not as a woman for a man but as a mother for her son. Don't ask me why. It hurt terribly not to be there for his funeral. I hope that wherever he went, he would know it."

When she had gone Helen and her daughters had just started to talk about her when the boys returned.

"Well," said David, his eyes shining. "Here are your two builder sons. We are not only going to build a summerhouse but we are to build it to our own design. What do you think about that?"

Deborah said, "I thought all summerhouses were like boxes."

"Not ours," William declared. "Not only that but we are going to play a part in doing things to the house. It's a lovely place. The house is enclosed in a park, if you know what I mean. There's a long drive up to it. It's brick-built and there are big pillars to the front door. On either side of a verandah are arches. It's four-storeyed and the windows are arched. Very unusual."

"And you saw – Mrs Dexter?" Lucy asked.

"There's no wife. At least, we haven't seen one."

The boys went to work regularly at Silver Acres. Lucy liked the evenings best, while David and William worked on painting the rag books and worked on the small theatres while she worked on her cushions and helped Deborah and Beth with the samplers.

One evening David and William came out of the sitting room into the kitchen, wanting ideas for a new storyline for the rag books.

David said, "We'll need one soon. Any ideas?"

Lucy, who especially enjoyed the evenings when they wanted ideas, said, "How about Bessie Baker, who had a cat who wore a funny hat?"

They all laughed but David wanted to know why the cat wore a funny hat.

"Because he fell downstairs and had a bump on his head. I think he's an adventurous cat. He swims, climbs mountains. His name is Clarence . . . I think."

And that was how Bessie Baker and the cat Clarence came into being.

Tom and Sarah loved the little stories, which gave them all confidence to do them. The girls put their sewing aside and cut the serrated edges of the pages while David and William did the drawings and the words.

They were then stitched up and by Saturday morning the boys took ten to the shop.

At midday a man came in a van to say they had sold out and could they have some more. More were promised for the following Tuesday but this, David said to the family, was where they would have to think about profit. They would soon be needing more special paint and also linen for the pages.

Lucy pointed out that they had plenty of coarse linen sheets they could use but said that as they were doing the sewing and missing out on their own work, what they could do with was a sewing machine.

The boys said they would ask around.

They went out and came back later with a machine in perfect working order and announced joyfully that an elderly lady they had done jobs for wanted it out of the way.

The books were finished and delivered.

Later that morning Helen said, "I think I'll lie down for a while."

This brought quick, alarmed questions from the girls.

What was wrong? Was she just tired or did she feel ill? Could they get her anything?

"It's all right," their mother said; she just had a little bit of a headache. She would open up the mattress.

Deborah and Beth rushed to do so for her and Lucy ran upstairs to get bedclothes and pillows. Oh, God, please, Lucy prayed, as she came downstairs again. Don't let anything happen to Mother.

They got her settled on the mattress and they all sat looking at her, noticing how pale she was. Within a few minutes she was asleep. Was it that she had had a bad night? Lucy wondered. Or was it something that one of them had said? Or was she doing too much work?

They all just sat watching over the most important person in the family. It had always been that way. Mrs Trippet's husband had been kind to her. Her mother had had no kindness from her husband. Lucy remembered a time when she had been small and had had a reason to hate her father: she had seen him kissing a strange woman.

That evening when the boys came home their mother was a little better. She was up but not doing anything; the girls would not allow it.

David said gently, "You'll have to take it easy, Ma, for a few days. Do you think you should have the doctor take a look at you?"

"No, there's no need. I'll be all right by tomorrow."

She had no colour in her cheeks and there were dark circles under her eyes. Lucy said, "I think we should have the doctor. We have the money. Also I think we should keep the bed downstairs."

They all thought this a good idea. Helen protested but she was overruled. The bed was made up and later

Helen agreed to go to bed, but refused the doctor. She had not been sleeping much recently, she said. Once she caught up on sleep she would be all right.

She slept during the day but after three days they agreed the doctor must be brought in. Mrs Trippet, who was looking after the twins, said she would ask her doctor. He was good.

Dr Tindell came to see Helen. He was easy to talk to and examined Helen thoroughly. He had allowed Lucy and Mrs Trippet to stay while he examined her but the other two girls had to go into the front room.

He put his stethoscope in his bag and said to Lucy, "Your mother is run down. I'll make her up some medicine, which she must take three times a day. I want her to stay in bed for four days and she's not to get up in that time. After that she can get up for half an hour and increase it every day until she feels well again. Perhaps one of you can call for the medicine."

"Yes, of course. Thank you very much, Dr Tindell."

The examination had exhausted her mother and she fell asleep as soon as the doctor had gone. Deborah and Beth came in, wanting to know what the doctor had said and Mrs Trippet said she would collect the medicine. The twins were staying with her and she had left them with Cook and Polly.

"I'll take them with me; give them some fresh air. I'll go in about half an hour. The doctor was going straight back home."

Lucy and the girls found it difficult to get down to some work, but knew it had to be done. Lucy was anxious to get on with making cushions and Deborah and Beth worked on the samplers.

Helen slept most of the four days and was up for half an hour on the fifth, then began to tremble after she had been up for twenty minutes. On the following day she stayed up an hour and a half. On the sixth day her colour began to return.

She said there was a big improvement and put it down to Mrs Trippet having given her a white of egg, whipped up and some port wine mixed with it. She managed a faint smile when she said this and the girls knew she was on the mend.

It took ten days before she was on her feet again but she was gradually getting back to her former self. She laughed with the girls one day and Beth said afterwards, "We might be able to go to the dance in the barn, not far from Mrs Taylor's shop, in two weeks' time."

"I could do with a dance," Lucy said, "I need something to wind me up. Who's running it?"

"It's just a local dance that's held every year. It's finding something to wear that bothers me," said Deborah. "None of us really has a decent dress, do we?" After a few minutes' silence Lucy said, "There were a lot of remnants in a box upstairs. We could make one each. How about it?"

Deborah said she had seen them but the pieces were not big enough. Then while they were still discussing the dresses Mrs Trippet came in. When she overheard their conversation she said, "I have a lot of dresses that used to belong to my girls. They're a bit thinner than you normally want for every day but I think they would do for dancing. There's also a big bag of shoes. They're summer shoes but you can have a look at them."

They all found a dress to suit them and a pair of shoes.

"Oh, a bit of fun at last," declared Deborah. "I can't wait. How long is it since we went dancing? Two years ago or three?"

"It was two years ago," Lucy said. "Dad was off the drink because he lost so many jobs." She pulled a face. "It wasn't long before he was back on it again, but I remember that night."

They talked about the boys who had crushes on them and to Lucy it seemed an age away.

The only boys they had a laugh with now were friends of Mrs Taylor's nephew, Fred, who came into the shop while they were there. They would give them dances.

Deborah said in a scathing way, "And I might be Directrice of a fashion house next year too."

"You could be if you made up your mind to it," David said, looking very serious. "You start a dressmaking business, you get people to work for you and one day you will say you are going to give a fashion show and you simply do it."

"You simply do it!" Deborah declared, hands at her waist. "A fat lot *he* knows about design."

"William and I have designed a summerhouse and we hope to sell many, and soon."

Deborah dismissed this with an airy wave. "You go on with your summerhouse and I shall plan my fashion house. It won't be this year, nor the next and it might not be the next but that is my aim and it shall be done."

"Good luck to you all," Lucy said, smiling.

The following week the girls began to alter the dresses they were going to wear for the dance. Lucy had chosen a flower-pattern dress with a circular skirt. Deborah had chosen a soft silk in sage green with a pleated skirt and Beth had chosen a pale blue cotton

87

two piece. The bodice fastened up to the neck and
it had a rather plain skirt. Neither Deborah or Lucy
thought it suitable but Beth liked it and that was the
important thing.

"So what are you lot slaving at?" William wanted
to know.

Lucy said, "They're dresses that have to be altered.
You two are invited to the dance and it's a good thing
that your Sunday suits are decent. And don't dare say
you can't come."

David and William grinned and told them they
would be there.

Chapter Seven

Fred Taylor and his friend Nat Johnstone showed Deborah and Beth the steps of the charleston in Mrs Taylor's shop on the moor, and the two girls came back to demonstrate it to Lucy. They all got into such a muddle they laughed helplessly and collapsed laughing.

Every now and again they would leave what they were doing and by the early evening they were quite good at the dance.

Deborah said, "We'll have to teach the boys how to do it."

But when David and William had a go at it they were excellent.

Who taught them? the girls wanted to know.

David grinned. "A maid at Silver Acres."

Their mother looked at them disapprovingly. "I don't think that Mr Dexter would approve of that."

"What the eye doesn't see the heart doesn't grieve over," William said, chuckling.

Mrs Trippet looked in, went out again and returned with a gramophone. "You need some music."

Their mother said, "Only half an hour. You all have work to do."

The gramophone was wound up and they danced to the tune, *If you knew Susie*. Lucy noticed that her mother's feet were tapping.

They had a half hour's practice with the boys for the next few nights, the boys taking turns partnering the girls. There was plenty of laughter and eventually they all flopped down, glowing with the effort.

Mrs Trippet said, "If I hadn't a bad back, I'd have a go. I used to love dancing when I was young."

"But this isn't really dancing, is it?" Helen said. "All that kicking and waving about."

"It's modern day dancing, Ma." This came from David who spoke in a sweet, reasonable tone. He went on to say that the waltz at one time was considered to be vulgar. It was the way the gentleman held the lady around the waist.

Mrs Trippet leaned forward. "And what about Queen Elizabeth the first who, in the old days, could kick higher than anyone else."

"Oh, dear," Helen said.

They all had a feeling of excitement on the night of the dance. The girls had had a bath and washed their hair and when they were ready to leave their mother said how nice they all looked, and Lucy had a feeling there was a yearning in her to come with them. She had been asked, it was a family affair, but she said her dancing days were over. She reminded David and William to take care of the girls and David promised and said they would be home before twelve.

"What a heavenly night," Lucy said softly.

It was a full moon and the evening was still. The barn was not far from Mrs Taylor's shop and they could see that lamps were lit.

It was so still that even from this distance they could hear the voices of the people making towards the barn and those inside who were tuning up their fiddles.

David said brightly, "Now, girls, you do know that you're not to go wandering off with a man in between dances."

"Yes, sir," they replied in chorus, with Deborah adding, "And we mustn't chew gum, must be nice to the older people who go and – "

"That's enough," William said, laughing. "I would say, 'enjoy yourselves', but be good and leave it at that."

There were people coming to the dance from all over the neighbourhood and by the time they reached the barn it already seemed nearly full.

They hung their coats on big nails knocked in the wall in an anteroom then went into the barn.

Older people were busy putting refreshments on tables near the wall: cakes, tarts, pies and rounds of cheese.

William grinned. "I'm looking forward to the break."

The girls had met different people in the shop, a lot of whom were there and waved at them. A girl said, smiling, "And these are your brothers. How about signing my card, sirs?"

This set a pattern for card signing. Mrs Taylor's nephew and his friends were there and they had signed the girls' cards before they had been there many minutes. And, in fact, before another ten minutes had passed their cards were almost full.

"A nice selection of men," Deborah enthused, "and not all of them farm workers."

Lucy had kept looking for Joel and saw him at last just coming in. He was wearing a grey suit and she thought he looked very smart.

"Hello, Joel. You managed to get here."

"Only just. Are the family with you? Oh, how about some dances?"

She handed him her card and he said, "Well, a popular lady. Dare I ask for two?"

"Of course."

He signed it and handed it back. By then David was waving to them and they went over to him.

There was more card signing then the menfolk started talking about farming. Lucy didn't mind. There was plenty to see.

A big man named Gimson, who was in charge of the proceedings, opened with a few words, saying it was good to see so many people there and hoped they would all enjoy themselves. Then he introduced the lady pianist, and the two men who were to play the fiddles.

There was a roar of approval.

"So take your partners for the first dance. We always begin and end, as you know, with a gentle waltz."

The little orchestra struck up with a Strauss waltz.

Fred Taylor had claimed the first dance with Lucy. He was a good dancer and he complimented her on her dancing. David danced with Deborah and William partnered Beth. Fred talked all the way through the dance but Lucy didn't really mind.

The next dance was a quick step, which she had with one of Fred's friends, then there was a lively set of lancers, taken with William, where a couple in their group caused a lot of fun by always going to the wrong partners.

By then the barn had heated up and she said she would slip outside for a few minutes to cool. William said he would go with her and she teased him, saying she hadn't any secret assignations.

92

"David told me to look after you," he replied happily. The barn had really filled up and they had to edge their way through. Quite a few people had come out and were strolling around but it was too cold to stay out without wearing a coat and they were about to go back inside when someone called, "Here's the boss's car. Didn't know he was coming tonight."

Lucy looked ahead to see a limousine approaching. She glanced quickly at William. "It looks like Mr Dexter's car."

"It does, it is." Mr Gimson, who had opened the proceedings, came to the door. And, seconds later, there was tall and elegant-looking Mr Dexter in evening dress stepping out of the car.

The two men shook hands and went inside.

Lucy said, "Did you know he was coming?"

"We weren't told anything. But I had heard he's done a lot for the people in the vicinity. In what way, I've no idea."

The men were on the platform and Mr Gimson said he knew there was no need to introduce Mr James Dexter, everyone knew him for the work he had done for the community, but Mr Dexter had come this evening to present the awards for the winners of the charleston Competition.

Everyone started to look around as though not understanding and the big man laughed.

"I didn't tell anyone about the awards because I didn't want them to go mad and be wearing themselves out practising before the night. The charleston will be the next dance and you might want to have a change of partners. Will you sign your names at this table below me, where you will be given a number for the dance? Mr and Mrs Powy will be the adjudicators. As you all know, they have won many dance competitions."

Lucy was looking at William and he said with alarm, "Don't ask me. I enjoyed fooling around at home and I'll enjoy it here but I'm not made of competition stuff."

As he was talking, Fred came up and said, "Would you like to do the charleston with me, Lucy? Beth told me you were very good."

"The girl you want is Deborah. She's as light as a feather."

"So are you and it's you I want."

"We–ll . . ."

"Then that's settled." He grinned and proffered an arm. "Shall we go and sign on?"

Some couples had already signed and were having their numbers pinned to their backs. Fred and Lucy were number twenty-one.

Fred stopped to speak to someone and Lucy began to look around for Deborah. She was unable to spot her, nor could she see Beth anywhere. She asked one of the girls she had met in the shop and she said she had seen Beth recently with a young man. Then she grinned and whispered, "She's probably nipped to the privy."

"Probably," Lucy said. The girl vanished into the crowd and Lucy was waiting for Fred when a familiar voice behind her said, "Good evening, Miss Lingard."

Her heartbeat quickened and she turned to see James Dexter.

"I hope you are going in for the competition."

"Yes, Mrs Taylor's nephew asked me to partner him."

"I'm glad, I hope you win." His smile was heart-warming.

"I was looking for your brothers. Oh, I can just see them. Will you excuse me? I hope to see you later."

She watched him edging his way through the crowd and thought how hard she had tried not to think about him. Now she would be thinking again how he had taken Beth and herself to the little café.

Her shoulder was suddenly grabbed and she jumped. Fred said, "Sorry about that. It was a friend I hadn't seen for some time. They'll be announcing the dance soon. I saw Deborah and her partner. He's an excellent dancer but the one I think will win is the chap I just met. He's Francis Cooper and his partner is Marian Stead. They've won numerous dance competitions."

The floor was being cleared and Lucy caught a momentary glance of Deborah and her partner. Deborah seemed quite cool, which was unusual for her.

Mr and Mrs Powy had a big welcome when they stepped on to the platform. Then the musicians began to play *Somebody Stole My Girl* and the dancing began.

People were shouting to the couple they wanted to win and at first the noise seemed deafening. Feet and hands were twisting, knees bending, shoulders swinging and bodies swaying. Then Lucy had a sudden feeling of lightness, as though she were dancing on air and her feet were not touching the floor. She was only vaguely aware of people leaning forward and urging them on.

Then the dance was over and the couples were trying to get their breath back while the onlookers were clapping and cheering.

There was a call for silence but it was some time before Mr Powy was able to speak. He said how much he and his wife had enjoyed the dancing and what a lot of talent there was among the dancers. Then his wife spoke. She said, "This was a great experience. Some of the dancers were as good as any I have seen in competitions in ballrooms and it has been difficult to come to a decision. We both agreed in the end, however, that Mr Nathaniel Johnstone and Miss Deborah Lingard should be the winners, and I ask that Mr James Dexter will award the prizes."

There was a burst of applause and Nat and Deborah were asked to come up and receive them. David and William were taking turns dancing Lucy up and down.

Nat and Deborah came to the platform, hand in hand, both excited, and each received a silver award of a dancing couple and an envelope.

The applause went on until Mr Powy held up his hand again. "There's more folks. There is a second prize. There are no awards for this, but we do have a present, given so generously by Mr Dexter." Mr Powy glanced at the paper in his hand and said, "The gentleman is Francis Cooper and the lady, Marian Stead."

There was more clapping then Mr Gimson announced there would be a break for supper.

They went to greet Deborah and Nat. Deborah's eyes were shining.

"I still can't take it in and look what I've got." She held up a ten pound note.

"Ten!" Lucy exclaimed.

"Yes, isn't it marvellous?"

David suddenly said, "Where's Beth?" and there was a minor panic. Beth should have been falling over herself to reach them.

They searched the barn then went outside. Joel had

followed them. "If you're looking for Beth she's with a friend of mine."

"Where?" David demanded.

"They said they wanted to go for a walk. It's all right, don't worry. He's a quiet chap, rather shy."

"They're the worst," Lucy snapped. She turned away and in the next second saw Beth coming towards them. She was hand in hand with a young man, looking up into his face.

David yelled, "Beth!" and she looked startled, then came hurrying towards them.

"What's wrong, what's happened?"

"What's happened? you ask. You do know you've been gone from us for over half an hour. Where have you been?"

"I've just been for a walk with Harold. We were talking."

"I suppose you do know that you've missed the dance competition that your sister Deborah and her partner won."

"Oh, that's marvellous."

"We were worried sick."

The young man stepped forward and apologized. "I'm at fault for keeping Beth out."

"Yes, you are," David said grimly, "*and* in future stay away from her. Do you hear?"

He grabbed Beth's hand and pulled her back into the hall.

Joel said, "I don't know why he's making all this fuss."

Lucy made no reply but went inside.

Beth had gone to hang her coat up and David was still laying down the law. Lucy said, in a low voice, "I think you've said enough, David. Don't take it out on Beth to relieve yourself of the responsibility you set yourself."

His shoulders sagged. "You're right." He turned to Beth who was near to tears. "I'm sorry. Ma told me I had to look after you girls. Come along, it's the supper break."

There were even more plates of eats on the table. There were ham and egg pies, fruit tarts, big iced cakes, lemon, chocolate and orange. There were also jugs of lemonade and two men were carrying in a barrel of beer.

With so many people talking at once it was impossible to have a quiet talk with anyone, so Lucy could only grip Beth's hand and say, "Don't worry, it's over."

Beth, near to tears, managed a smile and nodded.

It was a pity it had happened because Lucy didn't want much to eat and neither did Beth. Deborah was further along the table putting a piece of this and a piece of the other on her plate and talking all the time to the man who had partnered her.

Although Lucy tried to enjoy the rest of the evening most of the pleasure had gone. Joel had not come for his dances and he did not seem to be anywhere in the barn. Had he taken exception to her brusque attitude? Yet he should have known that she would be upset. And anyway, he ought not to have gone home without letting her know he was leaving. She had lost two dances.

By eleven o'clock she felt ready for home and suggested to David they ought not to be too late as her mother would wait up to see them back. He agreed; so did Beth and William but trying to get Deborah to go home was a very different matter, and it was only the fact of William pointing out to

Deborah that she had wept when they thought they might lose their mother that she gave in.

They said goodbye to their friends and left.

Deborah was full of talk. Imagine Nat and her winning. She would go to London with her ten pounds. Lucy could go with her. They would take the silk sheets and pillowcases to London. They could also take the cushions and lots of other things. Lucy had not had a chance to say a word and it was David who told Deborah to calm down.

"Calm down?" she exclaimed. How could she calm down when such a wonderful thing like this had happened?

"Deborah, will you listen to me for a moment?" David spoke sharply. "I don't want you to walk in at home and start talking like this. Ma's just beginning to recover – "

"But why shouldn't I? We've been planning for this, hoping to save for it and now we've no need to. We can go."

William said, "Will you shut up for a moment and listen to reason? All this has gone to your head. Ma is still not herself."

"The boys are right," Lucy said quietly. "You can save the money for the future."

"The future? You can do what you like but I am going to London."

David stopped and caught hold of her arm. "You will do as you're told. And we won't move a step from here until you agree not to mention the name London when we get home. I don't give a damn what happens to you but I do care what happens to Ma. We all do."

Deborah sighed. "All right, I won't say anything."

But within a few minutes of leaving the hall she was

talking about the dance and what a pity Mr Dexter had left, she would have loved to have had a dance with him. She was sure he would have given her one if she had asked him.

David groaned. "We can't win, can we?"

Helen was waiting up and she was delighted to hear the news.

"How wonderful for both of you."

Deborah held out the ten pounds. "I thought I might treat myself to – " She paused and they all held their breaths. She grinned and added, "To a new pair of boots." Breaths were released.

David told his mother that Mr Dexter had been asking about her and said he would call sometime.

"That was nice of him." Helen looked suddenly drained and said, "I'll hear the rest in the morning." She attempted a smile. "Bed is calling to me."

"Of course," David said, "William and I will make a start. Come on, girls, you get moving and no whispering in bed. Let Ma have a decent night's sleep."

Lucy had been sure it would be difficult to keep Deborah quiet but there was not a sound, and she thought that no doubt her sister would be going over all that had happened. Beth would probably be doing the same, as she herself was doing. It still irked her that Joel had gone home without saying a word. She had sat in the anteroom where the clothes were, not wanting them to know she hadn't a partner for two of the dances. She would certainly let him know when next she saw him.

James Dexter came into her thoughts. He had not danced with anyone. She would have to stop thinking about him. It had been obvious that he had not wanted to stay talking to her. Just a few words then he had made the excuse of seeing the boys. But James Dexter stayed in her mind. How attractive he had looked in his evening dress. He had said he would call and see her mother. Would he? He had done everything else he said he would do. Why did she have to keep thinking about him? She must be firm with herself again and put him from her thoughts.

Eventually, she drifted into sleep.

The following morning they were looking for Mrs Trippet who said she would be there after breakfast, to hear how they had fared at the dance. But it was nearly nearly eleven o'clock when she arrived and her expression was sombre.

"Joel's mother is ill. She's badly bruised; her face, her body. She says she fell downstairs but Joel is sure his father had beaten her. He has disappeared. A friend went last night to bring Joel from the dance."

Lucy said in a low voice, "And I thought he was being petty."

"I sent a telegram to Mrs Morrison's sister to ask her if she would come. She's a spinster and is someone that Mr Morrison would never allow in the house. She's a big woman and strong and is the only one Joel would have there with his mother." Mrs Trippet got up. "I've been there all night. I must have a sleep but I'll be back."

Lucy and her mother talked it over and her mother said, "I'm grateful that your father never hurt me while he was in drink."

No, Lucy thought, but there are other ways of hurting. She never knew how much her mother had known about all his women. That was something she had never discussed with them.

Mrs Trippet had asked that they should not mention Joel's mother and was surprised that no one was already talking about it. In a small place such a thing was usually rampant in a matter of an hour.

Then Mrs Trippet brought them news: Joel had heard from his father, who was full of remorse and told Joel he would make over the farm to him. He said he couldn't stand his wife any more and was going to emigrate to Australia; start a new life. If he didn't, he knew he would kill her. "Make sure," he said, "that you marry a woman with spirit."

"Joel at first, was full of anger," Mrs Trippet said. "He had tried to accept his mother's constant whining at how much her husband loved her but had now begun to see his father's reasoning. His aunt was willing to take her to live with her, but so far nothing had been settled. Joel thought his mother would never accept that his father was emigrating without her."

It was a week before Lucy went to the Morrison farm. Joel had asked her, through Mrs Trippet, to come and see him.

He looked haggard. Lucy said, "I would have come before but Mrs Trippet told me that you didn't want visitors."

"I didn't then, Lucy, but I realised I had to get down to a life of normality. Mother has gone to live with Aunt Maggie. She's a strong woman yet has tremendous patience. She's the only one who can do anything with Mother. It's only now that she's realised that my father doesn't want anything to do with her. She always thought she was the perfect wife."

"Will she stay with your aunt?"

He nodded. "Yes, she says she can't bear to live here without him." Joel paused then, reaching over, took hold of Lucy's hand. "I love you, Lucy, I longed

102

to see you. I fell in love with you the first time I saw you at the theatre show."

Lucy felt shocked. This was not the time to talk about being in love. She withdrew her hand gently.

"I'm fond of you, Joel, but I'm not in love with you."

"If we get married it will grow, I know it will."

"Married?" She stared at him. "I have commitments. My own mother needs me." She got up. "I'm afraid I must go."

Joel ran his fingers through his hair. "Forgive me, Lucy. I've rushed it. I knew a longing for you. Forget it." In the next breath he begged, "Please don't desert me."

"No, of course not."

Realising all he had gone through, she felt suddenly sorry for him. His mother having been beaten up, his father emigrating. She said, "Mrs Trippet told me that your father had made the farm over to you. You'll have a lot to do, Joel."

"Yes, that's the only good thing to come out of this. I signed the papers this morning. I shall fit the place out . . . new pens . . . oh, all sorts of things to be done."

There was a different note in his voice. A note of hope. Mrs Trippet had gone up the field to look at the ewes and the newly born lambs and came in now. "You have a good stock of lambs, Joel."

"Yes, we were kept busy." He was much brighter. "Only lost one ewe but her lamb is being suckled by a ewe who already had three little ones. I'll take you up and show you them, Lucy."

"Tomorrow," she said. "I have a lot of work on at the moment."

"That's a promise," Joel said, smiling now. "I'll look forward to seeing you both."

Mrs Trippet said when they left, "Joel looks a lot better. I got really worried about him."

"He asked me to marry him."

"No." Mrs Trippet stopped. "You didn't say yes."

"No, of course not."

"He's a nice lad is Joel. But if his mother decided to come home life would be hell for Joel."

"That wouldn't put me off if I loved him, but I don't."

"It *would* put you off," Mrs Trippet said grimly. "Mrs Morrison couldn't leave her husband alone. She fawned on him, always wanted to know what she could get for him. I can understand any man wanting to hit her. And he knows he won't be able to keep his hands off her if he stays. No, Lucy, leave it be. Joel will get interested in having the farm to look after."

Lucy left Mrs Trippet and went on home.

When she went in she heard voices and she caught her breath.

James Dexter. There was no car. When she went into the kitchen he got up, smiling. "Hello, Miss Lingard. Nice to see you again."

Deborah, looking excited, said, "Mr Dexter is going to take David and William to London."

"Do sit down again, Mr Dexter." Her mother had a graciousness that Lucy envied. He was waiting and she took off her hat and coat and sat down. He relaxed into the leather armchair.

"I was explaining to your mother that the boys have some excellent ideas on theatre workings and I was asking permission to take them to London in a week's time to meet a friend of ours, who owns some theatres."

104

Lucy said, "I thought they were building a summer-house."

"They are. I left the designing of it to them and they really astonished me with the drawings they did." He smiled. "I have another man I want them to meet." He turned to her mother. "I hope you will give your permission, Mrs Lingard."

"How could I refuse, Mr Dexter?"

"I have another favour to ask. My aunt who is here on a visit from Canada is going with me and would like Lucy to come too. We shall be staying with friends. Is this possible?"

Lucy looked up, startled, and didn't dare look at Deborah, who was so anxious to go to London. Her mother sat up.

"Well now, Mr Dexter, that is rather a different thing, The girls want to go to London sometime, but – "

Deborah interrupted, "That would fit in perfectly."

"Deborah, please." Her mother's quiet voice brought her to a halt. "I think this is something that will have to be discussed."

James Dexter said, "Of course." He was smiling and Lucy thought he had the most wonderful smile of anyone she had ever met. He got up. "I must go, I shall leave that part of it to my aunt." He shook hands with her mother and thanked her for allowing the boys to go with them, assuring her she would not regret it. He said goodbye to the girls and left.

Immediately Deborah was on to her mother to allow Lucy to go with them. "Think of the advantage; she will meet the people who are likely to buy cushions and silken sheets and pillowcases. What an opportunity. You must say yes, Mother, you must."

Helen said, "I'll give it some thought. No more for now."

A frustrated Deborah suggested the girls should go for a walk. Lucy thought she knew how she must be feeling, but Deborah, to her surprise, was all for Lucy going to London. "I am a designer," she said, "you have the business head. You will be able to bargain. You were the one who got us food on tick from Mrs Taylor. She told us how you had been so honest. She admires you very much. Now the thing is, you'll need clothes."

"Look, Deborah, we shall have to forget it."

"No." This from Beth. "I'm on Deborah's side. You are going and that is it. Mother couldn't refuse."

Deborah had it all mapped out. There was a piece of warm brown velveteen in one of the boxes upstairs. She had thought at first when she saw it that it would make curtains. "Now I think it would make a lovely coat and hat. I have a newspaper cutting of coats. There was one I particularly liked. I'll show it to you when we get back home."

By the time they did get home Deborah had Lucy's whole outfit planned. She was going to spend some of the ten pounds to get her some second-hand dresses and shoes. There was an excellent second-hand shop in Whitby. They would go the next day.

Lucy was quite prepared for her mother to refuse to allow her to go but when they got back from their walk she said, "I have to be fair, Lucy, you shall go with Mr Dexter and his aunt."

The girls were dancing around for the next minute then Deborah brought the newspaper cutting of the coats and they all got down to studying them.

"This is the one that I like," Deborah said. It had a

106

high yoke with pockets under the seams. The bottom half of the coat was plain and shaped at the sides. "There'll be pieces left to make a hat," Deborah said. "It will be in six sections, they'll taper to the crown and will have a small brim and a tassel from the centre."

They were bowled over by the quickness of her decision. She had helped to make their dresses, but had never made a coat.

A newspaper was spread out on the table and after measuring Lucy, she cut out a pattern and pinned it on her. Then she cut out the coat.

By the time the boys came home that evening it had been stitched up on the machine and they knew it was going to be a success.

The boys were jubilant. They were going to London. What about that then? They were on their way to success.

Their mother said quietly, "Many a slip between the cup and the lip."

Deborah told them triumphantly, that Lucy was going with them, and they said, "Wonderful, we should be celebrating."

It was quite a time and they would have spent the evening talking about it if Beth had not said quietly, "I suggest you all get down to some work seeing that you'll be away for two or three days in another week."

They saw the sense of it and while the boys did the rag books and Deborah, Beth and Lucy worked on the samplers, Lucy was aware it would be some time before they could dispense with the everyday things in their life.

Chapter Eight

Getting Lucy ready for London took until the Tuesday evening before they were ready to leave.

Everything that Deborah had organised was a big success.

Two dresses had been bought from the second-hand clothes shop and also a pair of brown leather shoes, glove soft.

One dress was made of heavy turquoise silk that fell in pleats and had a cowl neck. The other was a soft brown cashmere, with a pale fawn collar and piping.

The morning they were due to leave there were comments from her brothers that she looked a million dollars, and her mother said softly, "No one could pick any fault with you, Lucy."

Mrs Trippet had supplied her with a suitcase and a pale pink dressing gown. She felt she could go anywhere.

When the limousine arrived Lucy felt alarmed when she saw that James Dexter was not in the car. The woman sitting on the back seat introduced herself. "I'm Mrs Justine Dalton," she said, smiling, "James's aunt." She explained that an American business acquaintance had phoned the night before to say he had to return home the following day and asked if it was possible to see James before he left.

Mrs Dalton smiled. "So, I do hope you don't mind travelling with me."

William and David said, smiling, "It's an honour."

"Oh, yes," Lucy said, giving a small gulp at this beautiful woman in a squirrel coat and cap. She felt gauche in her presence.

Goodbyes were said and their mother and the girls waved them off.

On looking back after the journey to London, three things had impressed Lucy: Mrs Dalton having told her how lovely she looked – just like a model; the fact of having lunch on the train with waiter service; and being told about the lives of their host and hostess, Mr and Mrs Draycott.

"They are the most delightful people," she said. "They were brought up in the East End of London and knew one another from childhood. When they grew up Ernie had a job as a doorkeeper at a theatre and Grace sold programmes. They married and from then on progressed. Ernie now owns a number of theatres up and down the country and has investments in a number of companies. Their five sons are all in the theatre world. They are warm, generous people. They've been wonderful friends to James and to me. You'll all love them as soon as you meet."

She told them that after her husband died she was unable to settle and spent her life visiting relations. She would be staying one night with Ernie and Grace but going on to a cousin's the following day.

They all found her an interesting woman because she wanted to know what line the boys and Lucy were in. When they told her, she was immediately interested in William and David's drawings of summerhouses and more than interested when she

110

knew about Lucy and her sisters' plans. Lucy had brought cushions and silken sheets and pillowcases and wanted to get them from the guard's van.

They laughed and talked and Lucy felt it was worth coming just to meet Mrs Dalton.

Later she felt the thrill of coming to London for the first time. People strolling along pavements, the road jammed with traffic, buses, taxis, cars, vans, barrows. Then there were the shops along Oxford Street, hotels, restaurants. The taxi turned right before they came to Marble Arch underground and stopped at a four-storeyed house.

A maid opened the door to them, but Mr and Mrs Draycott were there in the hall to welcome them. They were both plump. Mrs Draycott's fingers were loaded with rings. She wore necklaces too and a large brooch was pinned at the neck of her dress.

She also wore a beaming smile as she greeted them. "Take your coats off. For the last half hour my husband has been looking at his watch and saying he wondered if the train was late."

Her husband, bald headed with twinkling eyes, teased her. "And weren't you at the window every five minutes, Grace, my love? I must tell you all that James arrived an hour ago. He's having a nap. Come into the sitting room and we'll have a cup of coffee." They both spoke with a slight cockney accent.

As they were about to go into the room James Dexter came down the stairs. "Well, and there you are. Did you have a good journey?" He stifled a yawn. "Travelling at midnight does not agree with me."

Mr Draycott said, "Come and have a cup of coffee."

Mrs Dalton asked James how he had got on with his American acquaintance and he said very well indeed, then added that they had both been invited to Washington.

"How nice. That will be something to look forward to."

"Mr Everett was so sorry not to see you." James turned to David and William. "You two look as fresh as if you had been having a swim." Then he said to Lucy, in soft tones, "May I say how well you look, Miss Lingard."

She murmured a thank you, aware that his gaze was still on her. "You look different," he said. "It's your hair."

Warm colour came to Lucy's cheeks. "It's loose. I usually have it tied back."

Mrs Dalton said, "James, you are embarrassing Lucy."

"Oh, I'm sorry, forgive me."

A maid came in and set out cups and saucers then poured the coffee, and Lucy was aware that he was still watching her. Then Mrs Dalton began asking about other members of the Draycott family and James turned his attention to them.

A few minutes later Mr Draycott said, "I wasn't sure whether you would want to go out this evening, but I did ask Mr Trent at the Grand to reserve us some seats. If you would like to stay in then I shall let him know."

His wife said she thought he ought to explain about the Grand.

And so Mr Draycott told them it was a theatre that had been built by the people in the East End. "It was small at first and they had turns; a comedian, sketches, singing, dancing. Later they wanted a larger theatre. They collected money and a larger theatre was later built. It still exists and is very popular. For a month they've been doing a musical and good it is too. They've had full houses for every performance. They are hoping to go on with it for a few more weeks."

Lucy and the boys said they would love to go and Mr Draycott said he knew they would enjoy the show. Mrs Draycott went to the kitchen to arrange to have dinner a little earlier.

When she came back the men and the boys were talking about architecture and she said to Lucy, "Now I want to hear about you."

Lucy told her about the items she had bought, hoping they might get orders, and when they were brought in for them to have a look at both Mrs Dalton and Mrs Draycott went into raptures about them. They both had friends who would want some. Lucy felt as if she were glowing inside.

When Lucy happened to mention the connection with the daughters of Mrs Trippet having sold the sheets and pillowcases to hotels for honeymoon suites in hotels, Mrs Draycott chuckled. "Well now, isn't that amazing. A friend of mine has a charming hotel in Stratford-upon-Avon and was talking the other day in a letter about wanting new silk sheets for their honeymoon suite."

Lucy felt that this was too good to be true. There had to be a snag somewhere.

It was just before dinner that Lucy had a chance to tell the boys how well things were going.

"That's great," declared David. "Before long we shall all be coming to London to live. Our ideas seem to be going down well."

Lucy wondered if her mother would need the country air and, would Beth want to leave? She had been mooning about a lot, her thoughts on the boy she had met at the dance. Also, could they leave Mrs Trippet who was such a good friend?

David, perhaps aware of her change of mood, said, "If things go well, both William and myself will have to be prepared to go here, there and everywhere. On the other hand it might not work out, so don't let it spoil your pleasure, Lucy."

"No, I won't." She smiled. "I'm going to enjoy myself."

They had an excellent four course dinner of the kind of food she had never tasted before. Lucy and the boys pronounced it delicious, out of this world. And Mrs Draycott beamed at them and said that was praise indeed.

The next excitement was going out to the theatre.

They went by taxi and Lucy had a tingling sensation in her stomach when she saw the bright lights and was aware of people out to enjoy themselves. And it was then that James started to pay her attention.

"Are you enjoying yourself, Lucy?" he asked.

"Yes, I am, I'm loving every minute. Everything is so different. There's a liveliness as though everyone were out for pleasure."

He smiled. "Wait until the morning when they are running hither and thither, most of them harassed, having to catch buses, trains, having to push to get on them. Not much pleasure then. I think you and the boys will enjoy the musical this evening."

"I'm sure we will. This will be my first visit to a theatre."

"The first time?" His eyebrows went up. "Quite astonishing. Is there any place in London you particularly want to see?"

"There won't be time to see everything, but I really would like to walk along the Embankment and see the

Houses of Parliament from the other side of the river. My mother said she had done this once and had never forgotten it."

"We shall do that tomorrow. Anywhere else?"

"There are so many places, but I would be quite happy to see the Houses of Parliament."

The streets were busy and Lucy could see queues standing outside the Grand. There were strings of coloured lights that flashed in and out. The taxi drew up at the stage door. There were buskers: a woman singing, the child with her holding out a bowl. A man further up the queue was playing an accordion, the tune, *Lily of Laguna*.

Mr Draycott put some silver into the bowl and James gave money to the accordionist. They then opened the stage door.

Once they were inside the theatre Lucy was caught up in the atmosphere and activity. There was constant movement beyond the doorman's cubby hole, scantily clad females were popping in and out of rooms, someone was hammering, others shouting orders.

The doorman acknowledged Mr Draycott and his wife, and said, "Good to see you again. Mr Trent's in 'is office, 'e'll be looking forward to seeing you again."

"Thanks, Charlie."

Further along the passage Mr Draycott knocked on a door and a man called, "Come in!"

The next moment the manager and Mr Draycott were embracing one another. "Ernie, it's good to see you – and Grace. How are you?" The others were introduced and Mr Trent, a tall, thin man, shook hands. He had such a grip, Lucy winced.

"It's been like a madhouse," he said. "The leading lady became ill last night, but although she's here today I don't think she's well enough. She refuses to let anyone take her place so – " He raised his shoulders. "Heaven help her if she collapses at the last minute. The curtains stuck when they pulled them last night but the workmen have put that right. I keep wondering what will go wrong next."

"Nothing will," Mr Draycott teased him. "Not now that we are all here to support you."

While they were backstage Mr Draycott was constantly besieged by one person or another. Would he come and look at this and that?

Each time he came back he said, "I told you, didn't I?"

Eventually Mr Draycott said they would get out of the way.

They stood in the wings for a while and judging by the noise people were coming into the theatre. They were rushing up the stone steps to the gallery and there was laughter and joking. Mr Draycott let Lucy see through a hole in the curtain and she saw people drifting into the stalls. Quite a lot were in evening dress.

They left then and went to the seats in the circle. Her glimpse through the hole had left her full of wonder, now seeing the size of the theatre, the red plush seats, the dark green velvet stage curtains and all the gilt around the boxes and the balconies had her full of awe. She had never imagined anything like this.

She had been to the picture palace once or twice but then they had sat in the pit with wooden tip-up seats.

They were in the front seats of the circle and she watched people coming in and looking for their seats. The programme girl came around and one was handed to Lucy but she felt unable to take her gaze from the people. She had entered a new world.

She was seated between James and Mrs Dalton and Mrs Dalton said, "I heard about the Grand Theatre when I was working here but I didn't get to see it until we knew Ernie and Grace. I was really impressed when I saw it."

Lucy was aware of James watching her and when she looked at him he smiled. "I've been watching the changing expressions on your face, Miss Lingard, and your wonder is a delight to watch."

"It's so new to me." A group of people came into the stalls and she leaned forward to watch them. "The women are so beautifully dressed, aren't they?"

"And the people in the gallery will think that *you* are beautifully dressed," he said.

She realised what he meant and she smiled. The next moment she became aware of the musicians coming in to take their places in the pit below the stage. There was a lot of activity, men tuning their instruments and getting the music placed on stands and it was some time before some lights in the theatre began to dim.

Lucy had a quick look at her programme and read that the musical was the story of a couple in love, he the son of a wealthy man and the girl from a poor family. Neither of the parents wanted their children to marry.

More lights went down and the orchestra leader raised his baton.

Then a lively tune was being played and the stage curtains were drawn apart to display a garden scene and couples in summer attire, strolling around, the ladies twirling parasols. Gradually they moved away and when the stage was empty another young couple came on, and judging by the applause it was clear they were the leading couple.

The young man had his arm around the waist of the young lady and they were looking into one another's eyes.

She said, with despair in her voice, "What are we going to do?"

The music changed and this time there was a sadness in it as he sang his reply, "They would reach for the stars."

It became a duet and Lucy was impressed with the singing. Just before the song ended the couple prepared to leave as older people came on. When they had gone a curtain came down and chorus girls came dancing on, all looking lovely in sugar-pink tights with perky little hats.

Their precision was perfect, the girls kicking above their height. At the end of the stage they turned and came back in single file holding one another by the waists, legs kicking out. Mrs Dalton whispered to Lucy, "That is to make you smile again."

Lucy could sense her pleasure. By the time the interval came the audience knew most of the story; how the parents were against the couple marrying. There had been talking, singing, with always the dancers to come in between the sad parts and Lucy was most interested, and wondering how it would all turn out.

At the interval James suggested they should go for refreshments and they went to the bar. It was busy and while they were waiting to be served James asked Lucy and the boys how they liked the show.

All three said how much they were enjoying it, with Lucy adding, fervently, "I do hope the couple can stay together."

William laughed. "I can't have that. I've fallen for Gossamer. She's so sweet and reasonable."

"And have you fallen for the leading man, Miss Lingard?" James was smiling.

"Not really. I think they should run away and get married."

"Do you want to know how it turns out?"

"No," Lucy said quickly, "it would spoil it."

The rest of the party laughed. Then James said, "What are you all having to drink?"

The women and Lucy said they would have coffee. The men had whisky and the boys decided to have the same. Lucy was glad her mother was not there.

People were milling around and the boys and Lucy were introduced to friends of the Draycotts. A young man said, "And who is this lovely young lady?"

Mr Draycott said, smiling, "Miss Lucy Lingard, our guest and not to be treated as one of your chorus girls." To Lucy he said, "This is Mr Trent's son, Gerald. A saucy rogue if ever there was one."

Gerald grinned. "Take no notice of him, Miss Lingard. I know you are a lady and shall treat you as one." He picked up Lucy's hand and kissed it. She blushed.

He wanted to know if she lived in London and she said, "No, the Yorkshire Dales. We are visiting Mr and Mrs Draycott."

When he asked for how long and she told him three days he said, "This is terrible. I want to see you again, take you out to dinner."

David turned to him. "Sorry, we have a very tight schedule."

"Not one evening?" Gerald was practically pleading.

119

Lucy said, "It really is impossible, Mr Trent. We are here on business." She was surprised at how glibly the words had come.

"I must see you again. You must give me your address and I shall come and see you."

Mr Draycott took over. "Some other time, Gerald, some other time. We are all busy on a project."

Gerald grinned and told Lucy he would see her later. Mr Draycott said, "I've never known Gerald be so serious about a young lady before, Miss Lingard. He's really smitten by you."

David said, eyeing Lucy, "Do you know something, sister? You *are* very attractive."

William called, "Lucy, your coffee is getting cold."

She went to drink it and was thoughtful. James said, smiling, "I think the show has got you in its grip. Don't take it too seriously."

She inclined her head. "I could imagine it would be something that happens in real life."

"And I would imagine the parents would pay the girl off to stay away from their son."

"How cruel."

James said, "The show is make-believe, a fairy story. Don't let yourself be carried away by it."

"If I don't let myself get carried away by it then I won't enjoy it. So why come to see it?"

He raised his shoulders. "It's not meant to be taken seriously."

"Of course it is."

They all joined in the discussion and all were on Lucy's side, then the bell rang to let them know that the show would be starting again. James laughed as they all got up.

"Now wasn't that interesting?"

"Oh, James, you really are terrible," declared Mrs

Draycott. "I had forgotten for a moment how you like to tease us."

They were all laughing, apart from Lucy, who had a feeling that he had been serious when he started the discussion.

James laid a hand on her shoulder. "Enjoy the rest of the show," he said softly.

"Oh, I shall, there's no doubt about that."

And she did enjoy it. There were the high tones, the amusing ones in the show. Some of the scenes were excellent. She particularly liked the scene of the fair. There was so much colour, so many lovely dresses and the singing was excellent.

There was also the sadness that the parents would not give in to the couple marrying.

Then the young man tells the girl they will run away and get married and Lucy thought, at last.

But the girl refuses, giving her reasons. If there was conflict between the parents there could be no happiness. She loved her parents. He said that he loved his too, but had they to be sacrificed because of their stubbornness? No, they would get married.

The girl still refuses. If they had children they would never have the love of grandparents. It would make for unhappiness.

The scene ended with them parting.

But in the background the wealthy couple had overheard the conversation and realised how sensible the girl was and what a sacrifice she was making.

The last scene was the wedding, with wedding bells ringing and Lucy, emotional, had a job controlling her tears.

The leading couple were brought back again and again and Mr Trent came outside the curtains and made a little speech, saying how delighted they all were at the response. And thanked them.

"Oh, wasn't it beautiful?" Mrs Draycott said, wiping away a tear as they started to move. "I could see it all over again."

James agreed it was a good show but Lucy was unable to accept that he was sincere.

They went to see Mr Trent and he took them to meet the leading man and leading lady, but they looked so much older than when they were on the stage and there was no warmth in them.

Not long afterwards they left and the last person she noticed was Gerald Trent, his arms around a chorus girl, laughing as he rocked her from side to side.

Lucy wondered if James Dexter been right when he said that the show was a make-believe, a fairy story? It had seemed so real.

Chapter Nine

When Lucy came downstairs for breakfast she found that Mrs Dalton had already left to visit her cousin, but would be back to return home with them.

The menfolk had all been for a walk and had just returned.

Lucy said, "You make me feel lazy."

"Not at all," James said, "You are on holiday."

Mrs Draycott smiled. "Come along, breakfast's ready."

During breakfast her husband decided, after discussion, to take the boys to an architect friend of his, which prompted James to say to Lucy, "And what shall we do? You haven't been shopping yet."

"I would like to look in shop windows, if you don't mind. Deborah wants me to jot down the latest styles and prices."

"Why look in windows? Go inside and browse around."

"Oh, no," declared Lucy. "I might want to buy something and I can't afford it. I shall be quite happy viewing the windows. That is," she added hastily, "if you don't mind."

"Not at all. Perhaps afterwards we can do some more sightseeing?"

Lucy felt a stir of excitement. "That would be lovely."

Mr Draycott was to go by car with the boys but James and Lucy were to go by taxi. Mrs Draycott said, "Now don't hurry back, see all you can. Why don't you all have lunch in town and do some more sightseeing." She laughed. "As long as you get back for dinner."

"It's a deal," declared James.

Arrangements were made to meet at Buckingham Palace at eleven o'clock and they parted, the boys looking as excited as Lucy felt.

The morning was bright but cold and again James fussed a little over Lucy. She really ought to have brought a scarf. Perhaps they could buy one.

She chuckled. "Oh no, you won't get me into a shop that way."

He said softly, "Do you know, I've never known a woman who only looked in shop windows? Take my aunt. Whenever she goes shopping she comes out of every one laden with parcels."

"Perhaps I shall be able to do that some day," Lucy said lightly.

"I hope so."

After a moment's hesitation Lucy said, "If there is time I *would* like to go to the Embankment and see the House of Commons."

"Yes, of course, there'll be plenty of time. I suggest we go there first."

Lucy gave a little shiver, but it was a shiver of pleasure.

She was enchanted with everything she saw. They crossed the river so they could view the Houses of Parliament and she thought it beautiful. The sun sparkled on the water and seemed to be reflected in the windows of the Houses of Parliament.

"What wonderful architecture. Sometimes I hear David and William describe a church, or a building and I can see now why they've become so interested. From this side the windows look like lace."

They stopped and James talked about the bridges. He explained how the Tower Bridge opened to allow bigger ships through and then began to talk about the old London Bridge, describing how there had been shops on them. He added wryly, "And where heads were hung, to warn people that their heads might be hung there too if they thieved."

"How awful."

"It was the only way to keep some sanity. People starved to death, as many do now. On one side the poverty-stricken and the other side the wealthy."

They stopped to watch the water traffic, busy little tugs, fruit boats going to the docks to sell to the steamers, lighters, coal ships. There was all the noise, the melancholy note of the tugs, the deep throated funnel of ships, the shouts of men, Big Ben striking the hour of ten.

When James asked her suddenly if she would like to live in London she stood, hesitant for a moment, then said, "I'm not quite sure. There seems to be so much more of interest in the city."

"On the surface, yes."

"Don't you like London?"

"Yes I do, just as I like New York for certain things and Rome, Paris, Buenos Aires, Amsterdam. I could go on and on."

She would have liked to have known what line of business he was in, but did not want him to think her forward. She said, speaking lightly, "You travel a lot. You could write a book."

"I've started one. What I need is a secretary to type it."

"I can't type," she said, still keeping her voice light. "But I could soon learn."

"Good. We shall have to discuss it, won't we?" His smile was enchanting. "Now then, shall we stroll along here for a while?" It was so pleasant, she could have gone on walking all morning, but they went back over the bridge again and looked more closely at the Houses of Parliament.

From a distance Lucy had seen the magnificence, the various towers, seen the intricacies of the work on the towers. Close to, she saw so much more, each tower a poem, the walls spoken of by James as "symmetry penned in stone – " He showed her where there would be a light when the House of Commons was sitting late.

They spent so much time there that they had to hurry to meet Mr Draycott and the boys outside the gates of Buckingham Palace.

Mr Draycott said that everything had gone well. His friend was impressed with the boys' work.

There were quite a few visitors standing around and Lucy asked James if they were waiting for the King and Queen to come out.

He had just told her that there were always people hoping to see them when suddenly there was a surge forward and in seconds a crowd was there at the railings, cheering. Lucy felt choked with emotion as she saw a carriage coming towards the gates. The gates were opened and she was lucky enough to have a wonderful view of the King and Queen as the carriage came through, King George inclining his head, acknowledging the waiting people and Queen Mary, raising her hand. Lucy waved but was unable to cheer. William was shouting with the others, "God bless you both." David was solemn. When the carriage began to go up the Mall, Lucy began to look for Mr Draycott and James saw them on the fringe of the crowd. She drew a finger across her eyes and made her way to them.

"Did you see them? Oh, what a special, special treat. Wait until I tell Mother and the girls. To think of all the times I might have come and never seen them."

An elderly woman standing close said, "I must have come a dozen times and at last I've see them. I can now die happy."

People round about laughed.

Mr Draycott suggested they have lunch then they could do whatever they wished. James explained they would do some window viewing first then meet again later to see more buildings, and Mr Draycott and the boys agreed.

It was after six when they all got back and Lucy and her two brothers talked Mrs Draycott to death. Lucy got in first with telling her about seeing the King and Queen. She said, her eyes shining, "Wait until I tell the family. They'll never believe it!"

James said solemnly, "And Lucy did an enormous amount of drawings of coats and dresses in shop windows to give to her sister who wants to have a salon in Paris eventually."

"Oh," Mrs Draycott said, "I have numerous cuttings from newspapers of bargains. I'll give them to you."

William said, "And we had a wonderful day too and went to Mr Draycott's friend the architect . . ."

Mrs Draycott said, "Do you think we could go

to using Christian names? It seems so stilted using surnames and we are good friends."

She was smiling broadly and Lucy thought what wonderful people they were.

After dinner, friends called unexpectedly but Lucy and the boys thought it a most interesting evening. Later, Lucy suspected they had been invited for her and her brothers' sake, Mrs Hall managing an emporium and her husband having a gardeners' shop and selling summerhouses.

Not only did Mrs Hall buy a cushion and a set of silken sheets and pillowcases, with a promise to give an order later, but Mr Hall wanted to see all the drawings of summerhouses the boys had done.

After they had gone the boys danced around and Lucy gave Grace a hug and said, "Oh, thanks a lot. How good you've both been to us."

"It's a pleasure for us," Ernie said, beaming.

Lucy felt sad that this was their last night. Her bedroom was bathed in a warm glow from the fire, shadows danced on the walls. She sat on the bed and tears welled. Why was she weeping? It had all been so wonderful. Was it because she had fallen in love with James and nothing could come of it? She gave a little sniff. She should be grateful. They had had a wonderful time. They were going back with orders and they really had had a wonderful time.

The musical of the night before had gone to her head. James had stated his feelings. He had said the show was make-believe, a fairy story. With a sigh she got to her feet and finished undressing. Tomorrow she would be back home. There would be all the fun of telling them about their trip. She had seen the King and Queen. That was really worthwhile. She had written a quick card to them the evening before and posted it that morning. The girls would be full of excitement.

But nothing could take away that feeling of sadness that her dream was over. Tomorrow they would be going home and slogging away again. She knew she was in love with James, but he was not for her.

Still, what was she grumbling about. What a wonderful time it had been. It would be something to remember for the rest of her life.

The following morning they were all solemn when Lucy came down and Grace told her that Justine, James's aunt would not be going back with them. She had been taken to hospital to have an operation for appendicitis.

"Appendicitis!" Lucy exclaimed.

"Yes," said James, "and unfortunately, I won't be coming back with you all. I must stay to see to Justine. The boys will look after you and I shall phone my chauffeur and tell him to meet you at the station."

The boys told him there was no need, but he insisted. William and David had a week's holiday and wanted to spend the next few days at least at home, so it was best they should go now.

Ernie and Grace saw them off at the station and Grace slipped a bag of small parcels into her arms. "It's sandwiches and flasks and small presents from us and James."

Lucy gave Ernie and Grace a hug. "You've both been so kind. We can't thank you enough."

"We've loved having you and we hope you will be able to come again."

"So do we," Lucy and her brothers said softly.

There were tears in the eyes of all of them when the train drew out of the station.

It seemed a much longer journey going back but

there was the chauffeur waiting at the end of the journey to take them home.

In the car the boys and Lucy decided they would not say anything about Mrs Dalton until the following day. They would say that James and his aunt had been delayed. They did not want to spoil the homecoming.

It was dark but as they approached the house the door opened and in the light from the lamp she saw her mother and Deborah and Beth with Mrs Trippet. They were all waving.

The next minute they were all hugging one another and all talking at the same time.

A fire of logs and coal blazed in the grate. The twins were not there and Mrs Trippet said they were sleeping at her house; they thought it would have been too noisy when they were all back.

Helen then asked where Mr Dexter was and they told their little story. By then Deborah was itching to know if they had sold the sheets and cushions and also, if Lucy had her drawings.

Mrs Trippet said "For heaven's sake let them get their coats off."

Lucy, smiling, said to Deborah, "Yes, to both questions," and took off her coat.

"Wow! Isn't that great, and how did you like London?"

"We had an absolutely wonderful time, but it's so lovely to get back home."

"And lovely to have you all back home," her mother said softly.

"How are you feeling, Ma?" This from David. "I think you're looking better."

"Yes, I am. But for goodness sake forget about me

and tell these girls what they want to know or they'll explode."

Mrs Trippet said, "I've made some tea, we'll sit down and have it and you can tell us all about it."

So they sat around the fire and Lucy told them first about seeing the King and Queen. "Just imagine being there at that moment. Oh, I shall never forget it."

Beth wanted to know if they were wearing their crowns and Lucy said no, the King, she thought, was wearing a naval hat and the Queen had worn a grey satin toque and a dress to match and had a fur stole around her shoulders. "I was so close to her, it was just so wonderful. The dress had a high neck and – "

Deborah said, "You can tell us about that later, I want to know how many orders you have for the silk sheets and cushions and did you go around the shops?"

Lucy showed her the orders they had taken and said there could be more. "I've looked in the windows of dozens of shops and got ideas for clothes for you." Then she said, "I think the boys must have their turn. They had some wonderful experiences."

They told their story and David said, "What Mr Draycott doesn't know about theatres and architecture isn't worth knowing."

The talk went on and it was some time before Lucy decided to tell them about Mrs Dalton.

"Oh, dear," said Helen. "What a shame. I do hope she'll be all right."

"They have the money to deal with it," William said, in a slightly aggressive tone.

"So what are you moaning about?" David asked. "You've had your share these past three days, having

131

wonderful food, going to the best theatre. You've been cosseted."

"All right, all right, I didn't mean anything. Honest, I didn't."

Helen said, "I think you are all tired. Lucy, go upstairs and see what we've been doing to two of the bedrooms up there."

They all went up and Lucy said, "It's warmer up here."

"There are fires on in the boys' room and in yours."

Mrs Trippet said, "We got two men to bring in the carpet and the furniture."

There was a wardrobe, a dressing table and a chest of drawers. A green carpet partly covered the floor and chintz curtains had been hung at the windows and to pull across the bottom of the bed.

"It's lovely," Lucy declared, "I can't believe it."

Deborah said, "Beth and I slept in the bed last night and we had a lovely night's sleep. No draughts at all."

Lucy had been thinking on the train how they could improve the house and here was a start.

Mrs Trippet said she must go, but told them, with a grin that she would be there after breakfast the next morning.

The family went downstairs and after Mrs Trippet had gone they sat talking until quite late.

Their mother was still sleeping downstairs, and when the girls went up for bed they were all ready for sleep too.

It was cold and wet the following morning and, dressing quickly, the three girls went downstairs to the warm kitchen. David and William had had their breakfasts and were ready to leave. Their mother was still sleeping. "And be quiet," David said in a low voice, "Ma still needs extra rest."

London, to Lucy, seemed suddenly remote, her experiences like a dream.

Deborah said she was sure she would not be able to do any work that day. Why couldn't they have a day off?

It was Mrs Trippet arriving with the twins at half past nine who roused them from their apathy. The twins came running in and they were picked up and given a hug. Lucy said, "We have a little present each for you," and gave them chocolate and a Union Jack flag.

They were more energetic than usual and Lucy guessed it was having the dog to play with and being with people who were not sitting most of the day doing embroidery. Why shouldn't they too have a day off to do as they pleased, and just laze?

But Mrs Trippet had other ideas. They would go to the farm and see Joel. He had done a lot of work while they had been away and had made quite a few improvements.

Lucy was willing but Deborah thought she would like a brisk walk over the moors and Beth decided to go with her. Lucy guessed that their respective boyfriends would be involved somewhere.

So the children and Lucy and Mrs Trippet set out to go to the Morrison farm.

The rain had stopped but the morning was dull. The twins ran on ahead and Lucy took the opportunity of asking about Joel's father.

"He's sailing for Australia in two weeks' time. He won't even go and see his wife before he leaves. He said he couldn't stand the upset. Joel says he looks terrible. Ill. So, how did you get on with Mr Dexter?"

133

"Oh, very well. He was kind to me." She changed the subject by asking if Mrs Morrison seemed settled with her sister and and Mrs Trippet said, as settled as she would ever be. When she started to ask her where James had taken her, Lucy mentioned the children, how animated they were.

"They need something to do, Lucy, instead of sitting all day, sucking their thumbs. I know you all have work to do and I know you do take them out for a walk, but I'm happy to be with them."

"Mrs Trippet, do you think that Mother is improving?"

"There's no doubt about that. Yesterday morning she was quite bright and kept saying she wondered what time you would be home. Last night she was looking tired but one expected that with all the excitement. She's tough, she's had to be. She'll be all right soon, don't worry."

Joel was up in the top field with a man who Mrs Trippet said was the vet. He had come to castrate the lambs, but judging by all the noise they could hear, they were having trouble. They were trying to separate the three lambs and get the ewe in the next field out of the way but she was grunting and pushing the vet away. Joel called, "Hang on a minute, I'll get a sack." He found one and pulled it over the ewe's head. He eased the animal into the next field and locked the gate. "You can get on with the lambs now," he said.

It was a bloodless castration and the job was done in no time at all. The ewe was released and the moment she was back with her family, the three of them climbed all over their mother, who had laid down so that they could feed.

The twins had been eyeing all this solemnly and

Mrs Trippet said, "Well, that's another job over, isn't it?"

Joel came to them. "Hello, ladies. Did you have a good time in London, Lucy? Go on over to the farm and put the kettle on. Mr Corrie will want a cup. We'll be with you in a minute."

The kitchen was spotless, the table scrubbed to a whiteness and there was a cosy fire burning. Lucy asked, "Joel's work?" and Mrs Trippet said, "Yes. And he cooks his own food. There's never a plate or a cup out of place."

Joel came in alone; Mr Corey had to attend to a cow at the next farm. Mrs Trippet poured the tea and he held his mug between both hands, watching Lucy as she talked about going to two theatres.

After a while Lucy said, "I'm sorry, I've been talking too much. You have work to do."

"No, you go on. I was up at four o'clock this morning." He grinned. "I think I deserve a rest, don't you?"

Mrs Trippet said, "He puts in too many hours in a day. He'll kill himself."

"Not me, I thrive on work." He held out his hands to the twins and when they came to him he put one on each knee. "You have your Union Jacks. You can wave them at me, can't you?"

Tom nodded. "Lucy saw the King and Queen."

"She did? My, she was lucky, wasn't she?" Joel looked at Lucy. "And did you approve?"

"Oh, yes, it was wonderful."

Sarah said, "I am going to be an actress."

The grown-ups exchanged glances. Joel said to Sarah, "And do you want to sing and dance?"

"No, I want to talk."

"Oh, you want to be a proper actress and be in a play?"

She nodded vigorously. Lucy raised her shoulders. "She must have got the idea when I was talking about *Reach for the Stars*. There are no actresses in our family. At least not that I know of."

Mr Davies came in to see if Joel wanted anything doing and Joel put the children down and got to his feet.

"Yes, there is, I have a list as long as my arm."

As he talked to the old man Lucy watched Joel and thought what a strong, good-looking man he was. He set Mr Davies to do a job and when he had gone he said, "Before you go you must see what I've been doing."

Lucy said, "Show us now."

He was eager to show them the new pigstyes and chicken runs he had made and talked with enthusiasm of all the improvements he wanted to make. Lucy laughed, "You're like our David and William; you'll always have a job to do. They'll never starve."

"Neither will I. I want a big farm and I'll get it."

When they left he walked to the gate. "It's good to see you all, come again and make it soon."

"We will," Mrs Trippet said.

As soon as the gate was closed behind him he was away striding up the field. Lucy said softly, "I'm glad he seems over the worst."

"As long as his mother stays where she is he'll be all right," Mrs Trippet said grimly.

Tom and Sarah ran on ahead as the family walked back home. As she watched them laughing and squealing, Lucy thought how good it was that the simple things in life could be so pleasing.

136

Chapter Ten

William was sitting reading an old newspaper that evening when David reminded him dryly that they not only had a theatre to finish that night but had some rag books to finish. Then he said to Lucy, "We'll soon be ready for a new story."

"I have one ready," she said, smiling. "It's about a little girl whose mother is ill and she has to look after the younger children. Her reward is winning the school prize for her work."

"Oh, the mums will love that. Come on, William, we must get started."

No sooner had the boys gone into the sitting room than there was a knock at the front door.

Lucy went to answer it and was surprised to see Harold Trenton, who had met Beth at the dance.

He was quietly spoken and said he had called to ask permission to take Beth for a walk.

David came out of the sitting room and said, "No." Their mother called softly, "Ask the gentleman to come in, Lucy."

He introduced himself, said he had met Beth at the dance and would like to get to know her better.

Helen, obviously impressed with his quiet manner said, "Yes of course," and told Beth to get her coat and hat. Then she said to the young man, "Only half an hour. It's getting late."

Harold smiled. "Half an hour it shall be, Mrs Lingard."

Beth went off happily with him, but David was furious.

"We know nothing about him. Anything could happen."

"Obviously you don't trust Beth," his mother retorted.

He calmed down. "I know human nature, Ma. Beth is besotted with him. I only want what is best for her."

"I know, David." His mother gripped his arm. "Beth will be all right. Don't worry. They will be back before they realise it. It's time the girls were courting."

Deborah and Lucy stared at her, no doubt remembering a time when Mrs Trippet had been there and her mother had said that young girls rushed into marriage too soon.

Mrs Trippet had replied wryly that some *had* to rush into marriage. She had married a man twenty years older. He was a good man, very kind, but there had really been no fun.

Deborah had said, "It depends on the man, doesn't it? Some are old at forty, but other men could be old at twenty."

William teased her, wanting to know where she had got all her experience from and added that she made it sound as if she had had dozens of men.

"And who says I haven't?" Deborah replied pertly.

Lucy knew there had not been many men in Deborah's life and, thinking of Beth and her boyfriend, wondered if she and Deborah were not just a little bit envious.

It didn't seem long before Beth and Harold returned. He left her at the door and she came in, dreamy eyed. "The sky is studded with stars."

Helen got up. "Now you are back, I think I shall have an early night. We were late going to bed last night."

"I think I am ready for bed too," Beth said, still dreamy eyed.

Deborah stifled a yawn. "I'm ready too."

William suddenly said, "Oh, I have something for you." He took a piece of paper from his pocket and handed it to Lucy. "I found this in one of the boxes. It should interest you both."

It was a list of country hotels where Mrs Trippet's daughters had sold silk sheets and pillowcases. Lucy handed it to Deborah.

"Well, this is great, isn't it? We must write to them all. It gives the prices charged by shops. Quite a big difference."

There was a lot of work ahead of them. There were the cushions and sheets and pillowcases to do that had been ordered by Mrs Draycott and Mrs Dalton. There would be no more lazing from now on.

Helen offered to write to the address at Stratford-upon-Avon that Mrs Draycott had told Lucy about and also to those hotels on the list that the boys had found.

David said that their mother was not yet well enough to write letters and Helen was annoyed. "It takes little energy, please don't make out that I'm useless."

David apologised and the letters got written and posted.

Three days later James was home. He told the

boys to tell Lucy that Mrs Dalton was a lot better, but was staying on another week longer. He also said to tell her that Mr and Mrs Draycott had so much enjoyed their company and hoped they would come again soon.

It had been an exhausting day's work. Lucy's spirits were lifted by the news.

"How nice of them, what wonderful people they were."

William said, smiling, "I think that our boss is very fond of you, Lucy. He's always talking about you."

Deborah's head went up. "What nonsense. Why should you think that he feels something special towards Lucy?"

"Because you haven't heard James's voice when he mentions her name," William replied with a broad grin. "So sort of, caressing."

"Stop it," exclaimed Lucy. "You shouldn't make things up like that."

"I'm not." William was serious. "David and I knew when we were in London that he was fond of you."

Their mother said quietly, "Well, seeing that nothing will come of it, I don't think there's any more to be said."

After tea the boys went into the sitting room and once the dishes were washed the girls sat down to their sewing again.

Before Lucy started she had another look at the list that William had given her then said, "Look at the date of these orders. They were paid for a year after they were delivered. That won't do for us."

Deborah said, "We shall have to state that owing to it being necessary to keep sheets circulating we shall need to be paid for them a month after delivery. They can't grumble at that."

"They will, if they've been allowed to pay a year later. We'll wait and see what reply we get."

The boys had been working on the theatres and had not gone to bed until four o'clock. Their mother got on to them when they were lighting the fire.

"This has to stop. You must have been neglecting your work at Mr Dexter's and it's certainly not fair that he pays you money for a job you are both neglecting."

The boys gave in but David said he was not going to stop making the theatres and the rag books. They needed the extra money.

The following morning there was a dense fog that Lucy found depressing. "All the joy of the holiday is gone," she said.

"We can talk about London," said Deborah, "it will make us feel good, or we can talk about Paris, where I am aiming for."

Lucy had to restrain herself from saying that she would never get there.

What did cheer her, however, was having letters from the hotels that her mother had written to, most of them saying that payment would be made a month after the sheets had been delivered. Some more said that payment would be made three months after delivery.

"We'll accept them all," said Deborah, "but they'll have to take their turn. We can't do more than we're doing."

When Mrs Trippet heard of the rush she offered to stitch up some of the hexagons.

Helen said when she knew, "How lucky I am to have Mrs Trippet for a friend."

Lucy looked up from her embroidery. "I would say we all were."

"It's different for me. In time David and William will be going to London. So will Deborah. Beth will get married and you – "

Her mother stopped and when she made no further comment Lucy said, "And what will I do, Mother?"

"Well, I should imagine in time that you will be – married to Mr Dexter."

"Oh, you do?" Lucy felt anger rising. "So we shall all walk out and leave you and the twins on your own. You must have a dreadful opinion of us all."

"No, no, I didn't mean that. You all have jobs to do. I don't want to keep you back."

"But you really did think we would all leave home?"

There was a silence for a moment then she said quietly, "You've all gone money mad. At first it was making rag books and samplers, now it's silk sheets, and you all talk of big money. David was saying he wanted to build up a big bank balance."

"Where is the fault in that? We've been struggling since we were children. And Mother," Lucy's voice dropped, "we appreciate all you did for us. No mother has been more loved than you."

"I know. I don't mean to be unkind. Perhaps it is that my body is at a low ebb. I worry in case I should go suddenly."

"Of course you won't." Lucy got up and put her arms around her. "The doctor said it would take time. You've been doing some of the jobs. You'll have to stop. Take it easy."

Tears welled in her mother's eyes. "I hate to be a trouble to any of you."

Lucy assured her she was no trouble, begged her to accept it and not to blame any of them if they wanted money. "The money is for all of us, to give us a better

142

home. I have no doubt the boys will go away but you can rest assured they would send money home."

Helen wiped her eyes. "Please don't tell the others how I've behaved. I feel ashamed now that I said anything. I think it was feeling so unwell; it magnifies things."

"I know. Now try and stop worrying."

They talked about general things for a while then Helen said, a little hesitantly, "Mrs Dalton did tell me that Mr Dexter was very fond of you."

"Mrs Draycott told me he was fond of the family."

"Mrs Dalton stressed it and said he would like to marry you."

Lucy felt her stomach muscles tighten. She said in a light tone, "He hasn't even hinted at such a thing and I'm certainly not ready for marriage." She paused. "I have too much to do."

"I wonder where you will end up?" her mother said softly.

Lucy wondered too.

The three girls were all working on the orders the following day when James called.

Deborah said in a low voice, "We musn't stop working," but of course they did. James said he had just called for a few minutes to tell them that his aunt had improved a great deal, but she would not be at Silver Acres until she was nearly ready to return home and she wondered if the sheet and pillowcase sets would be ready, also the cushions.

"When will your aunt be leaving?" Lucy asked.

"In about another fortnight."

Lucy gave a small sigh of relief. "Oh, yes, we shall be done by then. We are all working on them now."

He gave them a winning smile. "Then I must go and let you all get on with them."

Helen said quickly. "Oh, no, please. I haven't had time to thank you for taking Lucy and the boys to London. They had a wonderful time. They still talk about it."

"Well, that's nice to know." He became serious. "I feel that the boys are going to be in demand too. They have a wonderful gift."

Helen asked a little cautiously if it would mean them leaving home.

"I think it would, Mrs Lingard, but then it is their future."

"Yes, I do realise that. Thank you for telling me, Mr Dexter. I think the boys would have found it difficult to tell me."

He gave her a smile. "Probably, but you would not be neglected." He looked at the watch on his wrist. "And now I must go. I have a meeting. I shall let you know when my aunt is home."

When he had gone Deborah said cheerfully, "It was inevitable that the boys would progress. I hope I progress as quickly."

Helen made no remark. She straightened her back as though to face what had to come but Lucy saw the pain in her eyes.

Chapter Eleven

James and his aunt arrived home two weeks later.

The boys were full of it when they came home in the evening.

Mrs Dalton still looked really poorly. She had had a very bad time. Taken all the life out of her. She had said she would call and see them when she had recovered. Mr Dexter had said he would most likely call the next day.

Lucy had started working on the cushions, leaving Deborah and Beth to do the samplers, secretly thinking they would fetch more money if they could get them to the big houses. Actually, she enjoyed this work; she had to fashion the designs and before she started she could see the various patterns she would make. The two that had been made were both the same pattern, a diamond in the centre and lines leading from them. Lucy made four and each was different. Her mother and the girls were entranced by them, but neither of the girls wanted to make them. That was Lucy's work.

It was a week before James and Mrs Dalton called, a day when Deborah and Beth had gone shopping at Mrs Taylor's, taking the twins with them.

Lucy felt a weakness in her limbs when she saw the limousine draw up. Lucy concentrated on Mrs Dalton while James talked to her mother.

Lucy said, "You look well, Mrs Dalton."

"I'm fine now, but I have had a wretched time. I would not like to go over that again."

She went into details about the problem of the operation and Lucy realised she was uncomfortable in her manner. Why? She had been all right in London when they were all together. Was she conscious of being in poorer surroundings?

James was talking to her mother. He was quite at ease as he said, "We are sorry not to have called earlier. There was so much to catch up on when we returned. A massive mail to deal with and I realised how free I had been while I was away."

He looked immaculate in grey, the dampness of the morning making his hair curl slightly. He talked about Mr and Mrs Draycott and said what wonderful people they were.

Mrs Dalton was also in grey, a loose coat, edged all the way around with a matching-coloured fur. The hat was made of the same material as the coat, a small, head-hugging hat. She said they must come and see the summerhouse when it was finished. David and William had been working so hard on it while they had been away.

Helen said, "I thought the boys might have been taking it easy while you were away and scolded them."

"Oh, no, it was undeserved." Mrs Dalton was gushing now. "They are just so clever."

James turned to Lucy. "And how are you getting on with your work, Miss Lingard? The boys were telling me that you are working long hours to fulfil your orders."

"Some days it goes well and other days not so well, but I just accept it."

James said grimly, "I know that feeling."

The next moment Lucy realised he was studying her and colour came to her face.

Helen enquired if they would take a cup of tea or coffee and James got up. "No, but thank you for asking. We must be going. I have to see some business acquaintances at a conference in Scarborough this afternoon."

Mrs Dalton suddenly said, "Oh, the cushions and the sheets. I nearly forgot them. I'm sure there will be orders for more."

Lucy went into the sitting room to fetch them and after Mrs Dalton had settled the bill she said, "Don't forget, you and the family must come to Silver Acres and see the summerhouse when it's finished." She got up. "And now we must go. James has an appointment."

James smiled. "I shall let them know the date."

After they had gone Deborah and Beth came in and were annoyed that they had missed them. Deborah said, "Well, anyway, she got a bargain. I would have charged her more. They can afford it."

Their mother came in and Lucy told her quietly not to say any more about money, her mother didn't like it.

James had given the boys an afternoon off and when they started to go on about the money, Lucy shut them up. They took the hint and talked about the summerhouse. They would be pleased with it.

They then set to work on the rag books and later concentrated on the theatres.

Lucy felt a sense of unrest. Why had Mrs Dalton been uneasy? Several times she thought of going to ask the boys but each time she heard them talking quietly and did not want to intrude. Deborah and

Beth had been for their afternoon walk and had come back and were whispering together.

Lucy, for the first time, felt excluded, something she had never experienced before.

After a while Lucy got up, put on her hat and coat and left without saying a word. When she glanced back they were staring at one another as though to say, what's the matter with her?

She walked quickly at first, going in the direction of Mrs Taylor's shop. It was not that she wanted to buy anything and after a while she slowed down. How stupidly she was behaving, like a spoiled child. Her sisters had not been taking any notice of her but why should it feel necessary to leave?

She sat on a slab of stone in the wall where one could get over to the next field and she thought of her mother who had spent time alone when they were younger and had jobs in the evenings. Never once had she complained of feeling neglected.

Lucy looked around her, at the mountains in the distance, at the rocky road and the whitewashed cottages, settled at random. Away at a further distance was a lone farmhouse high on the steep side of a hill. There were no other buildings anywhere near it. It didn't even have a proper road leading to it, just a few narrow paths. All they bought would have to be carried up to it. How did they exist? From what she had heard a large family lived there.

And, no doubt, working and helping one another.

Lucy got up and began to retrace her steps. She should be working now. How childishly she had behaved.

When she went into the kitchen both girls got up and came to her, asking her if anything was wrong.

148

She smiled. "No, it was just a mood, but it's all over now."

Within minutes they were chatting away.

For the next few days it was all work. Two orders had come in for two pairs of sheets and four pillowcases. Her mother and Mrs Trippet helped, her mother saying she needed something to do. The sheets and pillowcases had to be hand-stitched, the top and bottom hems herringboned and then the broader hems embroidered.

The boys had had to abandon the making of the theatres for the time being, but they had managed to keep on with the rag books, but David now gave the impression that if their summerhouse was popular they would abandon making the rag books and theatres.

Sometimes they would come out of the sitting room when Mrs Trippet called in the evening and they would do their share of tale telling.

One evening, Mrs Trippet was telling them tales of her life when she was younger and worked in the racing stables.

"A rum lot they were," she said. "Men and horses. If a horse took a dislike to a jockey she would trap him against a wall and lean on him and he just couldn't get free. The boss would come and tell the horse to get off and that horse would look at the boss with such disdain you just had to laugh."

She told them about a time she had put a pound on a horse at a hundred to one. "It won and I jumped about shrieking and laughing so much that I fell and broke both my ankles. It was a lovely day!"

They all laughed.

Lucy suddenly thought that part of the pleasure in

working on the sheets and pillowcases was that the proprietors of each hotel sent the money by return. Money was important, no matter what her mother thought.

William slapped his knees and got up. "Well, we must get on with our work if we want to go places."

"Where were you thinking of going?" Helen asked quietly.

"Well now, Ma, we don't rightly know. But if we make a success of our summerhouses we're sure to be moving around."

David got up too. "But I can tell you this, Ma, we shall always be coming home to you."

Lucy could already see the pain in her mother's eyes and knew that she and the girls too would miss the boys.

The following evening David and William were telling them about a family from London who were staying with James and who had two beautiful daughters. They teased one another about which one they would ask out.

Deborah said, "You wouldn't stand a chance, not with the handsome James there."

"James has his eye on our Lucy," David said.

Lucy was annoyed. "I wish you wouldn't say such a thing."

"Because it's true. That's right, William, it is, isn't it?"

"He's always talking about you. Never fails to mention you at least twice a day." William was smiling broadly.

"Oh, stop it."

"They really are lovely girls." David was serious now. "I don't think I've ever seen any more attractive than they are."

Beth asked their names and both boys said in unison, "Rosalind and Stephanie."

"What beautiful names," Deborah said. "I wish I had been called Rosalind."

"Shall we have our tea?" their mother said quietly. No more mention was made of the girls.

That evening in bed Lucy wondered if James did like her. It wasn't the first time that the boys had mentioned his taking notice of her.

She slipped into a daydream. He was the wonderful sheikh in *The Desert Song*, a musical which Mrs Draycott had told her about but which they had not been able to see. He had picked up the girl and carried her into his wonderful tent in the desert, his robe flying away behind him. He was an impatient man, wanting to make passionate love to her. His lips were on hers, demanding when Deborah said in a whisper, "Nat wants me to go to a dance with him on Saturday evening at Whitby. He told me that Fred wants you to come. He'll ask you."

Lucy, annoyed at having her dreaming spoilt, said, "I don't want to go. I like Fred, but I don't want to get into a habit of going out with him."

"Oh, say yes, Lucy. Mother won't let me go alone with Nat."

Lucy, to quieten her, said she would think about it, but it was impossible to dream any more. Tent and sheikh and sand had vanished.

The following morning, having run out of salt she decided to go to Mrs Taylor's shop to get some. Fred might be there and she could tell him it was impossible for her to go Whitby with him, she had too much work to do.

Fred was behind the counter, his face one broad

grin. "Did Deborah ask you to come with us on Saturday night to the dance at Whitby?"

She told him yes, but added she wouldn't be able to go, she had too much work to do.

Mrs Taylor came in from the back, smiling. "Forget work. It's not a competition night. Just the ordinary dance. It doesn't start until eight o'clock. Nat's taking the car. Have a treat."

They both got on to her and in the end she gave in. "All right. I'll go." She forced a smile. "In the meantime I need some salt. I want to make some bread for our starving family."

They chatted for a while and Fred said that Nat would pick up Deborah and Lucy about half past seven and Lucy left.

Why had she been so weak! She enjoyed dancing but although she liked Fred she was not in love with him.

She had only gone a short distance along the road when a car drew up with a squeal of brakes, the door opened and Mrs Dalton called, "Hello, Lucy. I was coming to see you. Jump in."

Lucy said, "I can't believe it, I thought you had left to go to London for another fortnight."

"I changed my mind. I'm going to some friends in Edinburgh."

She drove a short distance then stopped at the side of the road. "It was you I wanted to see, Lucy. Our guests are out for the day. They've gone along the coast." She gave a brief smile. "The girls' mama wants husbands for them."

Lucy found herself saying lightly, "And is Mr Dexter going to take one for his fiancée?"

"He can't. He – " She paused. "He has a wife."

The sudden shock had Lucy feeling as though a

lead weight had dropped in her stomach. When she found her voice she said, "I didn't know. No one told me."

"Few people know. I shall try and explain the situation. James and Imogen met last year while they were in Cairo. She's a shy, rather gentle person. Her parents died when she was young and she had been brought up by two maiden aunts." She paused then went on. "James and Imogen were married in Cairo but, unfortunately – the marriage was never consummated."

Lucy looked up quickly. "Never?"

"No. James goes to see her every few months but she can't bring herself to . . . It's so sad. She had known nothing at all about sex. Her aunts had never told her. James had made up his mind the last time he saw her that it would have to end. He wants children. It doesn't mean that he will have to have a divorce. The marriage is simply annulled." She paused again.

"Then he met you, Lucy, and fell in love with you, but I don't feel it would be a suitable marriage. You do understand." Mrs Dalton spoke earnestly.

"Of course. It would never work. We're of a different class."

"You're a lovely girl, Lucy, you have a very nice family, it's just – James has to entertain, he mixes with moneyed people."

"I know, please don't feel embarrassed. I really do understand. If Mr Dexter had asked me to marry him I would have refused."

"You would?" Mrs Dalton kissed her gently on the cheek. "Thanks, Lucy. I'll take you home but I won't stay. I can come again."

"No, I'll get out. I don't get much exercise. I need a walk."

"Are you sure?" She looked worried.

"Yes." Lucy managed a smile. "Off you go."

Mrs Dalton swung the car around and Lucy waved until the car was out of sight and felt glad it had gone. She felt she wanted to hide herself in a deep forest.

Why had James not told her about having a wife? But then, why should he? It must have been humiliating to him to have his young bride reject him. She felt suddenly sorry for him. What a thing to happen. Why didn't his wife know about sex? Older girls at school had told her everything they could. At the time Lucy had thought it all rather dreadful, unclean. But when she had fallen in love and she was daydreaming she had thought it must be the most wonderful thing on earth. She had longed to be made love to.

Lucy decided not to mention anything to her mother and the girls about James's marriage, but with a need to talk to someone about it she went out to meet Mrs Trippet the following morning when she saw her coming towards the house.

"There's something I want to talk to you about, Mrs Trippet."

"Then let's go into the spinney."

They seated themselves on a big tree that had become uprooted in a gale one evening and so Lucy told her the tale of James Dexter.

"I knew you were in love with him," she said.

Lucy stared at her, "I've been so careful."

"It was after you had come back from London and were talking about him. Your eyes had taken on a gentle look, a dreaming, and I thought to myself, she's in love with him."

"I shall have to be more careful in future."

Mrs Trippet sniffed. "I'm bothered about Mrs Dalton. Who does she want for her nephew? One of the girls who's staying with them?"

"Oh, no, she has his welfare at heart. They are quite young."

"They come from moneyed people. They're gentry."

"No." Lucy would still not accept it and Mrs Trippet said, "Your mother speaks and act like a lady and when you went to London you looked like one."

Mrs Trippet pointed out gently to Lucy that Joel still loved her but she said, as she always did, that she liked Joel a lot but was not in love with him.

The end result of this change in Lucy's life was that she became determined to "become a lady". She would not wear a shabby dress again. She would learn to speak French. There was a Children's Encyclopaedia among the stuff that had been moved from the attic, which had some lessons in it. She would get Deborah to work with her. It would be a start, they could perhaps pick up a second-hand, more advanced book later.

Deborah was delighted: Lucy's decision brought a shine to her eyes. She would have to know French to put on a fashion show, wouldn't she?

Lucy just smiled to herself, feeling that she was starting a new life.

Beth at first was persuaded to learn with them, but after a few days became half-hearted about it.

Helen had made little comment initially but the evening Beth said she wanted to give it up said, "Learning to speak French could be an advantage to your children. I would have liked all of you to speak French in the hope that you would all go to university. The opportunity was not there, but I did make you all do your homework and was pleased with your good marks."

Beth stuck it out for a few more days then dropped out. She really had no wish to speak French, and if her children wanted to learn it later, wel' it was up to them.

Lucy had sorted out some better dresses and wore her hair loose. Her mother marvelled at the change.

When James called one morning, a week later, he remarked on it.

"I like you with your hair loose," he said. Then after a moment added, "Could we have a short walk together?"

Lucy went tense and was about to say she was too busy when her mother said, "It will do you good, Lucy, you've been working too many hours recently."

She went to get her hat and coat and, feeling uncomfortable, she left with him. James suggested they walk on the moor.

It was a while before James said, "I had to talk to you, Lucy. Justine told me she had told you I was married. She said she had explained everything. I would rather have told you myself. I fell in love with you from the first day of meeting you. I want to see Imogen and explain that this situation has to end."

Lucy glanced at him. "And if she happens to say she wants to live with you, what then?"

"I shall tell her it's too late. I've waited nearly eighteen months for her to give in. I still like her but I'm not in love with her the way I am with you. Never have been. I think I was taken with her shyness, her gentleness. Justine said that she knew you would never marry me and I want to know why."

"I'm not in your class."

"Class is of no importance."

"Oh, but it is, Mr Dexter. You entertain moneyed people. You have wealthy friends. You must know it wouldn't work."

"It would, Lucy, I'm not bothered about wealthy friends. We could live abroad. Lead a quiet life."

For a brief moment there had been a slight hope but his last remark had finished it.

"I'm sorry, but I don't want to live a quiet life. I want to enjoy it and it just would not work as it stands now. If you don't mind I would like to go back home."

He gave in and she knew he was hurt.

They walked back in silence and she wondered in a rather desperate way if she was doing the right thing. Had he felt humiliated for the second time? Rich man asks poor girl to marry him and she turns him down.

When they were near the house she stopped. "Mr Dexter. I'm sorry. It just wouldn't work out."

"If you say so." His voice was cold. "If you will excuse me." He raised his hat and walked away. His car was not in sight. Lucy walked on and into the house, regretting her brusque manner.

Everything stopped as she went into the kitchen and all eyes were on her, even the twins.

She took off her hat and coat then said, "You may as well know that Mr Dexter has asked me to marry him. I turned him down." She made no mention of his previous marriage.

"In heaven's name why?" Deborah demanded. "We could all be living in a big house, have plenty to eat and I could have had my dress shop in London."

157

"So, you think I should have married to provide you with a wealthy living? How despicable can you get?"

Deborah's face flushed red. "We're a family. You have to think of us."

Their mother said, "That's enough. Lucy has only herself to consider. There's no reason why she should marry Mr Dexter if she doesn't want to. It's her life, not ours. Remember that."

The boys spent the whole night in the sitting room. It was one of the quietest nights in the house that Lucy could remember. And at the end of it Lucy knew she had done the right thing.

Neither Deborah nor Beth spoke a word when they were in bed.

The following morning, however, was the same as any other morning, the girls coming down to the kitchen to get dressed in front of the fire and debating what they were going to work on that morning.

Lucy did come to one conclusion that day. She was going to study hard learning French. Deborah would work with her.

Two months were to pass before Lucy saw James Dexter again. They had not seen Mrs Dalton at all. They thought she had gone away.

Lucy had gone to the dance that Saturday night when Fred had asked her, but although she had enjoyed the dancing, she did not enjoy Fred trying to get his hand under her skirt that night on the way home in the back of the car.

He did humbly apologise to her when he saw her next and said it was the drink he had had, but although she accepted his apology she would not go again. Deborah was seeing Nat every Saturday evening and

158

Beth was seeing Harold. Beth lived in a dream world, wanting only to be married.

She had been well warned by her mother what could happen if she allowed Harold to make love to her. Beth had said, in a slightly shocked way, that Harold was not like that.

Deborah had also been warned but said that no man would have his way with her, she had a career to get on with. Lucy knew she was living for the day when she would have enough money saved to go to London and open her dressmaking business.

When Lucy said that she was no longer going to wear shabby dresses Deborah had said, "Good, I'll make you some new ones from the remnants in the box upstairs. I shall make you another coat."

A curb had to be put on her. There were sheets and pillowcases to be made, they needed the money. Making the coat could come later. But Deborah was forever scribbling down ideas and she certainly had a flair for design.

March had come in with torrential rain and a waterfall on the moor had rushed from a high level, splashed on to a level below and drummed into a pool. Lucy had thought it quite spectacular.

There was little rain in April and bluebells covered the floor of the spinney and there were clusters of purple and yellow crocuses in hollows and under trees. Lucy had a feeling of wellbeing, and her mother's health had improved tremendously. She joined in the French lessons and was glad when Tom and Sarah began to repeat certain words and often a phrase. They had a lot of fun over the lessons.

Helen and Mrs Trippet started to turn the soil at the back of the house and start a kitchen garden. When the boys protested at their mother working,

Helen said happily that she would certainly not do it if she did not feel like it.

To Lucy they were strange times. It was as if the formation of a new life was taking place. Now and again James would come into her mind, but when he did she put him firmly aside.

One day when she was out on the moor the air was crystal clear. It was possible to see at a great distance and a dark blotch at the foot of a mountain turned out to be a forest. She stood staring at it and it was as though it had just appeared. How wonderful. One day, when she had time, she must walk to it.

The boys seldom mentioned James except perhaps to say he had gone abroad for a week. But one evening when they came in they were excited as they announced that the summerhouse was finished and they were all to go and see it on the following Monday.

Alfred, the chauffeur, would bring the car.

Lucy thought that her mother would make an excuse but right away she said that the outing would be most interesting. Helen, who had seldom gone anywhere, had a decent black dress and a hat and coat. Deborah said she must lighten the outfit up and laid pale pink roses on the brim of the hat and, finding extra pieces of pink chiffon, made a long thin scarf with a fringe to wear with the coat.

Lucy was to wear the clothes she had worn for London. Deborah wore a dark grey coat and cloche hat with a big white bow at the side and and a white collar on the coat. Beth wore a light navy coat, hat and dress and accepted a handmade bunch of lily of the valley pinned to her coat.

And, as Mrs Trippet said, no one would have known that they didn't come from gentry stock.

They debated about taking the children for such a special occasion but the boys thought it wise to leave them with Mrs Trippet as no one had mentioned bringing Sarah and Tom. They were quite happy to be playing with Rags and to see Poppy and Cook.

Lucy was surprised that James had asked them to his house, seeing that he had not been near them since the day she had refused to consider marrying him, and although she told herself she was not worried about going, her stomach had been trembling all morning.

The car would be there at three o'clock and they were all ready to leave when it pulled up. It was a beautiful, clear day and Lucy showed them the forest in the distance. The windows were lowered and the scent of bluebells came from the spinney. Lucy felt strangely at peace. If James was cold with her it would perhaps be just as well.

The house was hidden from them by a thick belt of trees that surrounded the estate. The gates were open and they went up a long drive and stopped at this big, lovely house. Wide stone steps went up to a terrace.

James was waiting for them at the foot of the steps with David and William. Both boys were trying to control their excitement. James was courteous, helping the ladies out and saying what a pleasure it was to have them all there.

What surprised Lucy was her feelings for James. Her heart gave a lurch when she first saw him and she felt she wanted to go to him and tell him she was sorry. She did love him.

He motioned them up the stone steps to the terrace. They would have some tea and cakes first then see the summerhouse later. It was at the back of the house.

Lucy stared around her, impressed with the hall.

161

When she had asked the boys about the house they had said it was all right. David had remarked on the hall; it had suits of armour and there were portraits of descendants of the Dexter family on the walls.

What neither of them had mentioned were the beautiful paintings on the ceiling, all of them framed in carved white stucco. Nor had they mentioned the wide staircase that rose from the centre of the hall or the shallow marble steps that branched at the first floor into landings where the portraits hung. She just had time to catch sight of the suits of armour before they were led to the drawing room.

And there her attention was captured by two middle-aged men who were sitting talking on armchairs near a beautiful, low table. When they came in, both men rose and James introduced them as Mr Alvin Kermit and Mr Andrew Hamilton. Then he introduced the family, name by name.

The men bowed slightly and Mr Kermit said to Helen, "Allow me to congratulate you, Mrs Lingard, on having two sons with such excellent minds."

Helen acknowledged the compliment with a gracious inclination of her head and said how kind of them to say so.

The tea was brought in and James said, "Perhaps you could put your proposition while we eat."

While Mr Kermit picked at a piece of excellent fruit cake he told them how Mr Hamilton worked with him in his garden furniture business and how Mr Dexter had spoken to him of David and William's work. Mr Kermit leaned forward. "And we would like to have your sons come and work for us, Mrs Lingard. It would give them a good opportunity to gain experience of a business."

"I think so too, Mr Kermit. If this is what David and William want, I have no objection."

David and William wore broad smiles. Lucy noticed that her mother's expression had not changed but she sensed her ache of loss.

"How splendid," Mr Kermit said, also smiling broadly, and Mr Hamilton told her how delighted he was too.

Lucy had learned that young men were not often paid when serving an apprenticeship. Would her brothers earn a wage? If not, would her mother allow them to go? Their wages were badly needed.

Chapter Twelve

After tea they all went out to the back where the summerhouse was, and Lucy became aware of the vastness of the estate. Gardens, lawns, and beyond, hidden by trees, was more land which could be vegetable gardens.

They walked along a path, turned a corner and there was the summerhouse. It brought a gasp from Deborah.

"My goodness! How beautiful."

All the men were smiling with approval of the two boys' work.

It was round and domed, the dome being carved into patterns. The windows had tiny diamond panes and there was a wide front door that led to a rose arbour.

Helen said she must admit she had never seen such a summerhouse.

David remarked they hoped it was the first of its kind.

Mr Hamilton brought some papers from his pocket and showed them drawings that the boys had done for some other summerhouses. There was an oval one with trellis work on it and trellis round the edge of the roof. One was in the shape of a small castle with turrets and the turrets held bowls of food and water for birds. Ladders, which seemed to be part of the decoration, pulled out at the sides and tilted so that the bowls could be easily filled with food and water every day without much trouble. There was an oblong summerhouse with a glass roof with a tower on top which was beautifully carved. At each corner of the roof were hanging baskets.

"They're so unusual," Lucy said.

"That is why we are interested in having your brothers with our firm." This from Mr Hamilton who spoke gently.

Lucy liked Mr Hamilton. He was tall and slender and looked younger than his colleague. There were laughter lines at the corners of his grey eyes.

They talked of summerhouses and follies. What would David and William achieve when planning follies? It was so interesting having two young men who thought in the same way. Customers had so many different tastes. They had many to cater for. Both boys had said they had drawings of many more summerhouses at home.

Lucy wondered when they had done the drawings. They had never even mentioned them.

When they walked back she found James by her side and, taking the plunge, she said, "Mr Dexter, I understand that when young men are apprenticed they work for a year or two or more without pay. Will this be the case with my brothers? I ask because we need money to live."

"They will be paid a decent wage. They are to be taken into the firm. I would have thought you would have understood this."

How cold his words were. Lucy's cheeks burned. Why had she asked him?

She excused herself and dropped behind to be with the girls.

Deborah whispered with a sly grin, "Have you seen who Mother is with? Take a quick glance behind you."

Helen had Mr Hamilton by her side and seemed to be having an interesting conversation. She heard them both laugh.

And I am cast aside, Lucy thought. It was all right for James Dexter. He had never wanted for money, never known starvation. From now on she would put him out of her mind.

The family certainly had plenty to talk about when they got home, their mother having shushed Deborah when she wanted to talk in the car.

Deborah said, as she was taking off her hat and coat, "I want to know if the boys have signed anything. It's all too quick for me."

"No, they haven't." Her mother looked thoughtful. "I spoke to Mr Dexter about it. He said that Mr Kermit and Mr Hamilton were bona fide people. The boys would receive a wage, it's a good wage and would be paid every month. They will have rooms in Mr Hamilton's house. I don't like them going away, but knew it had to come sometime. What I don't like is the boys having been so secretive about it. They must have known this was coming up."

"I don't think they did," said Lucy. "I imagine it was a surprise to them."

Beth wanted to know why Mrs Dalton had disappeared and not returned again. Deborah said to Lucy, "No one would ever have guessed that he had asked you to marry him, would they? Stayed right away from you."

Helen got up. "I think we should decide what we're going to have for dinner this evening."

A voice from the doorway called, "Fish!" Mrs Trippet came in smiling. "And plenty of it. Polly went to the market this morning and a fisherman handed her this great big packet. She said she didn't know him but her face was as red as a poppy. She can go again." She got a dish out of the cupboard and tipped the fish from its wrappings. "There you are, all from the last catch, the man said. Some sole, haddocks, cod and herrings. Now then, how did you get on at Mr Dexter's?"

They talked so much that they were rushing to get the chips done for the boys coming home.

The boys were still all excitement and it was some time before their mother had the chance to ask if they knew about going to London.

"No, of course not." This from David. "We would have been exploding with the news. Mr Dexter arranged it. We're just so lucky." Then he sat on the arm of his mother's chair. "Look, Ma, I know this must have been a bit of a shock for you, but you won't lose out on it. William and I will send you money every month."

"One of these days I shall have to accept that you will all be married."

"That's not for ages and we're not going to talk about it."

Lucy asked when they would be leaving and was told in about two weeks' time.

"In two weeks?" Helen whispered the words.

The two weeks seemed to flash by. The morning they were due to leave, Mr James came in the car to see them to the station. Their mother insisted there would be no tears. It was not easy but they were all shouting good wishes and no tears were shed. The nice part of the day was that

James came back to say they were on their way. If there was anything they wanted to know they had only to ask.

The unpleasant part for Lucy was that he gave her a passing glance and she thought, God help me, I still love him.

The house seemed so empty after the boys had gone and it was only the fact that they both sent letters that kept them going. Deborah kept on building up a stock of samplers and David and William were still painting the rag books and sending them back home to be stitched.

The girls had been so busy they had dropped their French lessons and Lucy decided it was time to take them up again. Deborah said they needed a proper book; the Children's Encyclopaedia they had found in the attic was too young for them.

Lucy pointed out it was a good way of learning the language because they were getting the feel of the different way the French formed their sentences. She gave an example.

"Take this. 'Nous sommes fatiguées de jouer.' We would say in English, 'We are tired of playing.' The French are actually saying, 'We are tired of *to* play.'"

"Which is daft," Deborah said.

Lucy looked up. "You have to learn the French way of speaking if you intend to learn the language. Here is another example. 'Tout le monde se depêche.' To us that would be translated as, 'Everyone is hurrying.' In French it would be, 'All the world itself hurries.' It's no use saying what we want in broken English. We must speak in *perfect* French."

Deborah sighed. "All right, we'll learn it your way."

169

As time passed their knowledge of the language increased. They had many laughs when the twins would say, "Oui, mam'selle." Or, "La dame." Then they came out with numbers; "Un, deux, trois . . ."

Helen was delighted. "We shall have them ready for university soon."

Lucy felt it was worthwhile learning French just to see her mother's pleasure at the advance and interest of the twins.

Then came a letter from David saying, guess what? They had had orders for twenty summerhouses, in different designs and they were going to various towns to build them. How exciting life was. As soon as they possibly could they would come home for a weekend. Mr Kermit and Mr Hamilton were wonderful people to work for. It said at the end of the letter, *Mr Hamilton thinks that Ma is such a lovely lady*, then followed, *and so do we!*

Helen blushed like a young girl. Deborah said, "We'll be having a stepfather soon."

"Oh, no, they must never say such a thing, never," said her mother, but Lucy had a feeling that *she* might be the one to end up alone.

Mrs Trippet was quite excited at Mr Hamilton's remark and said that no man said such a thing without a reason.

Helen said, "You must never think such a thing, Mrs Trippet, I would never marry again," but Lucy noticed during the next few days that her mother took more care brushing her hair and had started to wear white collars on her black dress.

Joel had got into the habit of calling on them sometimes in the evening and Lucy found herself looking forward to his company. He always had plenty to talk about. There were the buildings he was putting up to house more cattle and he would tell them little snippets of tales about various animals. Recently he had told them about a stray kitten that kept sneaking into the kitchen and sat and warmed itself in front of the fire, but if anyone came near it then it would streak out again and they wouldn't see it for days.

"I think it's wild," he said. "The first time I saw it was in a drainpipe and it never moved an inch. But as soon as I moved it was away, like a streak of lightning. I would like to keep it, it would catch mice, maybe an odd rat, although Smokey might not approve." He said they had brought Smokey from their old home and the cat was old and not too keen on catching rats these days.

When Lucy took the twins for a walk they would spend time looking for the black kitten but never saw it once. Then one day when she came into the kitchen with Joel he put a hand back to restrain her. "Hang on a minute."

He went quietly forward then whispered, "She's here." Lucy followed and saw the kitten stretched out on the rug. Joel went carefully to her and although she looked up at him she made no move.

Then Lucy saw blood and when she mentioned it he said, "I think it's coming from underneath her. She's been hurt."

He went to get a towel. He picked her up and she had been cut in her stomach. Joel, talking quietly said, "Look in the cupboard at the right hand side of the fireplace, there's some bandages in a box. There is also a small bottle of ether, a suture and a needle. She'll need to be stitched."

Lucy was about to say the kitten needed the vet when Joel asked her to pass over the bandage, then

171

told her to stop looking so worried, he had stitched up dozens of animals.

A whiff of ether was given then he carried the kitten to the table and made the neatest stitching Lucy had ever seen.

"Poor little mite. I'll make a box ready for her. She probably ripped herself on a piece of wire."

He was so tender with the kitten that Lucy felt touched.

"I started out as a vet," he said, "but my father objected and to keep the peace I gave in. And I've regretted it."

The kitten soon came round and it settled in the box lined with a cushion. The cat examined it, sniffed around it and seemed to accept it. "Good," Joel said smiling. "Now I have only *one* person to come around to my way of thinking."

Lucy, guessing what was in his mind said, "Not today."

"Next week perhaps?"

"Perhaps," she answered lightly.

He grinned. "Don't think I shall forget."

At first Lucy regretted having said what she had, then she thought, why not? The boys had left home, Deborah would eventually leave. Beth would get married and if anything developed between her mother and Mr Hamilton, she would be on her own.

She liked Joel. She liked the tenderness he had shown with the kitten. Also, he was in love with her and had been for some time.

When she went to bed that evening she thought of James. Since they had been to his house she had purposefully kept him out of her mind. He had been unpleasant to her over the upset of his marriage; and had been unpleasant to her when she had asked about the boys' wages. No, she would let him slip out of her mind again.

It was not easy. There had been the nicer times when she had been in his company. He had seen that her scarf was around her throat on a chilly morning and had made a gift to her of a pair of gloves he had bought at Harrods, convincing her to take them only after quietly insisting it was for her own good in the cold winter months and that they could be considered as part-payment for the hard work her brother had done on the summerhouse, if she would rather not accept a gift from him.

That evening Lucy decided to go and see Joel. She needed to get James out of her mind.

He was sitting in front of the fire, reading the paper, the kitten curled up on his knee. She had walked in as she usually did and he turned his head when he heard her coming.

"Lucy, what a nice surprise." He put the paper aside and put the kitten on the mat. "How is she?" Lucy asked.

"Fine, she's being sensible, not going tearing about." He pulled up a chair. "Sit down."

"Just for a few minutes. I wanted to know how the kitten was."

He leaned towards her, smiling. "Are you sure you didn't want to give me your answer? And don't try and look puzzled. I know it's going to be yes."

"I'm sorry, but it's no."

"I don't believe it," he said softly and taking her by the hands drew her to her feet and pulled her towards him.

Lucy waited for a reaction and felt nothing. Girls had told her that this was the exciting part, when you would feel your body tense and there would be a warning tingle in your blood. Her heart was beating a little more quickly but that was all.

Joel put his arms around her and his lips covered hers. She did feel a tremor but nothing more. Then his lips moved sensuously over hers and his hand began to undo the buttons on her dress. She felt a momentary panic and tried to push his hand away.

"Don't, Lucy," he begged. "I need you, desperately."

Lucy came to her senses. She drew back from him then pushed him away. "No, it's wrong." She began to try and button her dress with fingers that trembled.

"It's all right," he said, "I won't force you. I thought you wanted to."

He turned his back to her and stood staring into the fire.

"Joel, I'm sorry. It was the way I was brought up."

"Yes, I understand." He turned suddenly to face her. "Don't think I thought otherwise."

"No." She left him and hurried out. Oh, God, how stupid she had been. She had wanted to know what it was like to have a man make love to her – and she had felt nothing. Well, practically nothing.

She had been told by girl friends that it was the most wonderful thing that ever happened. One girl said it was like a sunburst. Another said it was like an explosion and you would reach heights you'd never dreamed of. "Once you've tasted it, you want more and more," declared another.

An older woman had said, "Don't believe them, gal, they talk a lot of rot. Sunburst? Explosion? I pretend I've gone to sleep to get out of it, and as my man's usually on his last legs with booze I get away with it, thank the Lord."

When Lucy thought about the times when she had been daydreaming about James Dexter she realised she didn't feel any special excitement. She had felt tremors, but nothing like a sunburst or explosion. Perhaps she had not yet met the right man.

Deep down, however, she knew she was in love with James. Perhaps all these lovely feelings came when you were married. It was all so confusing.

The following day Deborah said to Lucy right out of the blue, "How about coming to London with me? You can keep on making the sheets and pillowcases. The boys are still doing the rag books. Beth will be marrying Harold soon and Mother will be marrying Mr Hamilton. You'll be on your own."

Lucy looked up quickly. "What's this about Mother marrying Mr Hamilton?"

"She's had a letter from him every day this week. Oh, she hasn't told us. It was Mrs Trippet who mentioned it to me last night when you went to see Joel."

"Why didn't you mention it?"

"In the mood you were in last night – lost in thought? What happened?"

"Nothing; and I'll believe mother is getting married when she tells us."

"Suit yourself, but I can also tell you that Harold will be calling to ask mother if he and Beth can get married. He's taking a chance and has rented a little cottage on the moors."

Lucy sat, thoughtful. If her mother did marry Mr Hamilton she would certainly consider going to London with Deborah. They would be company for one another. They would, perhaps, be able to see the Draycotts, just to call for a cup of coffee, not to stay for a meal. There were the shows to see. They could always go into the gallery at the theatres.

She smiled to herself. Why not? She would keep on with the sheets and pillowcases and cushions. Yes, she'd do that. It would be another life she would be starting. She had a feeling of excitement. She wanted to be married eventually. She wanted children, but first she would have a different kind of life.

It was then that Lucy realised she would be leaving Mrs Trippet. What would they all do without her? She decided, if there was an opportunity, she would ask her if she knew her mother's plans.

As it happened her mother forestalled her. She had woken from her afternoon's sleep. The twins were with Mrs Trippet, Deborah and Beth were out and Lucy had poured her mother a cup of tea and was about to light the lamp when her mother said softly, "Don't light it yet, Lucy, there's something I want to ask you."

Lucy felt her heartbeat quickening. "I have to ask you something, Lucy. So much depends on it. I heard Beth asking Deborah if you had said you would share a flat with her in London. Is this your plan?"

"Only if you were to get married again."

There was a short silence then her mother looked up. "He has asked me, but I wouldn't marry him and leave you here alone, Lucy."

"And I wouldn't have gone to London and left you alone with the twins." They hugged one another and both shed a few tears. Then her mother said, "Am I doing the right thing, Lucy? I'm very fond of Mr Hamilton, we've corresponded but I didn't want any of you to know that he asked me this week if I would marry him. It's like a young couple's romance. I took to him the day we met and he wrote to tell me how much he liked me. He's been a widower for seven years and I have only been a widow for a year. Would it be wrong to marry him?"

"Mother, I can't think of anything that would give us all more happiness. We all like him."

They talked for a while of all the changes that would have to be met then her mother said, "I know we shall all miss dear Mrs Trippet but she promises to come and visit us often."

The two girls came in from their walk and when they were told, Deborah showed her delight and so did Beth, knowing that she would probably now get permission to be married sooner than originally hoped, as her mother would need to know her daughter was in safe hands once Helen herself was settled in her new home.

Harold came that evening and Lucy had to admit that he was sensible in his line of reasoning. He was willing to start in a small way and build up. They were both very much in love and he did not want there to be a time out of wedlock when he might be unable to control his love. He said, "I had never imagined how strong love can be, Mrs Lingard, and I promise you shall never regret giving your permission for us to marry."

When her mother gave her permission, Lucy thought that the look of joy on the faces of Harold and Beth was something beautiful to see.

Mrs Trippet was marvellous. She said that Helen and Beth must have a double wedding. At first they talked about being married in the registrar's office in Whitby, but Mrs Trippet said how much easier it would be if they were married in the little church on the moor and afterwards they would come to her house for the reception.

Deborah began to laugh. "We are making all these arrangements and the poor bridegroom doesn't even know a thing about it."

Helen looked dismayed and clapping a hand to her mouth said, "Oh, dear, please don't tell him. I shall write this evening."

The following morning a letter was dispatched to Mr Hamilton, telling him she accepted his offer of marriage.

By return came two letters, one from the boys saying they were truly delighted to hear the news from Mr Hamilton and a letter from Mr Hamilton himself, saying that he and the boys were coming for the weekend. He would stay at Whitby. They were coming by car. The rest of the letter, her mother said, was private.

Mrs Trippet again took over, saying that she would put Mr Hamilton up and they would all have dinner at her house.

And Beth said quietly, that Mrs Trippet's heart must be breaking to think that so many of them would be leaving the house.

Helen was outwardly calm but Lucy would catch her mother looking into a mirror, patting her hair and smiling privately to herself.

Beth found a lovely piece of chiffon with flowers of all muted colours which was just big enough to make a scarf and on the Saturday when David and William and Mr Hamilton were due to arrive, Lucy draped it around her mother's black dress.

There was a delicate colour in her cheeks and she looked quite beautiful . . .

It was late afternoon when the boys and Mr Hamilton arrived and there was laughter and tears as they greeted one another.

Mr Hamilton said to Helen, "You look quite charming, Mrs Lingard. How good it is to see you again." There was no doubting the admiration in his eyes.

They were told the second news, that Beth was going to be married, and she showed them her engagement ring that had belonged to Harold's grandmother. She was hugged and congratulated and there were tears in her eyes because she was very proud of her ring with its small ruby heart-shaped stone.

After that the boys talked about their work and described what they were doing.

It was non-stop talk. Mrs Trippet told them that the children were learning French and Tom giggled and said, "Je suis" and Sarah said shyly, "Mademoiselle", and they were applauded.

Deborah later talked about how she wanted to go to London and start a dressmaking business and said that Lucy was going with her.

"Oh, that's splendid," said the boys, asking them all about where they would live and where they wanted to set up their business. Then William asked Mrs Trippet what she was going to do with the house and she replied, promptly, "Keep it for when you want to come for a holiday." Then she added, "It's possible that I shall carry out my ambition and start a small farm. Joel will give me some advice."

They went to Mrs Trippet's house for dinner and afterwards Mr Hamilton produced a ring, studded with small diamonds and, taking Helen's hand, slipped it on to her finger, saying he felt honoured that Helen had agreed to marry him.

Lucy found it a moving moment, her mother with a shy smile and Mr Hamilton looking as proud as if he had been accepted by royalty. There were more congratulations and they hugged their mother and said how pleased they were for her. Mrs Trippet was smiling too, but Lucy understood how she felt, knowing that all their lives were going to be altered.

Chapter Thirteen

On the Sunday morning David and William decided they must take Mr Hamilton to Silver Acres. After all, it was Mr Dexter who had brought their boss's attention to them.

After they had gone the womenfolk got down to the business of the weddings. Mrs Trippet's suggestion of a double wedding and offer to hold the reception at her house was accepted.

Helen's protest that it was far too much trouble was whipped aside and all was settled within the next few minutes.

Clothes were the next problem and Helen decided she would wear silver-grey. Beth wanted to be married in blue. No, she did not want to be a white bride, nor did she want a honeymoon. She would be pleased to be going to their cottage. No prospective brides could have looked more gently happy than Helen and Beth.

It was decided that Deborah would make the dresses but the date was not set for the wedding, this having to be discussed with the future bridegrooms.

Helen took the opportunity that morning to talk to her eldest daughter about her future husband. She told Lucy that Mr Hamilton's Christian name was Andrew and that although they would live in the flat in Mr Kermit's house they would buy their own house later.

"Andrew is not Mr Kermit's partner, Lucy, but his manager. I'm glad. I didn't want to be caught up in a social circle. It's really astonishing how this has all come about. We wrote letters to one another and simply found that we had similar tastes. He's so kind, Lucy, so generous. I felt somehow disloyal to you all when he suggested marriage, but knew I would have to lose every one of you in time. You do think I'm doing the right thing? I'm not marrying Andrew just for a home. I'm extremely fond of him."

Her mother's earnest expression had Lucy smiling.

"We all do, Mother. It's time you had some life and Mr Hamilton says that Surrey is a lovely place. And, not too far from London. We will come to see you."

Not long after this conversation Lucy found herself thinking what a close-knit family they had been. Now they were being torn apart. Beth would be left behind with her new husband; the boys were going to become travellers and she and Deborah were going to London to start a dressmaking business, starting from scratch. Would their business work out?

When David, William and Mr Hamilton came back they all seemed very cheerful. David said that Mr Dexter would be calling sometime next week. Helen asked if Mrs Dalton was there and he said no, she had gone to America to visit some relatives.

After that, all their talk was of summerhouses.

They were leaving the following morning, early. In the afternoon Mr Hamilton asked Helen to go for a walk with him. Mrs Trippet had kept the children with her after lunch and Deborah said she would sketch the wedding dresses. Beth stayed with her.

Lucy decided to sew a cushion and went into the sitting room. The fire was on and she sat in front of it, stitching. It was not easy to settle to anything. Would she be able to sell cushions in London? What they really needed was a small shop to start with. She could display the cushions, perhaps the silk sheets and what else? Would there be time to do anything else? She would be caught up in Deborah's fashion designs, but she wanted her own lines. She did not want to be seamstress for her sister. That is, if they managed to get customers. Lucy knew they were taking a risk.

She laid down her work. What she needed was a separate section that she alone would handle. What they both needed was staff. The more she thought about it the more she thought how foolish they were to even think of running a business. What Deborah needed was a seamstress, or perhaps two. And experienced people.

But what line could she be in? She liked making the cushions. Everyone seemed to like them and there were the samplers. But she would need to buy quite a variety of goods to go into that kind of business. She would need to look around a warehouse. It was not a small shop she wanted, but a small factory.

Lucy felt her blood racing. She had not realised it until now. She must tell Deborah.

Deborah was only partly listening at first, then she laid down her pencil and studied Lucy.

"You are talking about a warehouse. I want a small, exclusive business. You want to cater for the masses. I want to capture the attention of the wealthy."

"I know. Is it possible to combine the two?"

"No, I need you as a partner."

"I would merely be a seamstress and you could

183

easily get one from outside. I think that each of us should have our own work."

"No, you're letting me down. We've always worked together, Lucy. You can't do this to me."

"I have to. I don't want to work with clothes."

"Clothes? They're fashions! I want mannequins to show them."

"And so you can. You have the ability to design. You are good at it. Look at the coat and hat you made me when we went to London. Mrs Dalton said I looked like a mannequin. You have the flair for this kind of work. I haven't." Lucy's chin came out in a stubborn thrust. "I want to do what I feel I'm good at."

Beth said quietly, "Lucy's right, Deborah. The boys were both good at the one thing; they are already getting on. But if they hadn't been, there would have been quarrelling."

Deborah threw her piece of paper on the table. "I just feel let down. I don't think I want to go to London."

"Of course you do. You've been planning it for ages. I should have given you warning, but the whole thing just came to me. Give it some thought. We can talk about it later."

Lucy left them and went back into the sitting room, sure that Deborah would come round to her way of thinking in time.

She was right. Even before Helen and Mr Hamilton returned, Deborah came in to see her. "I think you're right, Lucy, even though I think we'll have a job getting the sort of place to please us both. But, I'm willing to try."

"I'm glad, Deborah. It may take time, but things have been on our side since we came here and I think our luck will hold. I think it might be wise to keep this to ourselves for the time being. It would serve no purpose upsetting Mother, for instance." The three girls were all in agreement on this point.

The date was set for the wedding on the first Saturday in May, which suited them all. Two weeks beforehand Lucy and Deborah decided to have two or three days in London to try and find accommodation and a place to work.

To her surprise, the week before they were due to leave, Lucy had a letter from Mrs Draycott saying that a little bird had told them of their plan and they were to stay with them. They would have a look around and see if they could find somewhere suitable. They were to let Ernie know when they were arriving and he would meet them.

Neither Lucy nor Deborah had any idea who had told them, but Helen was satisfied that her girls had friends in London.

They left on the milk train, and from the moment of Mr and Mrs Draycott meeting them at them at St Pancras they were on the trail. Mrs Draycott asked them to use their Christian names, Ernie and Grace. Grace had had a phone call from a friend the day before telling her of a warehouse with a small house attached which she thought might be suitable. She had gone to get the keys and that was where they were going now.

Both girls were in a state of excitement.

It was actually a shop with a warehouse behind it. The house was next to the warehouse. The three-roomed house was in a good state of repair and Lucy could immediately see the buildings' potential. Not so Deborah, it was not the sort of thing she had in mind at all.

Lucy pointed out that it was on a busy main road, not too far from the station, and Ernie pointed out that a lick of paint would work wonders. But Deborah was adamant. Ernie then said cheerfully that there were plenty of other places to view and they would go home now and have some breakfast.

They spent the whole day travelling around but although Lucy thought there were one or two possibilities, Deborah was not satisfied.

Lucy liked the first one and wanted it. But she was willing to try the following day. By then she knew that what Deborah really wanted was a place in the West End which was impossible, due to the high rents.

At the end of that day she said, "Well, Deborah, you will have to decide. We must go home tomorrow."

Deborah's shoulders sagged and she sighed. "I suppose we shall have to take the one we first saw."

"No, I won't share any place where you are not satisfied."

"Well . . ." She hemmed and hawed and Lucy said firmly, "No. You don't have to make excuses. One has to be happy in a work place."

Grace said, "Lucy is right, Deborah. Shall I tell you something? I have many friends, people with money, who have dressmakers in the East End. They don't worry if the dressmaker lives in a small house: it's the work they admire. They pay good money to be well dressed. *I* do. Why not take this place, go into it with a feeling of 'this is going to earn me money'."

Deborah was silent for a while then she looked up and said with a wry smile, "You know my trouble, don't you? I think I'm perfect and should be settled in luxury." She turned to Lucy. "We'll go in the morning and settle for the warehouse."

Lucy was just feeling a sense of relief when the front

doorbell of the Draycotts' house rang. Mr Draycott went to answer it.

There was talking and laughter then Mr Draycott came in, a broad smile on his face. "Guess who's here?" He stepped aside and James Dexter came forward.

For a split second Lucy was sure it had all been arranged but she knew when she heard Mrs Draycott say, "Well, why didn't you let us know you were coming?" that it was a genuine surprise. They embraced then she said, "And look who we have here."

He turned and, seeing Lucy and Deborah, his smile broadened.

"Hello, how nice to see you both. How are you?"

Draycott said, "After tomorrow they will be two enterprising young ladies who are going into business, in fashions and other beautiful things."

James turned to the girls. "Well, congratulations. You certainly are enterprising. Wait until my aunt hears about this."

Lucy, aware of his charm, said, her heart pounding, "I understand that Mrs Dalton is in America at the moment."

"She'll be back in two weeks' time. I must let her know so she can call and see you all."

Grace said she would make coffee and then James could tell them his reason for turning up so unexpectedly.

James was in an exceptionally good mood. He had not thought he would be back in time from a visit to America to get to a conference in England but he had managed to get an earlier sailing.

"It was worthwhile. I had dinner with some of my business acquaintances and decided I would give you a call. And how worthwhile this is too," he added, looking at Lucy, his expression soft.

Why the sudden change in him? Maybe he had had his marriage annulled and he thought she would fall into his arms. Would she?

Lucy was not sure, she only knew there was some stirrings in her blood, something she had not experienced before.

He talked business with Ernie and talked to the girls about their business, asking exactly what they were hoping to stock and telling them he would be pleased to help in any way he could.

Grace was all smiles. "Now, you could not have had a better offer than that, could you?" Lucy said no, but was determined that she and Deborah would keep their independence.

James said he would like to see the premises the following day. Deborah was all for it and that night in bed she spoke in animated whispers about how lucky they were that he had arrived that evening. They could really make something of the premises, especially if he and Mr Draycott would be willing to lend them some money. Lucy, annoyed, said they would struggle on their own; Deborah thought her quite mad and they all but fell out. Eventually Lucy said that if things became desperate she might agree to some borrowing, but they would really have to be desperate.

They all went to the estate agents the next morning and once more were given the keys. Ernie and Grace and the two girls watched James walking around the warehouse, tapping his chin with one of the keys. He looked at the rooms behind the warehouse, came back and walked to the window, then spinning round he said, "Yes, I think you have a very good place here."

Breaths were released and Deborah said, "Well, thank goodness for that. I was beginning to think you didn't like it."

James gave her a brief smile. "I'm surprised that it hasn't been snapped up before now."

Ernie said that the coal strike last year had upset things. It was only now that things were settling down.

James looked at the three-roomed house, remarked that there seemed to be no tiles missing and said he thought it quite presentable. It was when he offered advice on how to deal with the arrangement of the factory that Lucy realised how knowledgeable he was.

He would "put" small ledges on the walls of the windows so that items could be draped. He "arranged" sitting accommodation for the workers, "placed" any necessary sewing machines that Lucy might use – Deborah's clothing would be all hand sewn, of course. He suggested that white paint be used as much as possible to make everything light for working and soon, Lucy could hear the machines working and see all the activity. A slow smile came to her face. He was interested in her and that was all to the good.

Ernie and Grace had their offerings too. There were the three sisters they knew who were living in a small, cramped home. Hadn't their mother been saying what a pleasure it would be if they could get work, and together? Grace said she would see about it that day. They had enquired what the rent would be when they first looked over the premises and although it was more than either girl had anticipated Lucy saw it as now being quite reasonable.

The whole situation took on a rosy glow.

James stayed with them that day and so did Ernie. Both were mines of information. Grace knew some charwomen who would scrub the place out; she knew men who would whitewash the ceilings and strip the walls in the house. They had to be stripped in case there were vermin. Lucy and Deborah shuddered when vermin were mentioned. When Deborah declared she hoped there were no mice, Grace said cheerfully that there were bound to be mice, but a couple of cats would soon cure that.

James suggested that the walls of the warehouse should be distempered a silver-grey. He also said it would be best to have the rooms in the house papered and the room where Deborah would entertain her clients must be comfortably furnished. He also said that lighting in both buildings must be good. There must also be warmth; it would be no use having staff shivering.

At the end of that first day the girls were exhausted but satisfied, knowing that everything was going to go well. James had left for home late but gave his word he would call and tell their mother the next morning that they would be staying a while.

He kissed Lucy on the cheek before he left and although there was no sensuality in it she felt a wave of emotion sweep over her. And knew then that this was the kind of love she had been seeking. She herself had closed it out. As tired as she was that night she had some wonderful dreams and longed to see James again.

While the women were scrubbing floors and men were stripping the walls of the house Deborah and Lucy went round second-hand furniture emporiums seeking furniture for the house. Grace went with them and did a lot of bargaining. They concentrated only on the necessary furniture. They were prepared to buy comfortable items for the room that Deborah would use but otherwise there would be only the bare necessities. They bought a desk, a sofa, some chairs and a good, dark blue carpet, also small tables and chairs for the warehouse, which the man said could be stored until needed. There were plenty of curtains at home that could be used.

At the end of three days they went home, both girls eager to tell the family what was taking place.

They were all excited, what with the double wedding and hearing about Lucy and Deborah's venture. Later Helen wanted to know how they were doing for money and Lucy said, they were managing fine, yet knew their money was getting low. These last few days before the wedding they must do some sewing.

Helen apologised for being unable to help moneywise, Andrew had only his wage and they would be buying a small house soon. Lucy told her it was all right. The Draycotts and James Dexter had offered money if they needed it.

Deborah made the wedding dresses for her mother and Beth. She also made a new dress for Sarah and a sailor suit for Tom. Lucy sorted through some remnants and stitched some flimsy scarfs for the shop.

The morning of the wedding was sunny and mild. Although the banns had been read out they had not expected many people to be there. To their surprise the church was full and an overflow of people were waiting outside for them. Lucy felt choked.

Both her mother and Beth looked lovely. Her mother's dress was a silver-grey alpaca and her hat a grey straw, which she had had for years but which suited her outfit for the occasion beautifully. Deborah had put a ribbon band on it in pale blue, which matched Beth's dress in silk. This had a low waist and fell in pleats. She wore a cloche hat, with a pattern of beautiful hand-stitching done by Deborah.

Mr Hamilton, with Mr Kermit, who was to be best man to both grooms, arrived with the boys late the night before. The two men stayed with Mrs Trippet and the boys came home to sleep. David and William were to give the brides away.

It was intended to be a quiet wedding and Lucy guessed her mother was nervous when she saw all the people outside. But when they all came out, bride and groom were smiling. People called good wishes to them and confetti was thrown over them.

Cars were waiting to take them to Mrs Trippet's house for the reception, and the people there to welcome them were James Dexter and Joel Morrison.

James said, "Mrs Trippet invited us to welcome you and may we both congratulate you."

Lucy was pleased to see Joel there and also, of course, to see James. She thought how alike they were, both dark, both strong and broad shouldered.

Afterwards Lucy said that the reception could not have been bettered had it been held in a top London hotel. A whole ham had been cooked, a tongue, there were pies, chicken legs and a wide variety of cakes and trifles, as well as the two wedding cakes, and all had been been prepared by Mrs Trippet's cook and her servant Polly. They were congratulated and so was Mrs Trippet for her kindness in giving the reception. The only other guests were Harold's parents and his brother and sister, who were quiet but pleasant.

Joel was sat between Lucy and Deborah and on

Lucy's left was James, who talked most of the time to Mrs Trippet. She didn't mind. Poor Mrs Trippet would be left behind, which made Lucy ache every time she thought about it. After the reception Beth was going with her husband to their little cottage between Mrs Trippet's house and Whitby. Mr Kermit, Andrew, Helen and the twins were leaving after the reception, travelling in Mr Kermit's car. The boys were not leaving until the next day and would be travelling by train. Helen took only one suitcase with her; the other things would have to be sent on.

Before they were due to leave Mr Hamilton said he had a present for her and brought from the car a musquash fur coat. Helen wept. How lovely of him, but he ought not to have done it. He said gently, "Let me help you to put it on."

He wiped her eyes with his handkerchief and Lucy wanted to cry. They were going to be all right.

Although there were tearful farewells there were promises to come and visit the girls in London and Mrs Trippet promised to come and visit them when they got settled in their new home.

The only things the twins were interested in was a drive in the car which was just as well, Lucy thought. She only hoped they would settle down in their new home.

When they had waved them away Deborah, Lucy, Mrs Trippet and the boys went into the house. David said, "What an upheaval, I don't think I realised it until Ma and the twins left in the car."

"And I can't believe that we'll be settling in London in a few days' time," Lucy exclaimed.

"I do hope that you'll remember to invite me to your new home."

Mrs Trippet had spoken lightly, but her eyes were

tear-filled. Lucy flung her arms around her. "Of course we shall. How could we forget you? You've been the most wonderful friend any family ever had. What would we have done without you?"

"What indeed?" This was from David and there was a shakiness in his voice. Then William said he echoed this feeling.

Mrs Trippet gave a sniff. "Who wants a cup of tea?"

They laughed and it settled them and they talked while the kettle was boiling for the tea.

The boys were leaving the next morning and they all managed to be light-hearted about the parting, saying that after all they would not be far apart. James sent the chauffeur with the car to take them to the station. Lucy was disappointed not to see him.

The girls settled to doing some work. Mrs Trippet spent the first two days with them, helping them with sewing and she made them meals and ate with them. Lucy made scarfs and Mrs Trippet and Deborah did samplers.

When Mrs Trippet went home at night the house was like living in an empty barn, in spite of having a fire on all the time.

On the third day they had a letter from Mrs Draycott to say that all was going well and it might be best to wait until the weekend to come to London. There was also a letter from her mother to say she was missing them all terribly but everyone had been so kind and she was sure that in time she would settle. She said that the twins, as children often did, had settled in right away. They had a puppy each, given to them by Mr Kermit, and they were in their element. She ended the letter by saying she was sure they would all be meeting soon. Mrs Trippet had had a letter from Helen too. They talked and talked as they worked, but each day got worse and in the end they decided they would leave for London on the Saturday.

James took them to the station. It would have been a very sad sendoff if Mrs Trippet had not come to the station with them and kept up a lively chatter. She talked about starting a farm and how Joel was going to help her. James was lively too, saying he would make her a present of some of his chickens.

Joel had come the night before to say goodbye and he told Lucy he was not giving up on her. Although he was smiling, his eyes held a sadness.

Beth and her husband had popped in once or twice to see the girls but the couple were so besotted with one another Lucy felt a little impatient with them. They would be parting soon and it was a shame they could not spend their remaining time together as a family.

On the Friday evening only Beth came to say goodbye. Friends had called in to see them and Harold had stayed at home. All Deborah said about this was, "Folks surprise you, don't they?" and Beth was dispensed with.

Everything big, their sewing bags, the cushions and the curtains, had been packed by Mrs Trippet and had gone ahead by rail.

James, who had brought them with Mrs Trippet to the station, said, "Don't worry, I shall keep an eye on things. I shall be coming to London in ten days' time. I shall definitely call and see you both."

"I hope you will, Mr Dexter," Lucy said. "Deborah and I thank you for all you've done for us." Both girls hugged a weeping Mrs Trippet and climbed on to the train that drew into the station.

Steam hissed around them then Mrs Trippet whispered, "I love you all," and Lucy whispered back, "And we love you."

James had found them seats and after putting their luggage on the rack he turned to say goodbye.

He kissed Lucy on the lips . . . and for a long time afterwards she could feel their warm softness. It was special because he had only kissed Deborah on the cheek.

They waved from the open window until the train rounded a bend.

The girls were quiet for a while then Deborah said suddenly, "Mr Dexter kissed you on the lips. Is he in love with you?"

"No, he – he hasn't said so."

"I think he must be."

No more mention was made of James's name during the journey. They talked of the warehouse, the house, of the work they were going to do and Mr and Mrs Draycott. Later they spoke of the kindness and the warmth of the people on the moor who had come to say goodbye.

Ernie and Grace were there to meet them when the train drew into London and they talked in the taxi on their way to their new home, to have a look at it before going to stay overnight with the Draycotts.

Lucy was prepared for anything but when they arrived she and Deborah stood staring in astonishment.

The outside of the warehouse and house were painted white. The change was fantastic. The letter box and number on the house were black. Mr and Mrs Draycott were grinning broadly.

"All right," Grace said smiling. "So which shall we look at first?"

Both girls said the warehouse.

The walls were silver-grey, skirting boards white. There was blue lino on the floor, not new, but in good condition. Grace told them it was a small gift from them,

"Ohhh," breathed the two girls. "How lovely."

They went to see the house. The small hall and stairs had been laid with a patterned blue carpet and when they went into Deborah's office both thought it a dream with its dark blue carpet, its silver-striped wallpaper, the oak desk, the sofa, which had been recovered by Grace in a deep gold velvet. There were three paintings on the walls. One was of the moors, the other two were gardens.

Tears were not far away when they each give Mr and Mrs Draycott a hug. How kind of them.

Grace said brightly, "Now let us look at the other rooms."

All of them had been furnished, very simply, there was green lino on the floor in the kitchen, a cosy rug in front of the fireplace and a small fireside chair at either side. There was a teaset and dinner service, cutlery in the table drawer and pots and pans, Grace explaining that these had all come from James.

The floors of the bedrooms had been sandpapered and stained and had rugs in a rose pink. There was a double bed in each room, a wardrobe in each and a small dressing table. Each bed had a rose quilted cover.

Lucy and Deborah were speechless and Grace said they were not to say anything. They and James thought it was the least they could do. They themselves had thanked people in the past and they in turn could perhaps help other people in the future.

Lucy knew when they went downstairs that everything was going to work out all right.

Chapter Fourteen

When the girls were back at the Draycotts, Lucy was alarmed when Ernie told her she would need to borrow to get goods to sell.

"What have you now, Lucy? Cushions, samplers and some scarfs."

She said she had thought of buying some extra items from a warehouse. She did have some money left. When she told him how much, he dismissed it. "You are a business woman, Lucy. You need a wide variety of goods and you must be selling every day to make a success of it. Deborah comes under a different category. Her success will come from her ability to make clothes. We know she can do it. Grace has told her friends about her and three have promised to come and see her tomorrow.

"We'll take you to a warehouse. You'll have a big choice, but you must be selective. You will need to have a wide variety of goods. You'll need jewellery, things that make people want to buy for themselves *and* to give as presents. There'll be a choice of a hundred and one items. It's exciting buying, Lucy, but what you buy must be lucrative. I will lend you the money." He grinned. "Without interest. Or you can borrow from the bank."

Lucy looked at her sister. "What do you think, Deborah?"

Deborah said she would gladly accept Ernie's kind offer to borrow from him. It would save having to pay interest to the bank.

It took Lucy some time before she replied. "I think I would use the bank. If the business failed I don't want you and Grace to be the losers."

Grace said quietly, "You must think positively, Lucy."

Lucy smiled. "That's why I chose the bank."

Ernie grinned. "You'll succeed."

The following morning Ernie and Grace took the girls to the materials warehouse and Lucy thought it the most exciting time she had ever had.

Ernie had talked about having a choice of a hundred and one items and she felt sure he was right. There were handkerchiefs – men's, women's and children's; pieces of china, bowls and jugs – some coarse, some delicate; jewellery of every description: rings galore, brooches, earrings, necklaces, watches, cuff links.

There were photo frames and paintings. And there was women's wear, quite a good class of satin camiknicks in white, pale blue and pink. There were glass bowls with a snow scene encased and when the bowl was shaken there was a snow shower. Lucy laughed. She must have some of those.

There were some beautiful dolls with wax faces and big blue eyes. Lucy decided she would buy some and dress them herself. Two hours later she had bought six times what she had intended, but felt sure that everything would sell and could hardly wait to get the goods home and examine them.

When the goods arrived Ernie said, "I think you'll do well, Lucy, you knew what you wanted to buy."

The shop was screened off from the warehouse and Lucy arranged the window early that morning. One of her cushions was propped casually in a corner, some of the flimsy scarfs she had made were draped from a hook, pieces of jewellery were laid on the base, three samplers hung down the middle of the wall, the straps of a pair of white camiknicks were hung on a hook, with three others in different colours folded by the side of them. There were small blue patterned bowls in a circle and a round glass ball placed with the snow scene. A doll would follow later.

Deborah's prospective customers would not be arriving until later in the morning. Lucy waited for the sound of a group of people going towards the station or coming from it and, going to the window, picked up the ball with the snow scene and shook it, then withdrew. It brought a slowing of footsteps and voices saying, "Oh, look, the shop's open . . . we must stop by tonight . . ."

Lucy was satisfied. It was a start.

Deborah's clients were interested in her designs but only one gave an order for a dress. The woman had her own material but Deborah hoped to have rolls of material of her own in time.

That evening Lucy had five customers. Two bought pieces of jewellery, one bought a scarf on display, another bought the snow scene and, to her delight, a man bought the cushion for his wife.

Deborah laughed with joy. "We're on our way."

That evening Deborah cut out the dress she had to make while Lucy started another cushion, in spite of having several completed.

The following day, although people looked in the window, no one bought, which was a blow to Lucy. Grace treated it lightly.

"Give them time. They have to see what you've got. In another few days they'll be buying."

Lucy went two more days without a customer and was beginning to feel sick when on the third day there were ten customers.

Grace told her that her husband said she should have a name for the business. Lucy said right away that she had been thinking about it and suggested, THE GIFT SHOP. This was considered perfect and that afternoon a sign painter started on the painting of it. Lucy was on cloud nine; and although for the next few days the number of customers varied she stayed on the cloud. Especially when James arrived and took Lucy and Deborah with the Draycotts out to dinner at a small, select restaurant in Soho.

At the end of that evening there was no doubt in Lucy's mind that James was in love with her. It was clear in the way he looked at her, in the way he would touch her hand and her pulses leapt in response. She had never had such strong emotional feelings and she longed to be loved by him.

They talked a lot about the business and the success of it and Ernie talked about taking them to one of his theatres but nothing was settled. They went back to the Draycotts and ended up staying the night.

At bedtime when Lucy and James were alone for a few minutes he took her hand in his and said softly, "I must talk to you tomorrow. May I see you at the shop?" She agreed and his lovely smile made her heart beat fast.

Was it possible he was going to tell her he loved her, perhaps ask her if she would marry him? No, it couldn't be. He would not have waited until she was settled in the business. James would be a man who would want his woman with him. And she was not going to give up her work, even though she did love him.

Grace drove the girls to the shop the next morning and chatted happily, saying what a pleasure it must be for each of them to have their own business. Both Lucy and Deborah said they were enjoying it although Deborah did admit she thought she would have had more customers.

"Just wait until Mrs Arden sees her dress completed," Grace said, a twinkle in her eyes.

That afternoon, Mrs Arden was due for a fitting. It was also the day James was due at the shop. When James called, Lucy, who had been trying to sew, got up quickly and said, "Oh, hello, would you like a cup of tea?"

"No, I've come to talk to you," he said softly. "Could we go into the back?" She followed him slowly, her heart in her mouth.

He drew up two chairs and they sat facing one another. James took Lucy's hands in his and said, without preamble, "I fell in love with you the first time we met. Will you marry me, Lucy?"

"Marry you?" She was suddenly calm. "Has your marriage been annulled?" she asked, her thoughts clearing.

He nodded. "Yes, it was completed a few days ago."

"I've been in love with you, Mr Dexter, since I first met you, and I would like to get married. But could I keep on the business?"

"Oh, dear. Problems." His voice was gently teasing. "Yes, you can keep on the business. I shall be away a lot."

"I've waited a long time for the business."

203

"I do understand, but I warn you, Lucy. I do want children."

"So do I."

"Then that seems perfect," he said gently. "You are never out of my thoughts." He got to his feet and drew her to him. "When I saw you after we had been parted for a while, I thought how wonderful it would be to come home to you." He tilted her chin. "I need you, Lucy, want you."

His lips touched hers. At first he was gentle then his mouth moved sensuously over hers and and her pulses leapt in response.

"Lucy, Lucy . . ." He buried his lips against her throat and began to undo her blouse.

"I love you," she whispered in a shaky voice, "but we mustn't – " His hand cupped her breast and she began to know the meaning of the word sunburst. Everything was golden and her body was throbbing with an ecstasy she had never known before.

The next moment she was aware of running footsteps. "Deborah," she said on a moan. James drew away. The footsteps were near the warehouse door. Then Deborah was calling, "Open the door, Lucy, it's locked."

"Coming!" Lucy managed to get her blouse fastened and as she opened the door Deborah came rushing in. "Guess what, Mrs Arden is delighted with her dress. It's not finished but she knows she can get me customers. Isn't that wonderful?"

Lucy hugged her. "Oh, splendid!" Then James was calling, "And congratulations from me."

"Oh, Mr Dexter, I didn't know you were here."

James had moved out of the shadows and was standing smiling, completely at ease, while Lucy was having difficulty in controlling her trembling limbs.

Deborah, fortunately, was only concerned with possible sales.

"I'll get to Paris yet. We must take up our French again."

Then Lucy told her the news – that James had asked her to marry him. Deborah was delighted then she said suddenly, "What about the business?"

Lucy told her the arrangements and Deborah stared at him wide-eyed. "How wonderful of you, how generous. I can't believe it."

He smiled. "I was told I would not get her any other way."

They talked, they laughed and Lucy could hardly believe it was happening. "Just wait until the family hears about this," Deborah said. "And Mrs Trippet too."

James said he was going to the Draycotts to tell them the news and arrange a celebration.

Whilst he was gone, Lucy and Deborah talked about the business and wedding and how their plans would now develop. Lucy had reached an excited stage when she said she felt like closing the shop and just keeping on the warehouse.

"Oh, no," declared Deborah, "we'll need every penny. You're marrying into the aristocracy."

Mention of the word aristocracy had Lucy in a panic for a few moments then she said, "It will have to be a quiet wedding. At a registry office. I won't tell the family until it's over."

"You what? You'll do no such thing."

"Oh, but yes. James has already been married. His marriage has just been annulled. He won't want that in the newspapers."

"No, but – "

"I won't marry him under any other condition."

"Because you're ashamed of the family, is that it?"

"No, of course not! You're not thinking straight. Mr Hamilton had all the expense of coming here. Do you really think that he and mother will want all the trouble and expense of bringing the two of them and the twins to a big expensive wedding in London?"

James came back to say that the Draycotts had a friend visiting them that evening, and they wanted them to go over for dinner.

Their guest was a young relative named Adin Ramsay and right from the first moment of meeting a rapport was established between the young man and Deborah. He applauded both girls going into business and was especially interested in Deborah's side of the work because he was a tailor.

James had stopped to buy champagne and it was opened when he presented Lucy with a beautiful Victorian ring, a small diamond ringed by tiny rubies.

"Oh, James, it's beautiful. Thank you."

It was after this little ceremony that Lucy mentioned the wedding and James was all for it being quiet. He did say, however, on a note of pleading that they could have a honeymoon, even if it were just a weekend in Brighton. He was joking but Lucy said, "That would be splendid," and Ernie burst out laughing.

"What James had in mind was a couple of weeks in Cairo or somewhere similar."

James was smiling. "It was actually."

Lucy had to do some quick thinking. She would have liked nothing better than to go to Egypt but there was the business to think about. A fortnight away was out of the question.

"I really would enjoy a weekend in Brighton, or anywhere else on the coast."

"Oh, Lucy." James was shaking his head and laughing. "You and your business. All right, we shall go to Brighton."

Grace immediately stepped in. "Make it a long weekend and I shall help Deborah until you get back."

Then James said in a speculative way, "One thing we haven't discussed is, where we shall live. As I said, I shall be away a lot; then you, Lucy, can stay with Deborah. But we need an apartment in London when I am home. I have been thinking about making a move for some time. It is a little tiring having to go on to Silver Acres once I land in London."

Lucy was taken aback. She had thought they would live in the house next to the warehouse, but James was already suggesting places. Somewhere close to Green Park, perhaps, or Mayfair. Lucy was not consulted. The Draycotts thought it a splendid idea and James said he would look in at the estate agents the next day.

Lucy was anxious to discuss this with Deborah when they got back home, but it was almost impossible to get a word in: Deborah talked nonstop about Adin Ramsay. What a lovely man and just fancy, he was a tailor. He had asked her to walk out with him and she had agreed.

Lucy had thought him a very sensible person, and he was quite pleasant looking and had a warm manner.

It was bedtime before Lucy got round to talking about James, and then Deborah was still of the opinion that her mother should be told of her wedding. Lucy was adamant that she was doing the right thing. And there was no hope of discussing where she and James should live. Deborah was in a world where only she and Adin existed.

The next morning a letter came from her mother saying she had had a fall and had sprained both ankles. So now she was laid up. What a dreadful thing to happen. Andrew was so good to her. The boys had been over that very morning, but were going to a big house in Shropshire to make a very big summerhouse; *It has to accommodate over fifty people for a party to be held in November when the weather could be bad . . .* the letter went on.

Lucy handed the letter to Deborah. "I think that fate is helping me to have a registry office marriage."

"Well, I want a white wedding when the time comes and nothing will make me change my mind."

Lucy laughed. "That's a big change. I thought that marriage for you was when you were about forty."

"Ah." Deborah gave a cheeky grin. "That was before I met Adin."

Later that morning twenty completed samplers had come from Beth, with a letter saying how badly she had behaved.

Do forgive me, Lucy. I was so wrapped up with Harold. Still am. He's a wonderful person. We struggle a little but I don't mind that. How are you and Deborah? Is business good? Do write and tell me. (Mrs Trippet bought the samplers and read me the riot act for the way I had behaved.) Lots of love, your loving sister Beth.

"Well," Lucy said to Deborah. "That is the biggest surprise. But then Beth was always loving. Fancy Mrs Trippet telling her off. She's one person I would have liked to be at my wedding, but it just can't be. A letter is due from her any day."

It came the following day, It was all about the farm.

It was underway. Joel had been such a help. She had thirty chickens, two cows, a sow and ten piglets. Although she missed them all terribly she did keep busy. She hoped to visit them soon.

A PS said, *Joel sends his love. He still hopes to win you. His mother is poorly at the moment.*

Lucy hoped that Joel would find another girl. He often came into her thoughts. She remembered with fondness the day he had "stitched up" the kitten, and other kind deeds he had done for others.

The following day Deborah had four new customers and she was overjoyed. She decided to ask Grace if she knew of someone who would help with sewing and she recommended the three sisters she had mentioned to the girls as potential housemates.

When Deborah questioned, three? Grace said, "They only work together and they are excellent."

A few days later, Grace brought the three sisters to the warehouse. They were quiet but pleasant girls, and from their first conversation, Deborah realised she would be able to work with them. They were able to start that afternoon. While she was busy cutting out they did some sewing for Lucy. She was astonished at their speed. She thought herself a quick sewer but they were miraculous and absolutely delighted to get work. Their last employer had died of a sudden heart attack and they had been out of work ever since.

They stitched cushions and had completed three by the next morning. Lucy was delighted with the girls' work and hoped she could go on employing them too.

She had bought three dolls. She dressed one in a rose velvet coat and bonnet, a sprigged muslin dress and underwear, all hand-stitched. The second doll was in a ball gown of dark green satin and wore a headdress of golden feathers on a band. The third she dressed as a bride in a white satin dress and veil and was astonished when all three had sold after having been displayed for only an hour. Lucy bought more that day.

When she got back James was waiting to take her to the registrar's office and to look at an apartment in Mayfair which he liked. He seemed relaxed but she sensed he was impatient to have had to wait for her.

He had not attempted to make love to her again but when he brought her home after an evening out, there was passion in his kisses and she longed for the time to come when they could make love.

There was a wedding in progress at the registrar's. The bride was in white with a veil and for the first time Lucy felt she would have liked to have been a white bride.

When wedding arrangements had been settled for two weeks' time, James took her to see the apartment and she was dismayed at the masculinity of the furnishings. James did tell her she could order any furniture she wished but she decided that this would need a great deal of thought. James was anxious to fulfil an engagement.

The next day Deborah began to make her a cream dress and jacket and a hat, similarly stitched to the one she had made Beth, a beautiful creation. Yet again Lucy felt a slight yearning to be married in white. There were other nagging doubts and worries that went through her mind. And as the time drew near she began to feel detached, as if she were preparing for someone else's wedding. What was lacking? Romance? When Deborah returned after having been out with Adin there was a soft expression in her eyes as she would tell her the lovely things that Adin had said: "My princess" . . . "My own dear darling".

James never said anything like that to her yet she knew every evening how much he wanted her. And, she wanted him, desperately at times. She consoled herself that it would be different when they were married. James would feel he did not yet have the right to call her his princess. Or, perhaps, he was still suffering from the rejection of his first wife. Lucy wished she had met her, to find out what kind of person she was. But then her face might have intruded when they were making love. As it was she was just a vague image. A nothing woman, as it were.

It did not stop her, however, from wondering if he ever thought of Imogen, if he wished he could still be married to her.

Three nights before the wedding she was in bed when she found herself wondering if he was marrying her because he wanted children. No, of course not. She lay down again. She saw him the night before the wedding and he smiled and gave her a hug and told her in a teasing way, not to be late for the wedding. There was no kiss . . . nothing.

Ernie and Grace came the next morning to pick up Lucy and Deborah. The day was dry and reasonably warm, but Lucy felt cold and it cost her an effort to talk and to make it sound as though she were happy about the wedding. James was there with Adin and he and Deborah exchanged a shy smile at one another as though they were the bride and groom.

It all seemed so unreal at the registrar's office and as she repeated the required words, they held no meaning for her. "Do you take this man as your lawfully wedded husband?"

"I do . . ."

At the end of the ceremony James smiled and kissed her and a little of the ice in her melted.

The Draycotts congratulated them and so did Deborah and Adin.

Deborah was tearful. They went to a small café for a meal but Lucy felt that everything was rushed. They were going to get the train to Brighton and Lucy had to change into the coat and hat that Deborah had made for her when they were going to London for the first time.

Then they were saying goodbye, a taxi was waiting and James promised they would have a big get-together when they returned.

They all seemed jolly, except her. She smiled and waved from the taxi window when she felt like weeping.

At the station James hurried her along. They had only a few minutes to get the train. Lucy wanted to say, "For heaven's sake we can get the next one." A porter was hurrying ahead. He stopped. "This is your carriage, sir."

Lucy was aware of a lot of well-dressed people, waiting to say the last goodbyes. She was also aware that the carriage was quite luxurious. There was thick carpeting on the floor. Flowers on the tables. When James came back after seeing to the porter he said, "Well, we shall soon be on our way to Paris."

Lucy stared at him. "Paris?"

"Yes, my love," he said softly, "I shall take you to Montmartre, to the Sacré-Coeur, to the Place du Tertre where you will see the artists in the square. Tomorrow we shall go to the Palace of Versailles."

He had taken her hand and put it to his lips.

And she had thought him without romance.

She would make it up to him . . . on her honeymoon night.

Chapter Fifteen

That night in Paris they stayed at the Ritz, one of the most famous hotels in the world, where the suites were named after famous people who had stayed there, including Coco Chanel, Marcel Proust and Edward VII.

The suite they were escorted to was quietly elegant. Even the bathrooms were beautiful; the bath in the ladies' bathroom was painted on the inside with a balcony scene, where roses and foliage mingled. A girl sat with the back of her head resting against the shoulder of the young man. He had his arms around her. Lucy thought it so romantic.

Later, when Lucy went to take a bath, she was unable to turn on the tap. James went with her and turned one on. Scalding water drummed into the bath. He turned on the cold tap and she mentioned how she felt about the balcony scene.

"And the evening is just beginning," he teased her. He sprinkled essence into the water. "Don't dare be too long or I shall be in the bath with you." He kissed the tip of nose and left, laughing.

Lucy was tempted to linger in the cloudy warmth of the water but was afraid that James might keep his threat. She dried herself on a large fleecy bath towel, then put on her white lawn nightdress with its tiny tucks and lace, slipped into her dressing gown then, after releasing the water, fled to the bedroom.

She had been told that a bride must be in bed and waiting for her husband, and to her relief, she saw that James was not there.

After discarding her dressing gown she threw back the bedcovers and climbed into a beautifully warm bed.

Oh, what luxury.

Seconds later James came in, wearing a white towelling bath robe and drying his thick dark hair, which curled with the dampness. He smiled at her, rubbed his hair a little more then threw the towel over the back of a chair.

He came to the bed, then, taking off the bath robe, he stood for a few seconds then got in beside her. Lucy had seen her brothers naked when they were young, but she had not seen a man naked. Her face burned. She was surprised at the change from childhood to manhood and thought that entering her would be a very painful thing.

His hands teased her body, moving lightly over her skin. His lips moved over hers, gentle as before then sensuously and she responded at once. She was unable to do anything else. He played round the lower part of her body and she moaned with desire. She had no idea it would be like this. She wanted to shout but dare not in case it was not the right thing to do. How could her body have lain dormant for so long?

"I'll try not to hurt you," he whispered, as he entered her. His movements were unexpected and she was surprised that the pain was lost in the throbbing of her body, a throbbing that increased with every second. She automatically raised herself to meet the challenge and she knew a joy she had never known existed. James began to increase his pace and every tremor in her body wanted him to move more quickly. She was beginning to feel an ecstasy when suddenly James stopped, breathing heavily, and everything stopped inside her. What had gone wrong?

He said, his lips next to her throat, "I'm sorry, Lucy, it will be better next time for you. The throbbing inside you drove me mad."

"It was all right," she said.

"You are amazing, yet I know you were a virgin."

"When will the next time be?" she asked.

He raised himself from her and laughed. "In a moment or two. How wonderful you are."

She had been disappointed when the pleasure had finished. Now she was delighted to have pleased him. James rolled away from her.

"Of all the women I've been with in my life, you are the best, my darling Lucy."

The words, *all* the women, did not please her but the fact that he thought her the best, did. She said hesitantly, "How many women have you been with?"

"That is a forbidden question."

"Oh," she said.

"But I will tell you that you are the first one that I've experienced such vibrations with."

"Oh," she said again.

"And I want you again, now. This minute."

Her emotions responded at once. This time they climaxed together and she had never experienced anything like it. It was an explosion of joy and an ecstasy. Afterwards she felt bathed in a glow of warmth.

She could understand how a girl became pregnant. Why had his wife refused his pleas? She was no longer jealous of Imogen, just sorry for her, for missing such utter bliss.

It was a night of all nights. Going into a restless sleep then making love again.

They slept late, James having left word they were not to be disturbed. At half past nine he roused her with kisses . . . and wanted to make love again, but she laughed and, throwing back the covers, slid out of bed.

"Not until tonight," she said laughing. "We have a lot of sightseeing to do."

"So we have." He got out of bed. "I thought we would go to Versailles. You'll like it."

Over breakfast James told her about Versailles. He said that in the seventeenth century Paris was a rowdy, rabble-ridden city and that Louis XIV hated it and was looking for somewhere else to live. Versailles was the place he chose.

"It was marshy land and the Chateau must seem very big to people like us, but we have to remember that twenty thousand noblemen, servants and hangers-on, moved there with him. Vast mansions had to be built with avenues broader than some in Paris."

James then went on to say that they would go by car, lent by the hotel. And after he had described the gardens Lucy was anxious to see the Palace of Versailles.

She was taken with the Palace itself but she was utterly enchanted with the Hall of Mirrors and the 250 acres of grounds, which included glorious woods, lawns, flower beds, statues, lakes and fountains.

The leafy boulevards were also pleasant to explore but what really intrigued Lucy was the museum with numerous cosily furnished rooms containing paintings, weapons, exquisite porcelain . . .

The time she spent studying various items had James getting impatient. There was so much he wanted to show her that evening.

She felt exhausted when they got back to the hotel and thought that she would not be able to do another thing that evening, but when after dinner James asked her where she wanted to go she said at once, "To Montmartre."

He gave her a broad grin. "A good choice."

Lucy was surprised at just how much energy she had left. It was all up and down steps and when they climbed to Sacre-Coeur she had a feeling of awe. There was a lovely dome that they had kept catching glimpses of while they had been walking. With the high vaulted interior in the dim light it seemed so vast. Lucy became aware of women lighting candles and of others kneeling praying and felt a reverence she had never experienced before.

When they came out they paused at the top of the steps. Beyond lay Paris, twinkling lights giving a romance to even the poor parts of the city. James took hold of her hand and said softly, "It looks so beautiful when it's dark."

"Yes," she murmured, her eyes brimming with tears.

James took her to the market where there were many artists. Stalls were lit by naphtha flares, the flames twisting this way and that in the evening breeze. She loved the atmosphere of romance, young couples strolling along, their arms around one another's waists and stopping now and then for a kiss. Stall holders were shouting their wares, others wanting to paint the portraits of the passers-by.

James stopped at one stall and drew Lucy forward. "I have no photograph of you. Come along, this man seems to be quite good."

"No, no, some other time."

James gave in and they strolled about, James's arm around her waist, and Lucy thought she could not have been happier.

That night was similar to their wedding night. The next morning when Lucy was awake she found herself alone in bed. Where was James? In the bathroom. He came bounding in about ten minutes later, calling her "sweet lazybones". He was shaved and dressed.

He came over and dropped a kiss on her brow, saying, "That is all for the moment. I dare not caress you or I would be back in bed with you. It's a glorious morning and I want to walk with you among the arcades of the rue de Rivoli. They have some delightful small shops that sell beautiful blouses and the most exquisite perfumes. I shall buy you some of both. I'll leave you, and be in the dining room. A business acquaintance is here. Don't be long now."

Lucy washed and dressed quickly and went down-stairs, not wanting her husband to become deeply immersed with a business acquaintance on their honeymoon.

When she came downstairs she saw James standing at the reception desk. He was reading something and looked pale. As she drew near she saw it was a telegram.

She hurried to him. "What is it, James?"

He handed her the telegram and she read, *Imogen seriously ill. Stop. Can you come. Stop. David.*

He took the telegram from her and, folding it, put it in his pocket. "I must go, you can stay if you wish."

She was angry but tried to keep calm. "There's

no point in staying on my own. We had better go and pack."

When James had packed his bag he said he would go downstairs and find out the train times and settle the bill.

Lucy stood gripping the back of a chair. She did not believe that Imogen was ill. It was a ruse to get him back. Why were there not more details?

James came back saying, "There's a train at ten-thirty, We shall have breakfast on the train. Are you ready?"

"Yes, who is David?"

"Imogen's brother. We can discuss this later."

"Has this ever happened before?"

"No." The porter came for the luggage. "Shall we go?"

There was something about the whole thing that made Lucy think it had a false ring. How had the brother known where to find them? James must have told Imogen. But why should he? It had nothing to do with her. She would ask him later.

A taxi was waiting and when they had drawn away she said, "How would Imogen's brother know where to find us?"

"I've no idea."

"Did you tell Imogen where we were staying? None of my family knew."

"I refuse to be questioned."

How cold his voice was. Was he still in love with Imogen?

"Very well," she said, "we shall travel in silence."

"I didn't mean that. You have to remember that I was once married to Imogen."

"But she refused to be a wife to you. I was a wife, a proper wife and according to you a most satisfactory one. Now, the unsatisfactory one gets all the attention."

"Because she's seriously ill, for God's sake."

"Is she? I imagine you'll get home to see her looking pale and wan and falling into your arms."

"Will you stop it?" he said through tight lips. "Imogen could be dying."

"I shall be very surprised."

He sat up and stared straight ahead.

Tears welled in Lucy's eyes. All their beautiful honeymoon wasted. Perhaps when they were on the train he might relax.

But although James spoke to her when necessary there was no warmth in him. They had coffee and toast for breakfast and he sat staring out of the window.

After the meal he read and Lucy, exhausted after a sleepless night and all the upset, closed her eyes and slept.

When they reached London he saw her into a taxi to take her home and left her to go and see Imogen. He did not even say goodbye.

By the time Lucy reached home she felt ill. There was no mother to talk to, no sister Deborah to tell her troubles to nor a kindly Mrs Trippet. The telegram that James said he would send to Deborah was on the mat behind the door. The fire was almost out. She put some pieces of wood on, then when it caught she put on pieces of coal. She then made a cup of tea and sat huddled over the fire feeling utterly miserable.

At two o'clock she filled two hot-water bottles, put them in the bed and crawled up the stairs. She had nightmares throughout the night and tossed and turned, sweating one minute and ice-cold the next.

When Deborah arrived home at eight o'clock the

following morning with Grace and found the telegram she ran upstairs and found Lucy shivering. She called Grace. They refilled bottles, piled on blankets and an eiderdown, but it was midday before Lucy was able to tell them what had happened. She blamed herself for the rift but Grace and Deborah said they thought that James had behaved appallingly.

It was the following afternoon when James arrived and Grace told him what she and Deborah thought of him.

"Your wife is ill in bed, but you went rushing off to a woman who didn't even want to live with you?"

James head went up. "Lucy is ill?"

"She could have died if Deborah and I had not arrived when we did. How could you, James, your bride? She wanted to take the blame on her shoulders, but I hope we convinced her that the blame was yours."

"Imogen had cut her wrists. I had to go."

"But she was alive when you arrived."

"Yes, I . . . could I see Lucy?"

"No. She's still in shock. You sitting in silence all the way home. How could you?"

"Grace, I had to go and see Imogen. She's a lonely soul." He was pleading for understanding. "It was she who didn't want me there."

"Rubbish. She wanted you all right. If she hadn't she would not have told her brother where you were. Why did you give her your Paris address?"

He made no reply and Grace suddenly felt sorry for him. He was obviously still in love with the wretched Imogen.

Heaven help Lucy.

It was the third day after they returned that

James called again. Lucy was up and sitting in the chair by the fire, a shawl around her shoulders.

He said gently, "Lucy, I'm sorry. I didn't realise I would make you ill."

"It doesn't matter, it's not important. Nothing matters."

"It does, you mustn't talk like that."

She turned her head. "I don't care any more."

He reached out to take her hand but she withdrew it.

"Lucy, please don't ignore me."

"You ignored me. You just didn't care. The only one on your mind was Imogen. Did she die?"

"No, no, she recovered."

"How amazing. I thought she was at death's door."

He looked embarrassed. "David made her out to be worse than she was. She – cut her wrists. There was a lot of blood."

"So her brother rushed out and sent you a telegram."

"No, it was after she had been taken to hospital." He got up. "I'd better go."

"To avoid the awkward questions."

"No. Because I know you won't believe anything I say."

"Why should I? Any other man would have stayed with his bride. You could have phoned to enquire how Imogen was." Her voice had dropped. "I can't even have *my* marriage annulled."

James sat down again. "Lucy, I had hoped we could have got together again. Would you be willing to try?"

"Why should I?" she asked bitterly. "To ease your lot, so your friends wouldn't say, there must be

222

something wrong with you, leaving your bride of two days to go rushing to the woman who didn't want to live with you?"

"You've given me your answer, Lucy," he said quietly. "I won't trouble you again. Goodbye."

When he had gone, life came rushing back to Lucy. What had she done? She didn't want to be parted. She loved him still, God help her. She wanted him to love her, only her. What had she done? Lost him forever. Perhaps now Imogen had learned her lesson and would be willing to live with him as his wife.

She threw the shawl from her shoulders. She still had the shop. She would give all her concentration to her work from now on. It was no use sitting and feeling sorry for herself. That was all over.

Chapter Sixteen

Lucy had stitched quite a lot of hexagons together that afternoon when Grace arrived.

"Why, Lucy," she greeted her. "How good to see you working again. Has – James been?"

"Yes, and I sent him away."

"Wasn't that a little foolish?" she said gently. "What James is suffering from is guilt. He felt responsible because Imogen did not want to be a wife to him. He learnt a lesson, that although Imogen did not want to be a wife to him she did not want him to have anyone else. She cut her wrists but they were only small cuts."

Lucy looked up. "Who told him where we were?"

"We did, unfortunately. We were torn. David made it sound so serious. He is highly strung and was getting hysterical."

Lucy sighed. "I curse Imogen because she ruined a lovely honeymoon."

"Shouldn't you be feeling sorry for her, Lucy? She'll never get James to go running again to her. You two could have a wonderful life together."

"I gave of myself so generously." The bitterness was back in Lucy's voice. "And it meant nothing to him."

"It did. He told Ernie how much it meant to have you. Think about it, Lucy. Don't spoil your whole life for a bit of pride."

She said she would think about it.

Lucy thought about it a lot.

James came the following day and told her quietly that Grace had told him he had been a fool. "I know this might be hard to believe, Lucy, but I do love you. Won't you try?"

"We could but I still feel resentful."

"I'm prepared for that. I won't make any demands on you until you feel ready."

"Well . . ."

He thanked her for being so understanding. And that was it. He told her he would be out for the rest of the day and would call for her at five o'clock. She was a wife again, but he did not offer to kiss her. How would she take to living in a strange house? She had never lived outside of the house next to the warehouse since she had been in London, and now, that evening, she would leave her home for a new, unfamiliar one.

She need not have worried. He was there promptly at five o'clock and told her they were to go to the Draycotts for dinner. His smile encouraged her. Plus the fact that Deborah had also been invited. Adin was there too.

They talked of Paris, Ernie and Grace having been there three times. Grace said it was a pity that Lucy and James had not managed to get to the rue de Rivoli, such charming little shops they were. James talked so freely about them that it no longer bothered Lucy that he might have bought other women items from the arcades. He told them how he had tried to persuade Lucy to have a photograph done by one of the pavement artists and how she had refused.

"It's a shame you didn't have one done," said Ernie. "You are a very beautiful lady." Adin applauded this

226

and Deborah said she felt like packing up and going to live in Paris right away.

James laughed and told her not to be in a rush. People were crammed like sardines in the Metro morning and evening, and arrived home at night nervous wrecks.

Deborah, of course, would avoid all the jams by having her business in the centre of Paris.

"Where?" was the cry. Adin looked at her fondly, saying there would be no need for traffic jams, he was going to marry her and she would live at home and have babies.

Deborah stared at him. "Is this a proposal?"

"It is."

James said quietly, "You might have problems there, Adin. The girls decided when they took the business that they would stay for a certain time together to get it under way."

Adin raised his shoulders. "I am agreeable to that. I just want Deborah to say yes."

She said no, she loved him and thanked him for the honour, but said she wanted to build up her business.

Adin said in a peaceable way, "I'll wait as long as it takes, my lovely one."

Deborah gave him a smile and squeezed his hand.

This became a talking point later that evening when James and Lucy went to their apartment. James said, "I'm afraid that Adin will have a long wait. Didn't you say that Deborah said she wanted to do a fashion show?"

"She's longing for it. But that could not be for a few years."

"I don't know. She's doing very well, she has

227

several good customers already and the ones she has are recommending others."

"It's a hard world."

There had been no changes in the apartment since Lucy had last seen it but it had a softer look, possibly because of a fire burning and soft lights glowing. James carried Lucy's suitcase into the main bedroom, saying, "I shall sleep in the spare room until you feel adjusted, Lucy."

It was said in the most natural way and Lucy wished she felt adjusted but knew that it would take time. James offered her a drink but she said no, she felt ready for bed.

She wondered about Deborah and the business. Would she give in to Adin as she had done by returning to James? With a sigh she undressed and got into bed. This bed too had been warmed. She decided to put James and the honeymoon from her mind which was not easy. It took time before she began to drift off.

She awoke at seven o'clock and got up, wanting to get down to some work. James had told her there was a woman who came in to tidy the rooms and who would do any washing required. He also said she would prepare a meal if a note was left.

When Lucy went into the dining room she could smell bacon cooking. It made her feel hungry. To her surprise James was in the kitchen at the stove. He turned his head. "Good morning, did you sleep well?"

"Yes, I did. I should be doing that."

"We'll share it. Coffee is made. Sit down and have a cup while I do the eggs and tomatoes." Lucy poured herself a cup and walked to the window.

"Oh, we have a garden, I see."

228

"It belongs to the other people in the house too, but I'm told that a gardener comes to look after it. I haven't seen anyone in it."

"It should be lovely when all the flowers are out."

There was a sizable lawn with a border planted with clematis that had been trained to climb along the wall and other plants showing flowering. Lucy didn't know all the names but there were geraniums, lobelia and numerous other varieties, all blooming.

A shed at the bottom of the garden, said James, held garden chairs and two small tables. Lucy doubted whether she would ever have the pleasure of using them.

While the rest of the breakfast was cooking, James laid the table in the kitchen, saying it was convenient. They would use the dining room in the evening.

Lucy asked, smiling, if she would be allowed to prepare any meals. James, looking at her quickly and seeing her smiling, said it was something he was looking forward to. If she put what she needed on a piece of paper the cleaning woman would get the shopping. He didn't yet know her name.

When Lucy asked if he had a preference he smiled and said, "I eat what is put before me." Which was not exactly a help and she explained that she and Deborah had simple meals. He said that that would suit him fine. He added that he would let her know in good time if he would be away.

She made quite a long list and thought there would be times when she would have to leave the shop earlier than usual. She did not want to become known as a useless wife.

James ran her to the warehouse site and said he would pick her up in the evening at five o'clock.

As they were driving up to the door Lucy was sure she saw Adin leaving by the back door. If this was so, Deborah was asking for trouble. There was traffic in front and she could not be sure if it was Adin but she was determined to ask.

James dropped her off, said, "See you later," and was away.

Deborah, who was in her dressing gown, greeted her brightly. "Oh, it's like old times, isn't it, to be together again?"

Lucy took off her coat and hung it up. "Deborah, I saw Adin leave by the back door. He hasn't been here all night, has he?"

"Of course not. What would he be doing here?"

"Sleeping with you. Tell me the truth."

"Yes . . ." she said on a sigh. "It'll be a long time before we can get married and I wanted him as much as he wanted me."

"It's your life but he could land you with a baby and – "

Deborah interrupted. "He's careful."

"How many times have we heard that in our lives? I'm not going to say any more. James is going to pick me up at five o'clock."

"Lucy, I – I'll have a word with Adin. Oh, here are the girls."

Their staff, Ada, Jenny and Mary, came in by the warehouse. They were painfully thin girls, and although they didn't talk a lot to Deborah and Lucy they talked to each other, while they sewed at a lightning speed.

Lucy went out at the back of the house and opened the door connected to the warehouse and called, "Good morning to you all."

They were putting on their white aprons and

all looked up. Ada said, "Are you feeling better, Mrs Dexter?"

"Yes, top of the world. I wanted to make an early start. My husband will be picking me up at five."

"Oh, that's nice," she said, smiling shyly with her sisters.

Lucy withdrew into the shop to work and switched on the small heater. She found it difficult to get started and was glad when Grace arrived at nine o'clock.

"James phoned to say you had gone to work but I felt I must just call and see you. Did you get everything settled?"

"More or less. At the moment we're not sleeping together, but we will do later. It takes time."

Grace gave her a cuddle. "Don't wait too long. Now, what are you sewing today?"

"I shall dress the dolls, I think, when I can get started."

"I'll help you. Ernie is meeting James later."

They had some regular customers who congratulated Lucy on her marriage. It was a nice feeling to be missed.

During the afternoon she kept glancing at the clock. She must be ready when James called. She would miss the extra hours in the evenings when she had stayed late but perhaps James would not mind her doing some sewing at home.

At half past four Grace said she must go. Although she had left instructions with Cook, she liked to be there to supervise the dinner. "I would have liked to have taken some sewing home with me but Ernie will be in this evening and he doesn't like me knitting or sewing."

Lucy thought there were two lessons to be learned;

to see to the dinner and not to do any sewing if James was in for the evening.

James was prompt. He talked to Deborah while Lucy put on her hat and coat. Deborah was working late that evening. She had promised to finish a ball gown for a customer the next day. She smiled. "I shall have to resist Adin if he tries to persuade me to leave it to finish in the morning. There's always a snag to contend with."

"Then we'll leave you to it. Don't work too late. Ready, Lucy?" When they were in the car he said, "I think Deborah is making a mistake putting her work before Adin."

Was this a warning to her? Lucy wondered. She said, "She did prepare him that she might have to work some evenings."

"As long as she doesn't do it every evening."

"Of course she won't." Lucy had difficulty in controlling her temper, knowing that James was definitely warning her that she could not play about with *him*.

Then in the next breath he told her he would be going to Holland the following week, possibly for ten days, and Lucy felt a sense of relief. Perhaps when he came back they might get back to living a normal life. At the moment her body felt dead, with none of the emotions present she had felt in the first days of their marriage.

When they got home she found the apartment warm. Mrs Wainwright had not only done all the shopping but she had also built up the fire and prepared the meal. The potatoes had been peeled and were in a bowl of water, the onions and cabbage were cut finely and the liver was cut in slices and covered with a plate. A note from Mrs Wainwright said that she had boiled the pudding and made the custard, they would only need to be warmed in the oven.

"What a gem we've got," Lucy exclaimed to James. "Look at all this. And she put the guard to the fire. I'll soon get this cooked."

James said he would have a look at the paper. Lucy wished she could think of James as a husband and not as someone she had just met. That was the way she felt about him at the moment.

James praised her cooking and had an extra helping of pudding, which he pronounced as being delicious.

"It's just plain old-fashioned cooking," she said.

"And I'm all for it," he said smiling. "It suits me." Then more seriously he added, "I do appreciate it, Lucy."

She was touched by his appreciation, which she knew was genuine.

He said later he had work to do and would keep out of her way by doing it in the bedroom as it was complicated and it was then she asked him what his work was exactly. "You told me it was to do with the M.O.D. but what does that stand for?"

"Ministry Of Defence. I do a number of jobs. I must get started. I wouldn't mind another cup of coffee later."

She said she would bring him one. After she had washed up she would write some letters and, if she had time, she would stitch some cushion pieces. She felt pleased at the way things were going.

When she took the coffee in to James she found him immersed with a mass of papers. She said, "I think it would be better if we exchanged bedrooms. You would have more room to work."

He looked up and said, his expression solemn, "It would be better if we shared the bigger bedroom."

"Not yet." She fled and he called cheerfully after her, "Sorry."

The wretch. He knew how she felt. She was not ready to give in.

She settled down to sew, but found she was trembling. Was she being foolish in denying him his rights? Would he think of her as another Imogen? Surely not. No, he would have to wait.

But by bedtime Lucy was aware of tremors going through her body at the thought of James making love to her.

When he came in to have a drink with her before going off to bed he said, "Well, have you decided what we'll have for dinner tomorrow?"

She had not even given it a moment's thought. On impulse she said, "How about steak and kidney pie and apple tart?"

"Splendid. A drink?"

"No, thanks. Actually . . . yes, I've changed my mind. I would like a sherry."

With the drinks poured he sat down and began to talk about the work she had to do. "I don't want you to work too hard, Lucy."

"It's not a trial, I love it. I brought some sewing to do this evening, but I didn't feel like it, so it was left. I would never push my work."

"I'm glad. I was talking to Ernie today. He's taking Grace to Scotland for a holiday. Would you like to go with them?"

Lucy did not want to go. With Grace away Deborah would be on her own. She said, "I couldn't, I'm half expecting Mrs Trippet to come and visit us although she won't be staying with us. She has friends here."

This was true. Mrs Trippet had mentioned it in her last letter. "I wrote this evening to her and told her we would be delighted to see her," Lucy went on. "I told her about getting married. I also wrote and told Mother and Beth."

"It'll be nice to see Mrs Trippet, she's been a good friend," said James, nodding slowly.

"She has indeed."

James got up. "Well, I'll be off." He put down his glass. "I'll say good night."

"James, go into the big bedroom." Her heart was pounding.

"Only if you will come too," he said softly.

She hesitated a moment then gave a nod. "Very well."

He let her go first while he locked up and put out the lights and once Lucy was in bed James was no longer a stranger. He was the man she loved and wanted.

They had what James spoke and laughed about as a wild night and although Lucy was drained the next morning she was happy again.

When Deborah saw her she teased her. "Easy to see that all is well with you two."

"Yes, thank goodness. I wouldn't have wanted to go on living separate lives. How did you get on with Adin last night?"

"I resisted him. He wasn't pleased, but it's the future that I have to think about."

Lucy found herself wondering if Deborah was doing the right thing, then dismissed it. What would she herself do when James was away? Do housework? No, Deborah was right. They had to stick to a plan.

Two mornings later there were three letters for Lucy at the shop. Her mother was upset that she had not been at the wedding. If only Lucy could have waited a few weeks until her ankles had mended. But there, she could hardly blame her. Look how eager she had been to marry dear Andrew. She was so pleased they had gone to Paris. A beautiful city. It was so lovely to hear all about it. Andrew had his eye on a house and they would probably be moving in in a few weeks time. Then Lucy and Mr Dexter must come and visit them. The twins had settled in and loved Andrew. They all sent their best wishes. Love from them all.

Lucy read the few lines from Beth.

Well, and what a surprise. Lucky Lucy marrying money. Money was not important to them. They hoped to see them sometime. Love from them both.

Beth had changed. She had been a favourite with Lucy. Now she felt that Deborah had more tolerance and understanding. She picked up Mrs Trippet's letter, wanting to savour it and she was not disappointed.

My darling girl,

How delighted I was to have your letter with news of your wedding. And how lovely to know that you spent your honeymoon in Paris. Mr Dexter is such a lovely man. I just know you'll both be happy. I have a lot to tell you, but will wait until you come to see me.

With lots of love to you all.

Lucy smiled. A typical Mrs Trippet letter.

Over the next few days they suddenly had orders from several hotels in the country for their silk sheets. They had stopped making these once their material supply had run out but the orders meant that Lucy would now have to start buying rolls of silk. Her pieces for the cushions were going down and so were the remnants of flimsy chiffon for the scarves. She asked Grace for the addresses of the material

236

warehouses and the next day she went along to one. Grace went too.

The warehouse was huge, with such a variety of materials that Lucy spent far too much. When she complained Grace said cheerfully, "You are fixed up for months, you'll soon get the money back."

"Yes, in small amounts. I'll have to hope that Deborah will have a lull with her work and that I can get the girls to do some work for me."

Deborah kept them busy but Ada, who was the eldest, said that all the family would work in the evening for Lucy if she was willing. She refrained from saying anything to James about it and was looking forward to the ten days he would be away. There would be no rushing to be ready in time for James to pick her up in the evenings and she and Deborah could have lunch together again.

She drooled over her materials, the plain and patterned silks and velvets and the flimsy, flowered patterns of the chiffon. So did Deborah who asked for patterns to show her clients.

The day that James left for Holland, Deborah told Lucy, gleefully, that she had several more new clients. Adin was not so pleased, saying that dear Deborah was working much too hard. But nothing was going to put Deborah off and when she mentioned this to him they fell out.

When Grace heard the news she gave a sigh of relief. Adin's father was complaining that his son was neglecting his work and that was something he would not tolerate. It would be just as well if the couple had a break for a while.

Deborah was in a seventh heaven of delight. She missed Adin terribly, but she was achieving her object, building up the business.

She did make some lovely dresses and suits and employed two cousins of Ada's to make buttonholes and to do some very fine and intricate embroidery.

Although Lucy had been glad that James would be away for ten days she had to admit missing him terribly, even though she worked late at the business. And it was not only in a sensual way. She missed their togetherness in the evenings. They had had a telephone installed in the shop and he rang her every day to ask how she was and every time she told him she was missing him terribly. And always she would end by saying, "I love you, James, very much," and he would reply softly, "And I love you, my darling."

On the fourth day after James had left, a slender, attractive woman came into the shop and asked if she could speak to Mr Dexter. She was well dressed and had wide blue eyes.

Lucy was about to say that Mr Dexter was abroad when she suddenly caught a crafty look in the blue eyes and knew who it was. Imogen.

She felt strangely calm. "My husband is abroad," she replied firmly.

"Could you please give me his address? I am his wife."

"You are no longer Mr Dexter's wife. The marriage was annulled. I am now married to him."

"You are mistaken, I am still married to him. Please give me his address." There was a haughtiness in her voice.

"James and I were married some weeks ago," Lucy said firmly, "and you brought him back from our honeymoon by getting your brother to send him a telegram saying you were seriously ill and asking him if he could come."

She looked bewildered. "I don't understand. I've never been ill."

"You cut your wrists," Lucy said sharply and looked in the direction of her hands.

Imogen held them out. "You are mistaken. Look."

They were slender hands, slender wrists, without a mark on them. What was going on? Lucy's heart beat in painful thuds.

"You see," Imogen went on, "I was innocent when James and I were married and I was afraid to, well, to consummate the marriage. But now I've seen a specialist and am willing to be with him, as a wife." She stressed the word "wife".

Lucy, determined not to be taken in by this cheating woman, said coldly, "Do you have a brother called David?"

She nodded. "Yes, I do, but I haven't seen him for months. He goes to sea. He's in Japan at the moment. I had a card from him. I have it with me. I'll show you." She opened her handbag but Lucy told her not to bother.

"You are a very clever woman, but you don't deceive me for one moment. You sent the telegram, anything to get him to you, but he came back to me."

"I don't know what you are talking about. James told me to let him know after I had been to the specialist. I haven't seen him for weeks. Why won't you tell him I'm here?"

She was pitiful in her bewilderment. Lucy said, "My husband is away. I suggest you write to him in a week's time. And now, if you will excuse me." Lucy came round from the counter and opened the shop door. "Good day to you."

"I'll go," she said, speaking firmly, "but I shall be back."

239

And she left, her head held high.

Lucy sank on to a chair. Why had James lied about the cut wrists? He had said the cuts were small. Had he felt ashamed at rushing off and could not bear to tell her the truth? Imogen had said she had not seen him for weeks, which was also a lie. All this lying . . . for what purpose?

She needed to talk to someone about it. Deborah had a number of fittings today. Should she phone Grace? A trouble shared was a trouble halved. She picked up the phone.

Chapter Seventeen

Grace came over and Lucy told her the story of Imogen.

"The woman is mad," Grace said. "She obviously had not done anything to her wrists. She was the one who sent the telegram to James. Of course he wouldn't want to tell you. When he phones, you play it gently. He'll already be hurting by what went on."

"I'll try," Lucy said. "It won't be easy. I hurt. It seems awful to me that James had to lie about the affair."

"Wives suffer a lot of hurts, Lucy. I have, but if you want your marriage to work you have to keep a lot of things to yourself."

It was mid-afternoon when James phoned. Lucy told him straightaway about Imogen and then said gently, "I can understand you not wanting to admit that she hadn't cut her wrists. She's a dangerous woman, James, wanting you back."

He was furious and said he felt like coming home straight away.

"Don't, darling, that would be giving in to her. It's what she wants. You have business to attend to. I feel better for having talked to you. I love you, James, I always will."

"You are a wonderful person, Lucy, so understanding. If Imogen comes back just refuse to talk to her. Tell her when I'm home I shall deal with her."

There was some more talk but when James had rung off Lucy was glad she had not got on her high horse. Sensible Grace.

She had decided not to tell Deborah. She was busy, was a little uptight and it would serve no purpose.

Quite a lot of work was covered during the days waiting for James to come home. Letters came from her brothers saying how delighted they were to hear she was married. How sensible she had been in getting married quietly. They would not have been able to come. They had deadlines to get some summerhouses completed. Their mother was just so happy; she was enjoying entertaining and accepting invitations.

Thank goodness it had all worked out for them. She had a terrible longing to see them all and hoped it could be arranged soon.

Although she had accepted James's insistence that he would put things right when he came home, a tiny doubt niggled at her. He arrived unexpectedly one evening after she had come home and they went wordlessly into one another's arms. He stroked her cheek. "Oh, Lucy, how I've longed to see you."

"Why didn't you tell me you were coming home?"

"I suddenly made up my mind I couldn't stay a minute longer. I had to see you."

She had just made tea and she poured them each a cup and they sat over the fire, discussing Imogen. James said he had decided not to see her. "Let her come here and we can have it out. She had sent the telegram and used David's name. Yes, I know I let you think I had seen him. I thought it would be easier."

"She's unhinged."

242

"No, she's as sane as you or I. She agreed to the marriage being annulled."

"She insisted she was still married to you."

"Remind me later and I'll show you the papers."

Lucy told him about buying the new material but she felt he was not pleased about this. She told him about the letters she had had from her family and Mrs Trippet and he seemed quietly pleased. After she had seen the annulment papers and they had had a meal, he mentioned again the rolls of material she had bought and asked if it was wise to buy so much. It meant a lot of work.

She explained that Ada's family were sewing for her and he said no more. He seemed restless at times and on other occasions seemed detached. She asked him about his work in Holland and he told her it had gone quite well. He did not, however, enlarge on it and said he thought he would have an early night. He had left Harwich at midnight and hadn't been able to sleep; he added that he was not the best of travellers.

Lucy was not long in following him. James was asleep and it was not long before Lucy was asleep too. It was not until the next day that Lucy realised there were discrepancies in the stories of Imogen. She had said that her brother David went to sea and offered to show her a card he had sent to her recently. Grace had said that David had phoned them for James's address and that he was almost hysterical.

It was not possible for David to phone from Japan, so if Imogen did call at the shop again there was at least one definite lie she had told.

When James called to pick her up that evening she told him about Imogen's lie. He was thoughtful for a few moments then said, "I don't think we shall hear anything more from her."

Lucy found herself hoping that she *would* call. She very much wanted to tell her about the lie, let Imogen know how much she had slipped in James's estimation.

She was denied this satisfaction. At least for the time being.

Lucy and James slipped into a routine. She thought it a quite pleasurable routine. He picked her up in the evening and they either had an evening meal that Lucy had prepared and the Draycotts shared it, or they went to the Draycotts.

The only thing that started to bother Lucy was that after the first two weeks James became detached. He would go to bed early and there were a number of evenings when they did not make love.

When she asked him what was wrong he told her rather sharply that he was unable to make love to her every night, to which she replied, equally as sharply, that she did not expect him to do so, but pointed out that he had not done so for ten nights in a row.

"I have my work to think about, it's quite complicated." He sighed in an exasperated way, and Lucy put on a forced, cheerful manner.

"That's all right, as long as I know the reason. So, while you are thinking, I can do some work."

"I wish you wouldn't. I find it distracting."

"So, you expect me to sit twiddling my thumbs while you are thinking. It won't work, James. I've always been a busy person and I can't stop now."

"Then I'll turn the smaller bedroom into a study."

"Fine. I'll help you. The bed can go into the linen room."

"We can leave the bed in. I'll buy a small desk." He

244

spoke gruffly. He left to work in the small bedroom and Lucy sat down, feeling dismayed.

What had gone wrong? He had told her on her honeymoon that she had pleased him sexually, more than any other woman he had been with. Her heart skipped a beat. Was that the reason? He had not been able to make love to Imogen. Was he brooding about it? Did he feel a failure? Would she have felt a failure if she had not pleased him with her response to his lovemaking? Yes, she would.

What a miserable situation to have reached. And it was not something she could discuss with Grace. She did not want to make her husband sound a weakling. Perhaps he would make an effort that evening to make love to her.

But no. He was asleep and she lay wide awake going over the problem. Sex was not the be-all and end-all of marriage. It did, however, play a big part.

The following morning she felt bleary-eyed.

In the post was a letter from Imogen. Now what? Lucy thought as she split it open.

Dear Miss Lingard,

I must say right away that James belongs to me. He came to see me the other night to show me the annulment papers. But he did tell me that he still loved me and that he always would. The trouble is, he said, he doesn't know how to get rid of you, so I'm asking you to go back home and leave us together. We spent a lovely afternoon together making love and I was so pleased. I don't mind living with him. You can stay married to him. It doesn't worry me.

It was signed, *Imogen Dexter.*

Lucy felt as though all the blood was draining from her body.

"What is it, Lucy?" James asked.

Lucy handed him the letter. She could not stop trembling. She expected him to explode. Instead he sat staring into the fire, the letter in his hand. Her heart began to beat in suffocating thuds.

"So it's true."

"What? No, of course not. I did take the annulment documents but I never made love to her. Did you think I would?"

"You didn't tell me you had been to see her."

"Because I didn't want you to be upset. I told Imogen that I was married to you and I was staying with you. She seemed to accept it. It just seems to me that she must be a very sick woman."

"But is she? How do you account for your moods lately, wanting to work in the evenings, not making love to me?" Her voice had risen angrily and now he was angry.

"Good God, you must have a poor opinion of me if you believed all the trash that Imogen told you." He sat up in the chair. "How could you believe I would say to her that I was having trouble in getting rid of you? Such utter rubbish." He paused then went on more quietly. "I told you there were some complications with my work. It was important that I get them sorted out. I'm only human, Lucy. I can't be the wonderful lover all the time, but this doesn't mean to say that I had stopped loving you."

"No." She sighed. "I suppose I was expecting too much."

"Perhaps you were too. What we'll do is go and see Imogen together tomorrow and convince her that we are a happily married couple and that there will be no change.

Lucy felt that a weight had been lifted from her

246

chest and after an evening spent with the Draycotts they came away light-hearted. Grace said she would come over the next morning while they went to see Imogen.

Although Lucy was dreading meeting Imogen again she knew it had be tackled. And hoped that this would be the end of it.

Imogen welcomed James and made to kiss him, but he kept her away. She invited them in to a small but well-furnished house and sat beaming from one to the other.

So everything was settled, was it? Miss Lingard was willing to relinquish James to her tender care.

James spoke quietly but firmly. "It's settled, Imogen, as it was when I visited you last. Lucy is my legal wife and I want to stress that. I am staying with her."

All the joy went from Imogen's face and she was like a child who had been deprived of a doll. Why? she wanted to know. James loved her. They had consummated the marriage the last time James had visited her.

James and Lucy talked for half an hour but nothing could move Imogen from the belief that she was getting a raw deal. In the end she got up and said, her head up, "When you come the next time, James, do not bring this woman with you. She's not right for you." Lucy walked ahead when they left but Imogen was clinging to James and he had a job to get away.

"She has relatives, I must get in touch with them," he said grimly. "We must get this stopped."

They went to a house in the next street where an aunt of Imogen lived. She invited them in and after listening to the story said, "Just forget it. Imogen isn't mad. She likes playing around, having James

247

to come and call on her and to ask her if she is willing to behave as his wife. What floored her was him telling her he wanted to get married and have children. Imogen had been so confident that James would keep on coming to her and begging her to act as his wife it took the wind out of her sails. The only way to scare her is to tell her that you will inform the police of her behaviour. She's scared of the police."

They talked about Imogen and the more they talked the more Lucy became convinced that Imogen was of unsound mind, and she was doubtful that mentioning the police would stop her from making herself a nuisance. But time would tell.

James said, "We'll try and forget it and hope that Imogen comes to her senses."

It was a week later when James said one evening, "I think it's time we went back to Paris and finished our honeymoon. Don't you?"

He was smiling and Lucy stared at him. "Do you mean it?"

"Of course." Lucy jumped up and flung her arms around him.

"Oh, that would be heaven. When?"

"Tomorrow?"

"Great! I must tell Deborah and see how busy she is. If she's too busy I could ask Grace?"

"Close the shop."

"No, we have customers and I don't want to lose any."

"You don't need to pack any clothes. I am going to buy you everything you need. We are not going to stay at the Ritz but in a three-room apartment that I own."

"You've never mentioned it."

"No, it's where I take all my women." He was grinning broadly.

"If I thought that one of your women had stayed in it I – "

"Until a month ago, the apartment belonged to a married friend."

"Okay," she answered, laughing. "I never meet all these friends of yours. You are a mystery man, James Dexter. I must go and tell Deborah."

Deborah was thrilled about the news but thought she would let Grace know. She enjoyed her company.

She came off the phone to say, "Grace is thrilled too and will be over about half past eight tomorrow morning."

Immediately Lucy went running around, packing only the bare necessities and she had everything packed the next morning, ready to catch the eight-thirty train to Paris.

One of Lucy's greatest pleasures in their first few days in Paris was in going to their own apartment. It was on a first floor level with the bedroom and sitting room at the back, and with French windows that opened on to a balcony that overlooked the Seine.

She called, "Oh, James, it's gorgeous. How peaceful."

"It's up-river. Tomorrow we shall go into the centre and explore. Where do you want to go in the morning?"

"Where do you want to take me?"

"There is one thing you must see; Sainte Chapelle. History was one of my favourite subjects at college. The Chapelle is a beautiful piece of architecture. It's odd, it's beautiful. It was built in the thirteenth century for King Louis IV. I want you to think of it as a medieval casket. designed to hold relics. You go up a dark staircase. The chapel is – how can I describe it? Airy, like the heavens."

"Starry?"

"No, I'm giving the wrong idea. It's like a . . . like a fairy tale." He smiled. "I shall let you have your own impression, but I would just like to say that it's taller than it's wide and the walls have twice as much glass as masonry."

Lucy inclined her head. "Obviously a favourite."

"Yes, I was intending to keep it for the last when we were here before . . . but we won't go into that."

They went to the Chapelle first thing the following morning and Lucy was certainly impressed. James had described it perfectly. There was something mystical about it that she had not seen anywhere else.

It was almost entirely made up of very tall windows which seemed to sparkle in the light. The roof was arched and the lower part all carved oak. Lucy heard a man say softly to the woman with him, "This is one of the supreme achievements of the Middle Ages."

She came away feeling she had been in a dream.

They went next to an art gallery and when they came out James said, "I thought of taking you to the Folies Bergère this evening."

Lucy said, her head cocked, "I thought they showed living statues of naked women."

He grinned. "I thought it would be an experience for you."

"For you, you mean."

"So, you don't want to go?"

"Of course I do. I might learn something," she teased him.

"Your wish shall be my command. But right now

my wish is to take you back to the apartment and make love to you."

She flashed her eyelashes at him. "I am not objecting."

They were like giggling children as they made for the Metro.

It was the most wonderful lovemaking they had had, wild, then gentle and she wanted it to go on forever.

Afterwards they lay in a golden afterglow and James said lazily, "Something tells me we won't be going to the Folies Bergère this evening."

And they didn't because a friend of James called and they all went out to dinner. Although there was some talk of business Lucy came in for a lot of attention from the Frenchman, who was named Pierre Balmain. He would be about thirty, she guessed, and she learned that he and James had been to college together. She also learned that he was married to a beautiful woman who was twice as old as he. He put his fingertips to his lips. "A wonderful woman, you must meet her."

Pierre came back to the apartment with them and they talked until two o'clock in the morning.

Lucy and James slept late and it was a phone call that brought James wide awake. Lucy, still sleepy, heard him shout, "What! I don't believe it. We'll be home as soon as we can."

She shot up in bed. "What's wrong, what's happened?"

James raised his hand to stop her from talking. Eventually he replaced the receiver and got out of bed.

"That was Ernie. Someone has tried to set the shop on fire."

"Imogen," Lucy said bitterly.

"No, not Imogen, it could have been anyone. But we shall have to return home."

"I can't believe it. How dare she damage our shop?"

"Stop blaming Imogen!" James shouted the words. "Don't mention her name again."

They both got ready, both tight-lipped, and hardly spoke a word to one another until they were on the train. Then Lucy said, speaking quietly, "It could only be Imogen, James, why won't you accept it?"

"Because I know it wasn't. She wouldn't do such a thing. And please don't mention her name again."

"How much damage was done?"

"I don't know and I don't want to know. The damned shop."

This set Lucy fuming. And afterwards it was a silent, miserable journey. The second one of its kind.

When they arrived back in London Ernie and Grace were there to meet them.

James thanked them for coming and Ernie said, "It's the least we could do. Come along. We can tell you all about it in the car."

The men sat in the front and the women in the back. As they drew away Ernie told the story.

"No one is hurt, thank God. Someone threw bricks at the window, smashed it to smithereens, then threw burning paper inside. I'm afraid quite a bit of damage has been done. Deborah was late coming home and was about to undress when she heard the crash of glass. She ran to the window and saw a woman lighting paper and throwing it in. She ran downstairs in her nightdress and running outside saw the woman getting into a car. She drove off before Deborah could get to

252

her. Deborah called the fire brigade and luckily they put the fire out in minutes."

James was silent and Lucy said, "Can you describe the woman?"

It was Grace who replied, "Deborah will tell you."

When they arrived home Lucy wanted to weep as she saw the boarded-up window, but by now she felt like a block of ice.

Deborah looked as if she too had been drained of all her tears.

"Oh, Lucy," she said, "that this should happen while you were away. Everyone is shocked. I saw the woman, she was small and had fair hair. I wish I could have laid my hands on her, I would have killed her. All your work, just wasted. Rolls of material damaged. Every single thing has been affected. Your lovely cushions ruined, the dolls, the scarfs . . . well, as I said, it's all wasted."

There was a big fire burning in the grate but Lucy could not get warm. She said firmly, "I shall go to Imogen's and when I get her to confess then I shall go to the police."

James jumped up. "You'll do no such thing. Just leave Imogen out of this."

"Why should I?" Lucy stared at him defiantly. "If we let this go on she could end up setting the whole place alight."

"Lucy's right," Ernie said quietly. "She has to be stopped."

"No. There's nothing to say it was Imogen. I won't have her upset."

"Perhaps you won't, but I will," Lucy declared. "It's our business and I won't have it destroyed by an insane woman."

253

"Imogen is not insane and if you take this further I shall walk out and you won't see me again."

There was a silence for a moment then Lucy said quietly, "You are not the one affected, James. This business belongs to Deborah and myself and I shall do everything I can to protect it. If you are so much in love with Imogen, it might be the best thing if you did leave."

James looked at Lucy then, turning, left. Again there was silence.

It was Ernie who broke it. "I feel we should go, but we don't want to leave you in this state."

Grace asked the girls gently if they wanted to be left alone and both agreed it might be sensible for them to leave. Lucy thanked them for their kindness.

Grace put her arms around her. "Everything will come right in the end. James is obviously concerned for Imogen. We have to realise that he was married to her. Give him time, Lucy. We'll be in touch."

After they had gone Lucy thought that it would have been such a lovely completion of their honeymoon. She would, not, however, have James back until he had Imogen out of his system. She would go and see her, get her to admit that she was responsible for the fire.

She spent a fitful night and went to sleep only at daybreak. The pungent, leftover smell of the fire seemed stronger than the night before. Deborah offered to go with Lucy to see Imogen but she said she wanted to go alone.

When Imogen opened her front door and Lucy told her why she had come the innocence on her face told her it was not going to be easy.

"I don't understand why you think that I should

have done such a thing. I was at my aunt's all evening."

"The damage was done in the early hours of the morning," Lucy said grimly. "I know you are clever. What I want to impress on you is that I won't stand for this kind of treatment. I shall let the police know what happened, so don't attempt any more silly tricks."

Her smile died. "This is utterly ridiculous. I've never been near the shop since the time I spoke to you."

"My husband will probably come and see you, but don't get excited. He's trying desperately not to believe you're insane."

"I'm not insane." Imogen was getting agitated now. "I was never near your stupid shop."

"Time will tell." Lucy turned and walked down the path.

When she got back to the shop Grace was there. "I'm going with you to the warehouse to get you stocked up again. Ernie has told his men to put in a new window. You must get the business started again as soon as possible. And there's to be no talk of money. We shall see to that when you are under-way again."

For the first time since Lucy had had news of the trouble, she wept. She had always known it was good to have friends but she had not expected such kindness as this.

"Come along," Grace said, "off we go. We shall have the shop opened again by tomorrow morning."

Chapter Eighteen

Underlying the pleasure of stocking up again at the warehouse was Lucy's worry that James had not attempted to get in touch with her. She had been to the apartment but there was no sign that he had been there.

Well, it was not something she could do anything about. And the fact that he hated her having the shop did not stop her buying: she would not give the shop up. She and Grace came back laden and they worked like beavers to get everything organised again.

Lucy thought that she would be able to settle once this was accomplished but found she was still restless. That evening Adin came to take Deborah out. He kept repeating that they were fools not to chuck the whole thing up, so that by the time they left, Lucy, who many times enjoyed an evening on her own, was longing for James to come and take her in his arms. In her mind she relived their last visit to Paris and ended up with slow tears running down her cheeks.

At a quarter to nine Grace phoned and said she was sorry she had been unable to get over. They had had visitors, but she promised to be there the next morning. She asked if James had come back and when Lucy told her he hadn't, she said not to worry, he loved her too much to stay away. Lucy doubted it but refrained from saying so.

It was a long night.

The next day every time the handle of the shop door turned Lucy would look up quickly, hoping to see James but it was never him.

That evening when she closed the shop she went home, but the house had a deserted look. Mrs Wainwright had left a note asking if there was anything Lucy wanted and Lucy penned a reply, saying her husband was away for a while, but she would let her know when he would be back. She left her some money, not wanting to lose her.

Two weeks went by and Lucy gradually grew angry. How dare James ignore her? She was his wife after all.

Then one evening there was a knock at the front door. Deborah went to open it and came back, followed by James.

He was limping and looked as pale as death.

Lucy jumped up. "James, what happened?"

"I was involved in an accident. I thought it was time I gave you some money."

"Why didn't you let me know?"

"Because I didn't want to." His voice was cold, his manner aloof. He took an envelope from his pocket and laid it on the table. "I shall make a payment to you every month."

Lucy pushed it aside. "I don't want it."

"And I insist you take it. Never let it be said that I walked out and left you penniless."

"Oh, James, let us forget all this."

"I don't want to forget it. You refused to do as I asked."

"Does this mean that you are living with Imogen? Because if you are, I – "

"I'm not living with her, but I object to you blaming

258

her for the damage to the property." His voice held a harshness she had not heard before. He turned away and walked to the door. "Excuse me."

"James, wait." Lucy went after him, but he walked into the hall and left. By the time her fumbling hand had turned the lock he was stepping into a car.

Lucy saw then in the light from a street lamp that a woman was driving and Lucy closed the door and leaned against it. Oh, God, was it Imogen?

Deborah came into the hall. "Lucy, are you all right?"

She straightened. "I will be in a few minutes. James had a woman in the car. I couldn't tell if it was Imogen."

"He would have a nerve to bring her here. He did say he wasn't living with her."

"I feel I don't know him any more."

When Deborah offered to stay with her sister and tell Adin she could not go out that night, Lucy, though she was choked with gratitude, would not hear of it. When Adin came for Deborah, they went out together, after Deborah had said she would not be away long.

Lucy sat in front of the kitchen fire, finding it difficult to reconcile the James who had just left with the one in Paris, who had been so loving, so caring, so tender towards her. How sure she had been that she meant the world to him. And now? What was Imogen's appeal? Oh, yes, she looked very innocent, sweetly innocent, but she was a liar and a destroyer of lives.

How long would it take for James to become aware of this? Perhaps never. He would end up living with her because that had been Imogen's aim. She was sick. Why could James not see this? He was a sensible, intelligent man. Only not where Imogen was concerned.

Lucy asked herself if she wanted him back and she thought that yes, she did and that one day she would get him back. She was not going to let Imogen get the better of her.

The days went by, then the weeks and although her money came from the bank, James stayed away. How long could she go on living like this, not knowing if he had recovered from his illness?

At the beginning of May, Grace came over one evening and said, "Lucy, I did a bit of a mean thing this morning. I sat in the park at the end of Imogen's street and watched the house. I had to, knowing it was making you ill wanting to know if James was living with her. I had waited about half an hour when a car drew up and I saw it was James. He started to go up the path and Imogen came running out of the house and although she ran to him and flung her arms around his waist James showed little response."

Lucy tensed. "Did he stay?"

"About an hour. He came out alone, but as he was getting into the car she came running down the path and she was all animated as she stood talking to him. He got into the car and she leaned forward and kissed him on the cheek." Grace paused then added wryly, "I would say quite definitely that he's not living with her."

"But he visits her."

"Look," Grace leaned forward, "I'm hoping I can persuade you to go to the moors for a few days. You've lost weight, you're pale, you don't look as if you get much sleep."

"I'm all right."

"You are not all right. I shall look after the shop. Ernie has agreed to me doing so. You must get away from this atmosphere for a while. You are on your own too much. All day and all evening, wondering about James. I think he's behaved very badly. I had to force myself to stay away, but what I wanted to do was tell him what I thought of his behaviour."

"I'm glad you didn't."

"That's what Ernie said, but I do think he should have come to his senses by now. Will you decide to go away for a few days, Lucy?"

She knew a longing for the peace of the moorland, for the bracing country air, longed to see Mrs Trippet again, to see Joel. In Mrs Trippet's last letter she had said that Joel was going to spend a week with her.

"I don't know," she said.

"You are going. It's all settled. No, it's no use protesting."

"I'm not. I'll go." Lucy laughed, feeling a sense of relief.

At this, Grace began organising the holiday and two days later Lucy was on the train, feeling like a child who has been given an unexpected trip.

She was enthralled with the countryside. There were pastures golden with buttercups and in lower lying meadows a sheen of lilac lady's-smocks. There were trees with showers of May blossom and with the window lowered she could smell the sweetness. Oh, how lovely it all was. Later she came across a view that made her wish she was an artist and could capture the scene on canvas. Added to the buttercups and May blossom were snatches of bluebells in woods and spinneys and overall were the various greens of the unfolding leaves on the trees.

And much later when she arrived at Whitby there were Mrs Trippet and Joel waiting on the platform to meet her. After Mrs Trippet had given her a bear hug Joel said softly, "How good to see you, Lucy."

He wore a suit and looked older, more sophisticated than she remembered. She was surprised to find herself feeling shy with him.

He had a car. "Second-hand," he said laughing.

"It's lovely to be back. I had a feeling of coming home."

Mrs Trippet said, "That's why we are staying at the old house. You'll see a change in it. I've titivated it up a bit. I spend many an evening in the kitchen. And wait until you see all the sheep, the cows, the chickens. Joel has been marvellous, advising me."

Joel grinned. "Don't believe a word she says. She was telling me the way she wanted it, all the time I was trying to advise her."

"Rubbish," declared Mrs Trippet, beaming all over her face.

Lucy saw what they meant once they had passed her house and turned right after the spinney. "Oh," she exclaimed looking about her. Joel stopped the car.

"Well, there it is."

There were sheep in the fields, cows and their byres, and it seemed as if there were hundreds of chickens feeding in the yard.

"It's wonderful," she said,

"And we have pigs at the back," declared Mrs Trippet.

More surprises were to come. When they went into the kitchen Lucy stood open-mouthed, looking about her. The walls, the skirting boards, the dresser and every cupboard had been painted white.

"This is the farm kitchen," Joel said, grinning. "You'd better say you like it or you'll have Mrs Trippet on her high horse."

262

"I love it. So would the family." There were lovely patterned rag rugs and there were some thick blue tweed curtains at the windows.

There were two upholstered chairs on either side of the fireplace where a sizeable fire was burning and there were two oak-backed armchairs and a settee.

"You'll probably laugh when I tell you that I've had a dairy built on the back of the house. I spend more time in this kitchen than I spend at home. Today, however, we are going to my house for lunch. Cook and Polly are so looking forward to seeing you."

Joel carried Lucy's suitcase up to the room that had the built-in bed and she felt she wanted to cry for the times that had gone.

When they came down Mrs Trippet had made coffee and they talked about Lucy's family. "Mother hasn't managed to visit us yet and I'm glad because I didn't want her to know about James. She and her husband are very happy, they love their new home . . ." Lucy paused and was unable to go on.

"Come along now and have your coffee. You must ask Joel about his course. He's studying to be a veterinary surgeon."

"You are?" Lucy asked in surprise. "What about the farm?"

"If I succeed I'll sell the farm to the couple who are renting it now."

The good news took Lucy's mind off her own troubles and she settled down to enjoy tales of Joel's adventures.

It was a day of days; there was Cook and Polly's excitement at having Lucy back again and people from round about dropped in to have a word with her. Joel also took her to the farm to meet the couple who had taken it over, with the wife saying with a

263

laugh, "I thought it would be all cuddling lambs and feeding chickens and here I am, working like a young navvy."

"She loves it," her husband teased her.

When Joel and Lucy left the farm he said, "And now I want to know all about you, Lucy."

It was a soft morning with a light mist over the peaks. On the lower slopes the buds of yellow gorse were opening. Lucy took a deep breath then asked Joel how long it would take him to be a fully qualified veterinary surgeon.

"A long time. It's something I've wanted to do for years."

"And if you should fail what happens to the farm?"

"If I do, but I'm sure I won't, Bert and Janet who rent it now will buy it. Lucy, I want to know about *your* life. Mrs Trippet told me there were difficulties, but that they would soon be over."

"I hope they will, Joel. I'd rather not discuss it."

"Sorry." They walked on in silence for a moment then Joel said quietly, "I still love you, Lucy. Always will."

"And I love my husband and always will."

"I won't give up hope. I think that you and James Dexter are wholly incompatible."

Lucy bridled. "Although I came from a poor family, my mother taught us to always keep our dignity. I don't think of myself as being below the Dexters."

"I wasn't suggesting that. On the contrary. What I meant was, he had his marriage annulled and to leave you as well does not not say much for him."

"There were faults on both sides but I refuse to talk about it."

"I'll say sorry again and suggest we step out over the moors."

"Right, let's go."

It was a soft morning, with a light mist over the peaks. On the lower slopes the buds of the yellow gorse were opening. Joel said, "Oh, this lovely air. I don't feel I want to live anywhere else at this moment."

They walked in the direction of the little shop, but veering to the left. The ground was rough but the tufts of grass had a spring-fresh green about them and the unfolding leaves of a lone tree ahead was a delight.

Lucy said, "In the winter when we arrived here I found myself longing for the summer to come, but now I shall be spending it among the fumes of London traffic. But then I love the smell of the shop, with its various things. Did Mrs Trippet tell you that Deborah is doing very well in her line of business? I think she's feeling she'll soon be ready to go to Paris. She sees herself as owning a big fashion house and holding a show, which will draw designers of every kind."

"I don't know much about that line, but I wish her well. To wish for something is good, but to pull it off would be tremendous."

Lucy described all the friends she had made and he said, "Good for you. The next time I go to London I shall pop in and say hello."

Her heart skipped a beat, not sure she wanted him there.

They walked in silence for a way then Joel said, "I think we had better turn back. We'll never reach the mountains today." He was smiling and she smiled back and said she doubted it.

On the way back he told her some of the history

of the moors and she realised how knowledgeable he was.

By the time they were back at the house she had realised what a good and true friend he was and hoped he would come to London.

There was a letter for her from Grace who said she was sure that Lucy would want to know what was going on at the shop. Believe it or not they had had orders for six cushions! The inner parts of the rolls of material had not been damaged in the fire and she had the three girls cutting out hexagonals. The girls were real wizards. The designs were simply laid out and they had started stitching them! Amazing.

She said she knew Lucy would be enjoying herself and would keep her aware of any sales they made. The day had ended really well for Lucy.

There was a letter every morning from Grace during the next three days with news of the cushion sales and Lucy was quite happy to be able to relax when a midday telegram came from Grace saying, *James going abroad for six months. Stop. Leaving tomorrow evening. Stop. Wants to see you.*

Lucy felt a momentary panic. Then she told Mrs Trippet she would have to leave that afternoon to go home and explained why.

"I wasn't expecting James to leave so early."

Mrs Trippet said she understood and her sad expression told Lucy she had known that all was not well.

Joel had already left for his veterinary course and a taxi was ordered.

Both Mrs Trippet and Lucy shed tears when they parted and Lucy said she would write.

Lucy had phoned Grace and Grace met her at the

station. She said that James had not said whether Imogen was going with him but he had said he would call on Lucy the next morning at ten o'clock.

"And that's it, Lucy. He was cold, distant. I've never known such a change in a man. He was a stranger. It was impossible to get through to him. It's so sad. We've had some wonderful times together. Let's hope that going abroad will get some of the confusion worked out of him."

"Where's he going to?"

"No settled place. He talked about Egypt, about Venice, about India. I should imagine he'll be a travel wanderer."

Deborah was alone at home and said, after she had greeted her, "What a to do. It puts one off marriage, doesn't it?"

James arrived promptly at half past ten the next morning. He went straight into the fact that he was leaving for Egypt that evening and gave her a letter to give to the bank where she could draw her money.

She told him coldly she refused to handle it. He laid it down on the counter. "Please yourself what you do with it, the money is there for you."

After a pause she asked if Imogen was going with him and he told her no, he was going alone. His only concern was in seeing that she was provided for.

Lucy gave a harsh laugh. "Your concern? You don't give a damn what happens to me."

"I do." He spoke quietly. "I care very much, but I know we could never live together under the circumstances. The fact that you are determined to keep the shop on and also that you refuse to believe that Imogen is innocent."

"I only hope she doesn't come again and set fire to the shop."

James looked at his wife coldly. "I must go. Goodbye, Lucy."

He went to the door and she shouted, "If she does I shall go to the police!"

He left, closing the door quietly behind him.

Lucy fumed. It was all right for him, sneaking away. Well, there was one thing certain; she would never have him back again.

Chapter Nineteen

The next morning Deborah was up before Lucy. There was a determined look about her. She said when Lucy came down, "I've made the breakfast. My aim is now to get enough money together to be able to be able to start up in Paris. Would you come with me?"

"N – no. I want to go on running this shop and I have quite a lot of customers."

"You do as you wish, Lucy. I might have grumbled once that you had promised to come with me, but I think I have the confidence to start up on my own."

"I didn't promise to go to Paris with you. All I said was that I wanted to run a shop. We've both found what we wanted."

"Fair enough. I think I'll have to spend some money in a few weeks' time and go to Paris and see what I can find. I'll need to take up my French lessons again. Will you have a go with me in the evenings? I won't be going out with Adin. That's finished."

The coldness in her sister's tone upset Lucy. "You didn't say anything about Adin. What broke that up?"

"He's like James. He doesn't want me to work. They're both stupid. Would you take up French again with me?"

"Yes, but don't expect to learn fluent French in only a few weeks."

"I can, if I make up my mind to it. I have two fittings this morning. It'll be a pity to lose my customers but I can't take them with me, so – " She paused then went on. "The ones I would like to take with me are the three girls. They're splendid seamstresses but I think it would be impossible to pay three wages."

"I doubt whether their mother would allow them to go."

"I doubt it too."

No more was said about Paris that morning but during the afternoon who should walk into the shop but Imogen. Without any preamble she said, "Don't think you'll get James back because you won't."

Lucy was surprised to find herself quite calm.

"You are welcome to him. I don't want him."

"You don't?" The big eyes were wide. She looked disappointed.

"No I don't. Now, will you please leave me alone? You can't do any more harm because the police are anxious to find you."

There was no show of fear as Imogen's aunt had suggested. She simply turned away and left.

Lucy was still calm. She wondered if there would be anything that could upset her ever again.

During the weeks that followed they went through the French book in the evenings, discarding phrases they thought would never be needed and concentrating on the ones they thought would, such as work, time, her profession, meat, vegetables . . . As Deborah pointed out, what good was it learning to say, "Has the great diplomat arrived in Russia?"?

Lucy said, "You might meet a diplomat who's come from Russia!"

They collapsed in giggles.

There was a new closeness between the girls, both having suffered in different ways.

Adin had called twice, wanting to persuade Deborah to marry him. She saw him the first time but not the second.

"I still love him," she said in a low voice, "but I can never forgive him." She raised her head. "Would you take James back if he asked you?"

"I don't know, certainly not if he insisted that I gave up the shop. We all have a weakness and I think that James's weakness was in wanting to care for Imogen, who he knew had been hurt, and being unable to handle her habit of being possessive."

"He should get rid of that wretch."

"When are you planning to go to Paris?"

"I should think in about another month. I have some bills due to be paid. Now, how about my French when I'm enquiring about a shop with an apartment attached? I still don't know how to say that."

Lucy thought about it then said, "And what if the person in the shop replies in French? And don't forget, the French people speak very fast. I found I could make out very little of what was said. James spoke the language fluently so I didn't bother. I think you would be better off if you explained that you are English and speak very little French."

"And then find out there's no one who speaks English. I shall have to try."

To give Deborah her due she worked really hard at it and when another six weeks had gone by Lucy thought she might just get by. She had a natural ear for languages . . . which Lucy herself lacked.

In the past six weeks Deborah had worked until the early hours of the morning making herself some clothes. It was the middle of summer and she had

271

made a plain cream silk dress and a coat in the same material. The coat had a V neck, three-quarter-length sleeves and two very large pockets, quite close to the hem. She wore a cloche hat in a delicate blue and looked just like a model.

She twirled around. "Will I do?"

"Very much so. You look lovely, Deborah; you'll have to be sure that the property agent doesn't take you for a wealthy woman."

"I do have other clothes with me," Deborah laughed.

When Grace, who was taking them to the station, saw Deborah she said, "My goodness. What a beautiful outfit. You'll knock everyone cold. It's lovely, Deborah, I wish you all the luck in the world. I hope you meet a millionaire."

Deborah grinned. "So do I!"

She had booked in at a decent hotel for one evening and would look for somewhere cheaper for the next few evenings.

Lucy sensed her sister's excitement when they arrived at the station, but for her, Deborah's departure hurt.

They waited until the train moved out. Deborah's cheeks were flushed and her eyes sparkling. Grace called, "Enjoy yourself," but Lucy, feeling choked, could only wave.

Grace stayed with Lucy that day. Deborah had said she wouldn't write, she would save up everything to tell her when she got home. But Lucy gave her sister some money to phone her the following day, to let her know what was happening.

Letters came from the family, in answer to Lucy telling them about Deborah's venture. Beth said in her letter how surprised she was to hear of Deborah's trip, but added that she was more adventurous than herself and added that it was only now she had agreed to move from the little cottage which she loved, because she was expecting a baby. The rest of the letter was full of talk about the coming baby.

Her mother said in her letter how delighted she was that Deborah had branched out and was looking forward to hearing all about the Paris trip when Deborah returned. She said how contented she was with Andrew. The twins adored him. Lucy wouldn't recognise them. They were so sturdy, so full of fun. They were settling nicely into their new home and how good it was to know that they owned it. There was more news about the garden and how hard Andrew worked in it to give her plenty of flowers and foliage . . .

The boys wrote to say how excited they were to hear Deborah's news: it took guts to take to working abroad. Then they went on about the wonderful summerhouses they had made and were planning to make and said there was a competition they were hoping to enter and would be over the moon if they could win it.

Lucy was beginning to feel depressed. Not one of them had asked after her or how her business was faring. Or even asked about James. None of them knew he had left her.

When Grace came back into the room and Lucy told her Beth's news Grace said, "I hope this baby will settle her. It shouldn't have needed a baby to make her want to move."

Lucy sighed. "The family all seem to be the same, all of them wrapped up in themselves. They made me feel a failure. Should I have gone with Deborah?"

"Why should you go all the way to Paris when

you're doing so well here? James could return any day."

"I doubt it."

"He will come back to you, Lucy, don't ever think otherwise."

Lucy put James from her thoughts. Everyone was doing what they wanted. She loved working in the shop. She had made friends and they were important.

Deborah phoned about seven o'clock that evening. She was excited. Everything was going well. She had so much to tell Lucy, but she would have to tell her when she came home. She was going out to dinner. "I must go, 'bye."

"And that was it," she said in dismay to Grace.

"It sounds all right, we shall have to wait and see."

The day Deborah returned it had been raining steadily all day and it still was when Lucy and Grace arrived at the station to meet her. But when Lucy flung her arms around her sister it was as though the sun was shining. She was so excited. Grace said, "Well, let us get to the car and hear all about it."

The rain meant nothing. Deborah did. From getting into the car until they arrived at the Draycotts that evening she talked nonstop. It was such an amazing thing. Did they know who the woman travelling with her had turned out to be?

Grace offered jokingly, "A directrice of a fashion house."

"No, better than that, for me, that is. She was in charge of the seamstresses in a fashion house. What do you know about that? Could I have been more lucky? And, she spoke perfect English. Oh, how we talked. She examined the seams of the coat I had taken off and praised my stitching, said, 'Perfection'. She offered me a job right away but I told her my intention to be a designer and she immediately offered me some help. I could not believe it. She knew of an empty shop, and there was a living area attached. She went with me to look at it."

"And how did you fare?" Lucy asked.

"The rent was more than I had expected, but I took it and paid three months in advance."

Lucy and Grace said together, "Three months?"

"Honore, that is her name, told me that most people had to pay that much. I do have the first chance to take it for a longer period if things work out. And she has promised to get me some customers."

Grace looked at her thoughtfully. "She seems too good to be true. I can't imagine a woman in that position promising to get you customers."

"She seemed to think it would be easy. Did you know that it took thirty-five models to show four hundred and fifty dresses at a fashion show. Isn't it exciting? She can get me some seamstresses too, but I have to get the customers first. The rooms are partly furnished. Enough for my needs. Oh, I can't wait to get started."

"When are you planning to leave?" Lucy asked.

"On Monday, Lucy. It's no use paying rent and not making use of the place. Honore will meet me and take me there; she'll get food in for me. I'm sorry it's so sudden, but I just couldn't refuse such a chance, could I?"

There was a small silence and Deborah looked from one to the other. "You think I did wrong in renting the shop so quickly, don't you? I had to."

Lucy said, "Well, I hate to spoil your excitement, Deborah, but I do think it's strange that this woman is doing all these things for you. I feel there has to be a snag."

"I do too," Grace said quietly, "although I can't pinpoint it exactly. It has taken a lot of your money paying three months in advance. Does this Honore get a commission from the agent?"

"No, she's a really decent person helping me and you only think badly of her. You've spoilt my whole trip. But I'm still going and I'll prove you wrong."

"Perhaps we're being a bit too fussy," Lucy said quickly. "There are good people in the world. What would we have done without Mrs Trippet that awful night on the moors? And she's remained a good friend."

Deborah immediately brightened. "You would like Honore, I know you would. She's alone in the world. She has no family. I think she saw me as a sister."

"I should imagine so." Lucy saw that Grace was about to speak and she gave a slight shake of her head. Deborah was away again.

"Three thousand women buy from the collections and without good fitters, inspiration or not, the fashion houses would be bankrupt. Did you know that a ballgown could cost £2,000! Two thousand, just imagine, it's a fortune."

She knew the styles for the autumn; there would be loose velvet coats with fur collars of lynx, light fox and, wolf. Yes, she stressed the word wolf. Dresses of chiffon silk were to hang straight and full. Oh, yes, and there would be coats of fine kid and wraps of chiffon and patterned ninon and oh, all sorts of things, she just couldn't remember them all.

She became sleepy in time and Grace insisted they stay the night. She would get them home early in the morning.

276

When Deborah was asleep in bed Lucy and Grace discussed the situation, but got nowhere. If they kept harping on about this woman Honore, Deborah would be more and more upset, and she was decided about going back to Paris. In the end Lucy said, "I'm afraid we shall have to let her go. If it doesn't work out right she'll just have to come back."

During the next five days Deborah worked hard at finishing off some work for her customers. They had said they were sorry to lose her but Deborah was still on a high and rushed around at the last minute getting her things together ready to leave

When they went to the station Grace insisted on Deborah taking some money so she could phone Lucy after she had arrived to let her know that all was well.

Lucy was in a fever of worry and it was late evening when Deborah phoned to say that everything was fine; Honore had made them a lovely dinner and had talked about two customers who were interested in her work. The people were coming to see her the following day, so Lucy could stop worrying. Everything was marvellous. She would write to her the following day.

There was no more word for six days and Lucy was frantic with worry. "Something has happened," she said to Grace. "Deborah said she would write the next day. She could have phoned. If I don't hear by tomorrow I must go to Paris."

That evening there was a phone call from Deborah and Lucy listened to a distressed Deborah give a garbled account of what had happened. Everything had gone wrong. There were rats in the building and she was terrified of them. She had been to see the man who had handled the rent and he told her not to worry, he would get a man to come and see to it, but so far no one had been. Honore had said she was madly busy and would try and see her the following day. When she did come there was a prospective customer with her and while Deborah talked to the woman Honore had cleared her handbag of money and taken her new clothes.

Both women had vanished into thin air and when she went to the shop it was empty and Honore's address was an empty house.

The only money she had left was her train fare, in a bag tied around her waist under her clothes. She would have to come home. She gave Lucy the time of arrival and rang off and Lucy guessed she had had no more money to spare.

And Lucy was left with a day of worry. Had Deborah eaten? How long had she been without food? Oh, why had she gone?

She phoned Grace who came over and who tried to console Lucy. A girl like Deborah who would tie her train fare around her waist would also have put enough money away for food. Lucy must stop worrying or she would make herself ill.

While they waited for her to arrive that evening, Lucy said, "Heaven only knows what she will look like."

They were both shocked when they saw her stepping off the train. She had lost a lot of weight, there were dark lines under her eyes and she was wearing an old dress with a cardigan on top.

"Oh, my love," Lucy said, her voice breaking as she held her close. "What has this woman done to you?"

"I'll never trust anyone again," Deborah sobbed, "you and Grace were right about Honore. She was a bad egg, a very bad egg."

278

"Come along," Grace said gently, "let's get you home and get you something to eat."

In the car Deborah talked nonstop. She hadn't had a bite to eat since breakfast when a woman in the house next door took pity on her and gave her a slice of toast and a drink of coffee.

Grace raised her eyebrows. "I was wrong. I thought you would have put money by for food with the money you secreted away."

"I did, but at the time I wasn't reckoning with being without any money at all in my handbag. I swear that when I can afford it, I'll go to Paris again, I'll find Honore and leave her without any money or any item of clothes to wear."

"That would never happen. An evil woman like that will be ready for any emergency."

"I noticed that she had two big bunches of keys in her bag." Deborah's tone was bitter. "I bet she would have keys for a lot of empty shops and houses, and other people sharing in the profits."

When Lucy asked her why she had not gone to the police she said, "I did and although they didn't laugh at me I knew they thought I was a fool to do what I had done. You two saw what could happen but of course I couldn't. I feel such a fool."

"You needn't. It's happening all the time."

Deborah asked only one thing, that no one should know exactly what had happened to her. If anyone asked they would say she had had a good look around but could not find anywhere to live that was suitably priced, perhaps she might go again.

Lucy and Grace agreed to this.

Although Lucy had managed to keep Ada and her sisters in work she could not give them the employment that Deborah had been able to give them, so they were pleased to see her back. Her customers too were delighted to have her home again.

Lucy wrote to the family to tell them the news and they all wrote back to say that Deborah was wise not to pay too big a rent and the only one Lucy did not like lying to was Mrs Trippet. But it was no use lying to one and not to the others.

Deborah settled back to work and although she was not exactly happy again she did put on a bright face generally.

What surprised Lucy was her dedication to learn some French every evening, saying she would never go back to Paris until she was more fluent in the language. She also accepted Adin back again, although they only went out on a few occasions and she stressed it was only on a friendship basis.

Lucy felt that her life was in a rut. She enjoyed her work, but the evenings were a drag to her and at times when she went to bed James would be in her thoughts and she would torment herself wondering how it would all end. It did not seem fair to her that the rest of the family should be so settled yet in spite of doing what she wanted to do, it should all end so badly.

Then one Saturday morning, to her surprise, Joel walked into the shop. He was grinning broadly. "Surprise, surprise!"

"Oh," she gasped and the next second he had lifted her from her feet and was swinging her around.

She said, when he put her down, "What brought you here?"

"To see you, what else? You had been on my mind for days and Mrs Trippet said when I talked about you, well go and see Lucy." He spread his arms. "And here I am. Where are we going today? Into the city?"

280

She laughed and shook her head. "Not on a Saturday. It's my busiest day. But just a minute, I must let Deborah know you're here." She rang a bell that connected with the house and in seconds Deborah was there and was being hugged by Joel.

She kept giving little yelps of joy. "How wonderful to see you," and in the next breath asked the same question as Lucy. "What brought you here?"

"To see you and your beautiful sister of course."

Deborah said right away she would ring Grace and find out if she was free for the day. Lucy protested that Grace would have her own arrangements but Deborah rang and Grace said she would be delighted to come right away.

"So there you are," she said beaming at them. "You and Joel can spend the whole day together. You can spend the night at our house."

Lucy glanced at Joel and for the first time was aware of the hard animal vitality of him. It sent a throb of desire running through her. She felt surprised and ashamed and busied herself tidying away her sewing.

She changed into a pale blue silk two-piece that Deborah had made for her and carried a cardigan in case the evening became cool.

Joel parked the car and they went on the buses and became tourists viewing the sights. He said on the bus, in a low voice, "I hope you forgave me for the way I behaved, the last time I saw you, about Mr Dexter."

"I thought it wise to forget it."

"Thanks, thanks a lot. It won't happen again. I simply got carried away."

They changed buses and Joel took Lucy's hand and had her dodging among the traffic.

281

"You'll have me killed," she gasped.

He grinned. "Then we shall die together. Where to next? Shall we have a coffee? There's a café over there."

They had two cups and two cream cakes and again talked about Joel's work, about the people at the farm who seemed to be settling in. "They're a nice couple."

"What happens if you succeed in your exams?"

"Let them have the farm. If I fail I shall keep them on until I do. I'm determined to be a vet."

Joel had not mentioned his mother until then and when she asked after her, he said she was in a low state, and added that he only marvelled that his aunt had such patience with her.

They bussed and they walked and every time they walked Joel held her by the hand and swung their arms now and then, saying, "This is just great."

James had not been mentioned until the early evening when they came home. They had had dinner out but Lucy asked lightly if he would like anything to eat. Joel laughed and said she must be joking, then took a breath and added he was worried about what was wrong between her husband and herself.

Her heartbeat quickened. "Everything's fine. James is abroad, Deborah told you. He'll be away for several weeks." She forced a laugh. "I don't think he would be pleased if he could have seen the pair of us gallivanting around London."

"We weren't doing anything wrong."

"No, of course not, but if somebody told me that James was with another woman, holding hands and laughing all the time I would have been upset."

"Would you, Lucy? I doubt it. You never once mentioned his name to me. I found it unnatural. Now tell me. What is wrong? And no make-do story. Tell me the truth. I won't repeat it to anyone. I give you my word."

Lucy sighed. "Very well. This is it."

She told the story briefly, about their honeymoon, the intrusion of Imogen and of her destroying the warehouse stock and trying to set fire to the premises. "I wanted to go to the police about it and this upset James. He left me but he didn't go back to Imogen, not to live with her. I think she was very possessive and he decided to go abroad. To protect me," she added quickly.

"That is what you want to believe, isn't it?" he asked gently. Would you have him back, if he asked you?"

"We all make mistakes."

"It's an unforgiveable mistake. Remember this, I still love you, Lucy, but I certainly won't pester you. I hope I can come again."

"Yes, of course," she said softly. "It was a lovely time. It was fun."

Chapter Twenty

The following Sunday was one of the longest days Lucy had ever known. Adin had invited Deborah to his home and Lucy had pressed her to go, saying she had a lot of work to do.

She had gone for a long walk and tired herself out. What a difference it had been to the previous Sunday. She missed Joel's company, and asked herself if she had been a fool not to let him kiss her when he had clearly wanted to. No, she had been sensible.

She went to bed early but, unable to sleep, lay listening to the sounds in the house. She heard Deborah coming home, humming quietly; she heard her going into her room, then into the bathroom.

Normally Lucy never heard her cleaning her teeth but she did tonight. There was a click of the lamp going off then there was silence.

Lucy hated the silence. She needed to hear sounds of activity to keep her mind off her problems. Sleep eluded her still. Then there was a sudden sound that came from downstairs and she drew herself up in the bed, listening. Had Deborah allowed Adin to sleep on the settee? Surely not. There was no further sound and she lay down again.

Eventually she drifted into sleep, an uneasy sleep that made her feel that someone was in the house. But every time she lay tense, listening, everywhere was quiet. Sleep eventually overtook her and the next time she roused it was with the strong feeling that something was not quite right. Was it smoke she could smell? The smell of paraffin? The only paraffin they had was in the room at the back of the warehouse, for the few lamps they had. She would not be able to smell it from here. The next moment she heard what sounded like wood crackling and noticing a light beyond the curtains, she threw back the sheet and, going to the window, pulled back a curtain.

For a second she stood paralysed as she saw the reflection of flames on the yard. Oh, my God. The place was on fire. She ran to the door and flung it open and saw that there were no flames at the bottom of the stairs.

Deborah. She ran along to her bedroom and grabbing hold of her yelled, "Fire!" She had to shake her awake. "The house is on fire. Get up!"

Deborah rubbed her eyes. "Wh – what?"

Lucy threw back the cover and pulled her out of bed. "The house is on fire! Come on, we have to get out." Then realising that her sister had not taken in what she had said she began to pull her to the door. Deborah resisted her, she wanted to go to bed. Lucy knew then she had been drinking. She got her to the stairs then to her horror saw there were flames at the foot of the stairs.

"Stay there," she ordered and ran to the bathroom. She ran the bath taps over two towels, turned the tap off and ran with the dripping towels to Deborah. She threw one over her head and put the other one over her own head. "Now, we'll have to hurry." She took her sister's hand and pulled her down the stairs. She intended to go into the sitting room and out the back way, but there were flames in there. Flames were licking the front door and she turned to the kitchen. This was alight too, but there was a space they could get through. Smoke was choking her. The curtains were alight, the cloth on the table was alight. She was making for the door when Deborah tripped and fell.

Smoke caught Lucy's breath and her breathing was ragged as she tried to get Deborah up. She seemed knocked out and she had to let her towel slip as she helped Deborah to her feet. It was then she heard the clanging of a fire engine's bell. Oh, thank God for that. She got Deborah to her feet but couldn't move her and as she stood trying to balance her a piece of burning curtain fell over her head. She screamed but no sound came as she tried to claw the burning pieces from her. They were on her head, her arms, her back.

The last thing she remembered was the sound of the front door been broken down; then she fell into a black void.

When she regained consciousness she had no idea where she was. All she was aware of was pain, excruciating pain. She was moving, something under her was swaying. Seconds later a voice was saying, "We'll soon be at the hospital and they'll give you something to ease the pain."

"My sister?" Her voice was a croak.

"She's all right."

Lucy blacked out again.

It was daylight when she next woke and she was in a bed. That's all she knew at first. Then she heard a voice say, "I think she's coming round, nurse."

Nurse? What had happened? She saw then that her arms were bandaged from her shoulders to the tips of her fingers and that a nurse was leaning over her.

287

"How do you feel, Mrs Dexter?"

"What happened?" Lucy's voice was no more than a whisper.

"There was a fire. The doctor will be here in a few moments."

Lucy suddenly remembered Deborah and became agitated. "My sister. Is she all right?"

"Yes, you saved her any damage when you collapsed and fell over her. You will be seeing her after Doctor has had a look at you. Ah, here is now."

The doctor came over to her bed with a nursing sister and some students. The doctor was an elderly man who spoke gently.

"Unfortunately you suffered some burns, Mrs Dexter, on your arms, your hands and your back, but they will heal in time."

"My face?" she croaked.

"And that too will heal in time. You are not to worry, you could have been burnt much more if the fire brigade had not come when they did."

The doctor got up then and spoke to the students but she was unable to hear what he said. The doctor then came back to her and said, "Your burns will be dressed later, but I want you to try and sleep now. I shall see you again, soon." He smiled at her. "Just think, it could have been a lot worse."

A younger nurse brought her two pills and held the cup of water to her mouth. Afterwards Lucy asked her if her face was very badly burned and the nurse said, "I can't see. It's bandaged."

Bandaged? Oh, God. Was she disfigured for life? She tried to shout for someone to come and tell her, but she began to feel drowsy and a minute later had gone into a drugged sleep.

The lights were on in the small hospital room when

Lucy next opened her eyes and the first face she saw was Deborah's who was sitting beside her.

"Oh, Lucy, you're awake." Deborah began to cry. "It's all my fault, if I hadn't had too much to drink this would never have happened."

"It's all right, it wasn't your fault, it was the fault of whoever started the fire. It wasn't just a chance thing. There must have been paraffin spilt everywhere."

"There was. Imogen did it." She paused. "But it trapped her. She's dead. The men found her in the warehouse."

Lucy stared at her. "Dead? Oh, no."

"I think it's a good thing she's gone, Lucy. If it hadn't been for you falling over me and saving my life I wouldn't have been alive today."

Lucy said, "Poor James. He loved her."

"Rubbish. You can forget him. You've had people from all over asking after you. Mrs Draycott and her husband came and she's still here. Customers have asked after you and I've written to the family to let them know and to Mrs Trippet. Joel is in Scotland doing his exams."

"Oh, Deborah, this is terrible."

"Now don't you start worrying. All you have to do is to get better."

"Do you know if my – face is all right?"

"I don't know, Lucy. They took you straight to surgery. I'll try and find out. The doctor is very nice, not a bit snooty like they usually are."

"No, don't ask him. I'll find out when they do my dressings."

"They've done them, while you were still sleeping. I think they probably thought it would be better for you."

Deborah left her for a while because the doctor

was on his rounds and came to see her, but she came back later.

In the meantime the nurse came to say that a Mr and Mrs Draycott wanted to see her but they could only stay a few minutes. Lucy was tearful when she saw them and Grace was too. Ernie kissed her but told her she was not to say much.

Lucy asked, what was she going to do when she came out of hospital? There was no home, no shop to go to.

Ernie and Grace told her she musn't worry: she could come to them and her stock was insured. Then Grace told her quietly that she had let James know and also what Imogen had done.

"He was very distressed, Lucy. He said he would be home as soon as possible. He'll be coming to see you but that won't be for two or perhaps three days' time. You'll perhaps feel a little better by then."

Lucy began to cry and the nurse told Grace and Ernie they must leave, they could come the next day for a few minutes.

The thing that worried Lucy the most was wanting to know if she would be disfigured. When she had asked the sister she had said, "We'll know more in the morning when they dress your burns."

The next morning the nice doctor told her that the burns would heal naturally, then he said, "Your hair will soon grow again," which startled her.

She had not thought about her hair being burned as it had been soaked by the wet towel. So, she was going to be a bigger mess than she had thought.

Lucy saw herself without the bandages the following morning. Not all her hair had been burned, only the lower half, and the skin on her cheeks was burned. Her hands and arms had also suffered, but the doctor assured her that the skin would renew itself, given time.

Although still in pain she was calmer when her mother, Andrew and the boys arrived. They were all distressed.

"Don't worry," Lucy said, "it could have been worse."

"That dreadful Imogen," declared William. "It's a good job she died."

Their mother, weeping, asked Lucy how she was keeping.

"Not too bad." She looked at David who said gently, "Hello, sis." Then Andrew touched Lucy's hand. "We would have been here sooner but we had to arrange for someone to look after the twins."

William said, "I know I'm not like the others, I can't find it in my heart to forgive this Imogen. I still think she deserved to die."

"I can't help but feel sorry for her." This from David. "She must have been sick to do such a thing. Where is James?"

"He's – abroad. How long can you all stay?"

"As long as you need us." Helen dried her eyes. "We've all been a little selfish, wrapped up in our own lives. We're so glad that Deborah is all right. She's in the big ward. She's full of praise for you, Lucy, said you saved her life. The nurse wouldn't let her come in with us. We've promised to stay only fifteen minutes. We musn't upset you."

"I feel a lot better than I did yesterday. Don't go yet. Please."

"No, of course not, my darling. You must come and stay with us when you're ready to come out of here."

David said, "And you must come and stay with us

for a while." His smile warmed her heart. What a cold feeling she had had until then. She noticed then how much younger her mother looked. Now that the fine bones on her face looked fleshed out she was quite beautiful.

Lucy by this time was tearful and the nurse came bustling up and asked that her family would leave, adding, "You can see her later."

Helen lingered a moment. "We all love you," and she kissed her on her bandaged cheek.

For a while Lucy could not stop crying then Deborah was there, saying that tomorrow she would be going into the big ward, where it was more cheerful.

After a while they fell silent but it was right. There was now a greater closeness between them.

Flowers kept arriving from people whose names she didn't even know. Then, at visiting time, who should be ushered in by a smiling nurse, but James. "Your husband, Mrs Dexter. What a lovely surprise for you."

It was a shock. For him to see her bandaged like a mummy. He looked so serious and she was unable to say anything but, "You managed to get here."

He had brought a big bunch of roses, not red for love but pale pink. The nurse, still smiling, took them and said she would put them in water.

James sat in the chair and apologised for not being able to get to her sooner. Then, "I'm sorry, Lucy, for what has happened to you. Sorry about Imogen."

Lucy looked away. "Oh, yes, I knew you would be sorry about Imogen." And she, who had also felt sorry for Imogen, said, "She got what she deserved."

She saw the pain in her husband's eyes and wished she could have taken the words back. "Imogen was sick," he said. "That was why I went away. I thought if I was away she would leave you alone. I was proved wrong."

"You should have known what she was like," she said, a bitterness in her voice, "you had known her long enough."

"She was certainly not mad when I first knew her, nor later when I called to see her. It was not until she knew I was married to you that she changed."

"Very convenient."

"Lucy, you must believe me. That is the truth." He spoke earnestly but she was unable to tell him that she believed him. Imogen had left her body cruelly damaged.

"I really did leave you because I thought it would help you."

"You didn't, you left me because you wanted her. You loved her, you always had and always will."

"No, Lucy, you are wrong."

"You left me as if you hated me. You were cold, distanced from me. It wasn't me you loved but her."

"You are wrong, but I must go. The nurse told me I musn't excite you and you're getting upset. I'm sorry I've hurt you. I hope you will agree to see me again when you're feeling better."

"Don't bother. I don't want to see you again, ever."

He stood hesitant for a moment then turned away and left.

When the nurse came back she found Lucy sobbing uncontrollably and tried to soothe her. "Now then, you'll soon be home. Come along, stop crying," and Lucy was unable to tell her what was really wrong.

When she was calmer she wished she could have taken back every word she had said to James.

She spent a restless night, going over her friendship with Joel, thinking about her family, who were so settled in their lives. Her mother had a man to love her, Beth had Harold and Deborah had Adin.

James had tried to be kind to her but she knew he still loved Imogen. Their affair had gone on too long for him just to forget her. Look at the number of times he had visited her, wanting her to be a proper wife to him. And all the time she had refused.

Lucy still wished she had not been so unpleasant to him.

She was running a high temperature the next morning and visitors were barred, but by the evening her mother was allowed in. She was upset. "They did let me have a peep at you this morning when I came, but you were so ill. I'm so glad you've improved this evening. Andrew has had to go home, urgent business, you know how it is, but I shall stay until you're better."

"No, Mother, you go home too, you have the twins to think of, I'm over the worst now. I think it was the shock of finding the house burning and then James arriving. I must have got excited and my temperature shot up."

"Of course it would. I shall stay until tomorrow anyway then see how you are. You definitely look better now than you did this morning."

Lucy said she was sure she was on the mend, then Deborah came in and she was fidgety, wanting to know what to do for the best. "I'm well enough to go home," she said, "but I have no home to go to. What do I do? I wished I hadn't rushed back from Paris."

Their mother said she had done the right thing and

294

told her she would have asked her to come home with her, but then Lucy would have no one to look in on her.

Lucy said immediately, "Go with Mother, Deborah. I have the Draycotts, who have asked me to stay with them until I get pulled together."

"And you have James," her mother said. "You won't want to be parted from him until you have to when business calls."

"No, of course not."

And it was arranged when her mother did leave that Deborah would go with her.

If it had not been for Mrs Trippet arriving just after the bell went for the end of visiting, Lucy was sure she would have burst out crying again with all the emotional events of the past few days.

"Oh, my darling girl," Mrs Trippet said. "They didn't want to let me in but I told them I had come all the way from the Yorkshire Dales. They've allowed me five minutes. How are you?"

Lucy's eyes filled with tears, but they were tears of pleasure.

"I want to hug you and I can't. I was away when Joel came back and I didn't get Mrs Draycott's letter until I arrived home. I got dressed, asked Mr Davies if he would look after the animals for a few more days and here I am."

"Oh, Mrs Trippet, you're a sight for sore eyes. There's so much to tell you, but . . . here's the nurse."

Mrs Trippet begged for a few more minutes and the nurse said, "Well, if the matron happens to look in, you haven't seen me."

Grins were exchanged and the nurse left.

Lucy told Mrs Trippet as much as she could about

the tragedy and Mrs Trippet said, "That poor Imogen. It certainly is a tragedy when a woman is willing to kill because of jealousy."

She then wanted to know how James had taken the news and Lucy was saved a reply by the nursing sister coming in.

"Sorry," she said, "but I'm afraid I shall have to ask you to leave. You can see Mrs Dexter tomorrow."

Mrs Trippet got up right away. "Thanks for letting me have these few minutes. They meant a lot to us."

When Lucy was alone she made up her mind she was going to get better as soon as she could. She would get a bigger and better shop somewhere, and buy more goods. She would make a success of herself. Deborah could share it if she wanted, but if not, she would manage on her own.

She felt a great deal better the next morning and Mrs Trippet was allowed in to see her, being a far-distanced visitor. They had left the bandages off Lucy's face and when she saw herself with her burnt cheeks and short hair, straggly at the ends, she laughed. "What a mess."

"In another couple of weeks you'll be back to normal," soothed Mrs Trippet, "then I hope you'll be able to come and stay with me."

"I'll be with you as soon as possible and afterwards I'm going to look for a larger shop and stock it."

"What is James going to say to that?" Mrs Trippet teased.

There was a silence for a moment then Lucy said, "I'm going to tell you something but I don't want you to tell anyone else. James and I have parted. Even my family doesn't know."

When Lucy had told her all the details Mrs Trippet scolded her.

"You're being very foolish, Lucy. James is a caring man. He was worried about Imogen. He did what he thought was best. He's a closed-in person, because of his unhappy childhood, then he falls in love with Imogen. They marry and she won't consummate the marriage. Can you imagine the effect that would have on him? Then he meets you, and the marriage is annulled. You go to Paris for your honeymoon and you have to return after two days because Imogen has cut her wrists, or says she has. He finds out that she has been lying and later, what does he do? Takes you back to Paris to complete your honeymoon and, as you said yourself, you were deliriously happy. Now all that means nothing to you. He went back to Imogen to save you harm. And you turn your back on him."

"I know I did the right thing." There was a stubborn thrust to Lucy's chin.

"Well, I won't go on about it any more. Grace says she'll see you this evening. I shall have to go. I'm only allowed ten minutes. I might get a chance to have a peep to see you this evening. 'Bye for now, darling girl."

She kissed the top of Lucy's head and gave her a last wave as she went around the door.

After she had gone Deborah came in looking joyous. "I'm allowed out today. Isn't it great? Adin's going to take me to the Draycotts. I wish you were coming with me. I've decided I'm going back to Paris. Grace had insured the furniture and stock in the warehouse against fire and we'll split the money when we get it." Lucy wanted to say that all the stock was hers but stayed silent. She had saved and added the money that James had given her for her keep. She had plenty.

Her mother came with Grace that evening and told Lucy that now that her daughter was looking so much better, she would go home the next day.

"I'm just aching to see the twins," she said, smiling. "It's as though I had been away for months. That's how a mother is, Lucy, caring for the youngest who are unable to take care of themselves."

"I understand," Lucy said, trying to accept that the little ones were more important to her mother than she was. She could have been burned to death. But she wasn't, she thought; and she was itching to get back to work again.

She said to Grace, "I hope I shall soon be out of here."

"Don't try and rush anything, Lucy. Your whole body suffered a great shock. The doctor will tell you when you're fit to leave. You'll come to us; and don't forget that Mrs Trippet wants you to go and visit her. She's a lovely person."

"Yes," Lucy said softly. She would enjoy a visit to the Yorkshire Dales. Oh, how wonderful it would be.

Chapter Twenty-One

Deborah was on her way to Paris when the doctor told Lucy she could go home. One of her arms had not been healing and they had done a skin graft. The rest of her had healed very well but the scars looked ugly and she was full of despair that her face, her arms and her hands would never look normal again.

"Just be patient," said the doctor, "and keep on telling yourself daily that you are improving every day." She went to the Draycotts with a lighter heart.

Grace and Ernie could not have been kinder. There was a pile of letters awaiting her, from her mother, her brothers, from Mrs Trippet and a great many customers, all wishing her well. There was nothing from James although Grace said he rang every day to enquire how she was.

"I don't want to see him," she said, and Grace made no reply.

The following day Lucy was restless, waiting to hear from Deborah who had said she would ring early evening. She rang after six o'clock, saying she had been to some bona fide estate agents and seen several apartments she thought were possibilities. She was not bothering with a shop. One flat she liked particularly was in a house close to a busy shopping centre. There were three rooms, all large, one she could turn into a fitting room, and as the apartment was on the ground floor she could put a notice in the window, saying she wanted customers who were looking for designer clothes, all handmade, at realistic prices. There were curtains at the windows and carpets on the floor, which belonged to the owner of the house. Deborah could rent the rooms for a modest sum a week.

"I think I shall settle for it tomorrow. I can't see any snags. I need furniture, but there's an emporium not far away. I'll ring again tomorrow and let you know how I get on."

Deborah had not even asked Lucy how she felt, she was so excited.

The following morning Grace took Lucy for a tour round the local shopping areas and she eventually saw a shop to let that appealed to her. It had double windows and was in a busy street. The people had moved out the day before. The owner of the sweet shop and tobacconists next door told her they had sold large toys, dolls prams, tricycles, big dolls, forts and expensive games.

"They were too expensive for the people in this area," she said. "We sell boxes of chocolates but we also sell chocolate buttons, liquorice allsorts, humbugs and that kind of thing. You have to if you want to make a living. Our main line of trade, mind you, is the tobacco trade."

Lucy smiled. "I'll remember that. I may be taking the shop."

"Oh, how nice, what would you be selling?"

"Drapery, table linen, bedlinen, ladies underwear, threads, elastic, fasteners, jewellery, oh, everything in the drapery line . . . and little extras like cushions and snow scenes in a glass globe."

"How interesting. You should do well on this road.

Try and have some sort of sale bargain every week and you can't go wrong."

"Thanks, I'll remember that too."

The woman had been polite enough not to mention the scars on her face, but would probably wonder if she was going to serve in the shop. Yes, she was, and she hoped it would not put anyone off. By the time everything was sorted out the marks would have healed even further.

Grace had waited outside while Lucy had been talking to the owner of the sweet shop and when Lucy came out and told her what had been said, Grace nodded. "I feel you have a winner here. I've been around to the back of the shop. There seem to be some rooms above the shop and stairs up to it. Let's go and have a word with the agent."

They learned there was a four-roomed flat above and a room behind the shop. Lucy thought the rent satisfactory so they took the keys to inspect the premises.

They were pleased with the shop; there was plenty of shelving and big drawers underneath. The room at the back was large and had a small stove to heat a kettle. From there they went up the stairs that led to the rooms above. Here there was a small kitchen, but the sitting room and two bedrooms were large. They had all been recently papered and the paintwork was white. Lucy was in raptures over the flat.

"Oh, I can make a nice home here. I shall take my time buying the furniture. We must let the agent know that I want it."

When they went round to see him, he thought she was in the right line. The only other drapery department was part of a larger store. Competition was a good thing. Lucy paid a month's rent.

She came out jubilant. "It'll be splendid to be working again." She had paid Grace back the money she had lent her and was anxious to start stocking up. By the evening, however, she was drained, and was in bed early.

The next day they spent part of the morning at the wholesalers and rested during the afternoon. In the evening she made scarfs and cushions, with Grace helping her. She had left her goods at the wholesalers and that weekend, at Grace's suggestion, decided to go and see Mrs Trippet.

"You need a break, Lucy, before you start a full-time job. I shall help you, but the doctor did tell you to take it easy."

She phoned Mrs Trippet, who said she would be overjoyed to have her. She would be at Whitby station to meet her.

The journey tired her but as she neared the Dales and opened the window and smelled the sweet, cool evening air she felt she was half way to being strong again.

Mrs Trippet was there with a taxi, explaining that Joel was on his course and would probably not see her on that visit.

When they were home she said, "There you are now, sit in the armchair." She plumped up a cushion. "I put a bit of fire on, it's a little cooler this evening. I must say you're looking a lot better than when I saw you last. Your skin is healing beautifully."

"My hair looked terrible at first, all frizzy on the ends but the hairdresser trimmed it yesterday and it's made all the difference."

It was like old times and Lucy wished, in a way, that she was back to the days of the family sitting around the fire; how close they had all been then and

302

how distant they seemed now. She felt, however, that Mrs Trippet would always be close.

She asked about Deborah and Lucy told her what had happened and said she thought the setting was right. Already she had had visits from prospective customers.

"She'll get to the top, that girl," declared Mrs Trippet. "She's made for bigger things. A career. I know she said ages ago she would put on a fashion show one day and I bet she will. How about her young man? Does she still keep in touch with him?"

"Yes, Adin went to Paris to see her last weekend. He said she looked great. But his aim is marriage. And Deborah won't marry him until she's achieved her object."

"And how is James?"

"Grace says he asks after me but I haven't seen him."

"A piece of cake, Lucy?" Mrs Trippet spoke gently, seeing Lucy was near to tears and trying to take her mind off James.

"No, thanks, Grace packed me a huge lunch and I'm not really hungry yet."

"You will be by supper time. I have a nice piece of cooked ham."

It was amazing the things they found to talk about and how, whenever the talk got close to family, Mrs Trippet would find another subject to talk about.

At nine o'clock Lucy knew she was ready for bed and had to excuse herself.

The next morning she fed the chickens and the pigs then went for a walk on the moors and found herself stepping out quite joyously. After a while she sat on the stump of a tree and looked around her.

The stark outlines of the mountains were softened by the sun and there was a lovely feeling of peace in the stillness.

Suddenly there came the song of a blackbird followed by a thrush competing for supremacy and above them a cawing of rooks started as though determined to spoil the sweetness. It was like life, she thought smiling, one person wanting to get the better of someone else. Suddenly she sobered. Like Imogen? Lucy got up and walked on. She must forget her.

Ahead she came to the shallow river and saw two colts playing in the water. One went up to the other and nudged the head of its companion. The other splashed about then nudged its head against the other's, and they neighed with high spirits. Lucy's humour returned.

She had several changes of mood that morning. She came to a mountain of boulders. The sun had gone in momentarily making it look gloomy and Lucy remembered the terrible evening when they had reached this place during the snow storm. Her face had been numb against the driving icy particles in the snow. David had found the shed and then Mrs Trippet had come.

The sun was out again and chasing across the boulders. The storm was forgotten.

During Lucy's four day visit she must have met everyone in the valley. They tramped the moors during the day and spent each evening talking. Lucy thoroughly enjoyed herself. On the fourth evening she said, "I'm ready to go back now and do some work. I hope you understand, Mrs Trippet."

"Of course I do, my love. I shall miss you terribly, but I do think you look a great deal better. Your skin is healing wonderfully. It's this air."

304

"I know," Lucy said softly. "I shall miss you, but work is as necessary to me as it is to you."

"That's because we're two loners, Lucy. Both lost our men. How do you feel about Joel?"

"I like him very much, but I can't go further than that."

"And James? Where does he fit in?"

"Nowhere at the moment. All I can think of is the shop. By the time I get it stocked up and opened I think I won't be so conscious of my burns."

"You needn't be now. And I mean it."

Joel phoned while she was there and asked if he might come to London to see her when she had a break and she said, "Yes, of course, it will be lovely to see you." What else could she say? It was an emotional farewell the next morning and Mrs Trippet said if she needed help in the shop she had only to phone.

When the Draycotts met Lucy at the station they both marvelled at the change in her. "You look splendid, Lucy," Ernie said and Grace echoed this. "I just can't believe there could be such a change in such a short time."

"It was the bracing weather," Lucy said smiling.

When they arrived at the shop the next morning Grace confessed to Lucy to moving in some pieces of furniture. "You can clear them out when you buy your own, we just thought it would be nice for it to look liveable-in if you wanted it."

Lucy was overwhelmed at their kindness. Grace said quickly, "The furniture was given to us by friends. They wanted to be rid of it and I thought it would give you a chance of having all you need and therefore give you time to look round for what

305

you really want and fixing up the shop in your own time."

"I just can't thank you both enough. I'm lucky to have such good friends." Lucy had a job to get rid of the lump in her throat.

The rooms were carpeted and none of the carpeting was shabby. Some pieces of furniture she would have chosen herself. Everything went swimmingly. In the shop boxes fitted into the shelves perfectly and bedding lay snugly in the drawers. Lucy had Ada and her sisters making cushions and two weeks later she was ready to open the shop. The windows were tastefully done but Lucy had had a poster made to go on the window saying:

THREEPENCE IN THE SHILLING OFF ALL GOODS ON OPENING DAY.

"Aren't you being a little generous?" Grace asked.

"No, I want to capture customers. Mrs Smith at the sweet shop said I should have a special bargain every week."

"It cheapens the shop."

"No, I want to capture customers. And, to quote Mrs Smith again, 'Women in fur coats love bargains.'"

Grace grinned. "I do too."

They opened on the Saturday and half an hour before opening time six women were queuing outside; two wore cotton dresses and a cardigan each, two were well dressed, and the other two were elderly women dressed in black. All the women were talking to one another.

"Well," Grace declared. "You might have something. But I still think you'll be losing money."

"I couldn't possibly. I shall make something and if it brings customers in that's all I'm interested in."

In another ten minutes more people had arrived, some with children.

Grace took off her apron. "I'm going to see if Ada and her sisters are available to help. What we have to be careful of here are shoplifters."

"That is already arranged. They'll be here in a few minutes." Lucy smiled. "That women next door is a mine of information."

"I'll say she is."

As Grace spoke there was the sound of clattering footsteps coming into the shop from the back and there were Ada and sisters, all wearing navy dresses with white lace collars and their hair tied back and showing wide navy ribbon bows.

Ada grinned. "Ma's suggestion. She said if we were going to be shop assistants then we had to look like them."

Lucy laughed. "How sensible. I think now we'll be able to cope. Keep your eyes open all the time and if you bring any boxes down make sure each one is put back before getting another one down."

When at nine o'clock Lucy opened the door there was quite a crowd outside. They all came rushing in and most of them wanted something out of the windows. They were mostly items of jewellery and Grace and Ada handled the people there while Lucy coped, with the other two girls, in the shop.

Although the majority of items that were being bought were small, they also sold sheets, tablecloths, camiknicks and a woman who looked as if she would only have coppers in her purse bought two cushions.

Other customers were coming in all the time and it was not until after eleven that trade slackened off a little.

They were all hot and a little breathless and Grace went into the kitchen to make a pot of tea.

The three girls were excited. Ada said, "It was good, Mrs Dexter, wasn't it?"

"It was and I think you all did splendidly, just as if you had been serving in shops for years."

They were steadily busy all day and at eight o'clock when trade had really slackened Lucy said, "We're closing. I think we've all had enough."

The girls said they were not a bit tired, they had thoroughly enjoyed it and Lucy paid them and told them she would probably have them again the following Saturday, that is, if they were free.

Ernie had come at lunchtime and brought fish and chips for them all and they had eaten them from the paper with vinegar and salt.

Grace said laughing, "It reminded me of our younger days when we would have a penny haddock and a pennyworth of chips at dinnertime on a Saturday. I enjoyed them today as much as I did then. Did you hear the girls say that it was a special treat, they usually just have chips on their own?"

"I know, but they are beginning to fill out," Lucy said, "they were so skinny when we first employed them."

"So, was it worth all the rush and hassle?" Ernie asked.

Both Lucy and Grace declared it was. Lucy held up a bundle of notes and she pushed a big basinful of small change towards him.

"How about that, then?"

"My goodness, you have done well. Much better than I thought. That's the kind of money worth working for. Come along, I'm going to take you both for a meal." They said they didn't think they had the strength to go so he said, "Right, I'll get us each a meal from the restaurant along the road. What would you like?"

They both said anything would do and Ernie returned with a plate of lamb chops and vegetables for all of them, which had them exclaiming, "Excellent."

Monday was a much quieter day but a lot of people stopped and looked in the window and Lucy was satisfied with the number of people who bought. She tidied the shop after the Saturday rush and Mrs Smith looked in for a natter.

"Everyone was talking about you on Saturday and saying what a happy and friendly staff you had. Nothing was any trouble. They especially liked you, said you were a lady and all of them wanted to know if you were the one who was burnt in your other shop. They saw it in the papers."

"Yes, I am the one."

She made tea and the two of them sat in the shop drinking the tea and talking.

Mrs Smith said, "Well, I certainly take my hat off to you. A lot of women would have hidden themselves away. I consider myself tough but I might have been tempted to hide away too."

"You wouldn't, Mrs Smith. You are a business-woman too. You've already taught me a lot."

"I'm glad of that little compliment. When you have seven kids and a fussy husband there's not much room for that sort of thing."

"Seven children?" Lucy stared at her. "Where are they all?"

"Only one is allowed into the shop when it's open. That's the eldest lad. He's left school. The others help when the shop's closed, filling up and that sort of thing. Their Dad is strict with them, but they all love him. He's a good man."

Lucy thought about this a number of times during the day. Seven children, and Mrs Smith managed to cope with the shop and her family. And she had thought it would be impossible to run a business and have just one child.

Grace came over in the afternoon and when Lucy told her about Mrs Smith's children she said, "When we were young, there were folks with ten and more children who ran businesses. Yes, it can be done. Ernie and I brought up our boys under those conditions. It's just a question of discipline. Without it a business would fail. Were you thinking of James?"

"No, not at all. He doesn't come into this."

But even as Lucy said it she knew he did. He wanted children. And she was denying him his right. Over the day she kept thinking about it and eventually came to a point where she decided it was his own fault and dismissed him.

That night, however, she had a dream that brought back all the horror of the fire and eventually she got up and made a hot drink. This had to stop. She must keep James right out of her mind, otherwise she would make herself ill and she would not be able to run the business.

Things went well in the shop. She employed the three girls in the shop each Saturday and they loved it. She had a regular Saturday sale bargain which really drew the people in. What did surprise Lucy was the number of cushions she sold. She charged ninety-five pence each normally and on the Saturday she reduced them as a special bargain she sold them for seventy-five pence each and sold twelve. And it was not all the higher class people who bought them.

Some were buying them for wedding presents, one for a birthday.

It kept Ada's family employed making them.

Lucy had kept dolls from her stock, seeing that there was a toy shop a little further up the road, but one day she felt she wanted to dress a doll with handmade clothes. She made three and sold them in two days.

She spoke to the owner of a small toy shop further up the road and he said, "Sell all you can, Miss Dexter. They don't do me any harm. My dolls are of the cheaper variety. And the best of luck to you. You've brought a lot of customers to the area and we are all benefiting from it."

"Well, that's good to know," she said smiling.

"My missus bought one of your cushions last Saturday; she's been harping on about wanting one for ages, but I had to explain I couldn't afford a quid for a cushion. Then they were reduced on Saturday and she said she was having one, even if we had to starve for the rest of the week!" He grinned. "It wasn't as bad as all that, but she got it and now she sits cuddling it every night. It's a bonny thing, I must admit. I only hope she doesn't fancy one of them dolls or we'll be bankrupt."

Lucy laughed. "I tell you what. I'll make her one and you present it to her."

"No, I couldn't. She'd know it's the last thing I'd buy her."

"Then just think of all the love you'll get in return!" Lucy replied and left, chuckling.

"By heck, yes," he called after her.

Lucy took pains with this particular doll. She liked dressing them in old-fashioned clothes and dressed this one wearing a rose pink velvet coat with a cape and a bonnet, which the doll wore over a white muslin dress with long puffed sleeves; under this were two lace-edged petticoats, a flannelette one and a pair of knickers that reached just above the knees.

She had finished it by the Saturday and she wrapped it and sent Ada with it to the toy shop and, in case the wife was in the shop, to say it was the item Mr Henley had ordered for her.

Half an hour later a tubby little woman came into the shop, her face radiant. "Oh, Miss Dexter, my husband said he had ordered this doll from you. Must have cost the earth. First thing he's bought for me without me telling him what I wanted. It's just so beautiful, I'll treasure it. You don't know what this means to me." Her eyes were moist. She gave a sniff and drew a hand under her nose. "Thank you. I think I'll call her Rose."

And away she went.

Lucy found herself thinking how much pleasure it had given a person and for what, for dressing a doll.

Just before they were closing Mr Henley popped in to thank her. "It's given Milly so much pleasure, how much is it and I'll settle up for it?"

"It's a gift, Mr Henley. It's given me pleasure."

His eyes opened wide, then he smiled broadly.

"If there's anything I can do for you, just let me know."

"I will, I promise."

"Men don't think, I know I didn't. I'm very grateful to you."

A deeply moved man left her and Lucy found herself thinking about James again. Men don't think, Mr Henley had said. Had James not been thinking when he went back to Imogen? If he came again . . .

But James did not come again.

Joel did, however. He stayed for a long weekend and with Grace looking after the shop he and Lucy toured London, seeing the sights. Joel did not mention James or wanting her to be with him, and she was not sure how she felt about him.

The following week there was a long letter from Deborah. She had some wealthy clients and now employed three seamstresses. Soon she would have to be looking for larger premises. She was going to the top, she knew it. She had three men friends, but she still preferred Adin. He was jealous of her other boyfriends and wanted her to give them up. What he would not accept was a marriage with Deborah continuing to work. And she would not give up her work, not now that she was a success. She had worked hard for what she had. Lucy agreed.

The summer was over and the days grew colder. Every morning when Lucy opened the shop, dead leaves from some trees at the end of the road lay piled in a corner of the doorway. Lucy swept them up but before long there would be another pile. She was not as busy in the shop as she had been in the summer but she was satisfied with her takings.

One afternoon she was sorting out the deep drawers and when the bell above the door tinkled she closed the drawer and turned to the counter with a smile.

The next moment her heart was beating madly.

James was standing there, looking serious.

"Hello, Lucy, I was wondering if you could find time for us to have a talk? I feel it's necessary."

She hesitated a moment then said, "I close at four o'clock on a Wednesday. It's nearly that now. If you could . . . well, have a little walk around and come back, just after four, we could go upstairs."

"I'll do that."

She was trembling when he left. Did he want a divorce? Or did he want them to get together again? And did she want to go back with him? How could she ever trust him again?

After clearing the things away she stood a moment, trying to pull herself together. Then she went upstairs, put the kettle on, and after tidying her hair ran downstairs again.

James was there right after four when she was about to close the door. She took him upstairs and by then the kettle was boiling.

"Sit down," she said, "and I'll make some tea."

She wished she knew what he wanted to talk about then she might stop trembling. She brought out some cake and poured the tea.

Then she said, "So, what is it you wanted to talk about, James?"

Chapter Twenty-Two

James took a drink of his tea then set the cup down.

"We are man and wife and living apart. It seems rather foolish, don't you think?"

"No, I don't. You left me because you thought I had maligned Imogen. She came to the house to set it alight knowing that Deborah or I would be in it and could be burned to death."

"You can't blame a sick woman for her actions, Lucy." He spoke quietly.

Anger rose in her. "She had done it before and why? Because she was jealous that I was in your life."

"It wasn't jealousy," he persisted. "If you had known her when we were first married. She was a sweet person, so quiet, so shy."

"Sweet? She was all acid, playing on your feelings. She didn't want you to make love to her. She kept you hanging on for two years. And you kept going back, wanting to explain how much you loved her and were willing to wait until she changed her mind."

"I didn't. It wasn't until I told her I wanted the marriage to be annulled and marry you that she changed. She was sick then, but I had not realised it."

"But you did leave her and you married me. Then when she set the shop alight and I was unsympathetic towards her you walked out."

He became angry then. "You are so hard-hearted. Have you no pity at all for a sick woman?"

"I don't think so. We had a hard life. But we all loved one another as a family, and did our best for each other."

"I never had that privilege."

There was a stir of emotion in her and she softened a little towards him. "I know that her fault was jealousy."

James got up. "Isn't that your fault, Lucy?" He spoke quietly.

"No, it isn't." She felt mad again but tried to calm down. "I feel I'm a reasonable person, but there have to be limits. Why should I take the blame for Imogen's madness? She should have been having treatment, not allowed to be out and trying to burn a shop down! If Deborah and I had been killed, would you still be feeling kindly towards Imogen?"

"I would have felt more responsible than ever." He picked up his hat. "I'm sorry you can't see my side of it and I don't think there's any more to be said. Excuse me."

At the door he turned and she thought he was going to say something but after giving her a sad look he left.

Lucy stood, thinking how utterly arrogant he had been. He had not come to ask her to forgive him for the way he had behaved, or to plead with her to come back to him, but to make out that she was the one to blame. What a nerve!

She was too angry for tears but by the time Grace came they were on her lashes.

Grace, concerned, asked what was wrong.

"It's that Imogen. I'm never going to be rid of her."

"I think this will have to be talked over later. Dry your eyes. I'm taking you home for dinner."

Lucy was unwilling to go. She did not want things talked over. She knew what James had said and she would certainly not change her mind. But Grace said she was not going to leave her in this state and Ernie would wait for his dinner until they got to the house.

It was not until after dinner that the three of them got down to their talk and Lucy was shown there were faults on both sides.

Ernie looked at it from the man's point of view. He had come from a poor but loving family. This was something that James had never known. He had met many women in his own circle, most of them looking for a wealthy husband. Then he had met Imogen and she was, to him, a delightful creature. He wanted a family and was shocked when Imogen did not want to consummate the marriage. He persisted, feeling sure if he could overcome her fear that he would have the perfect mother for his children.

Grace said many of the things she had said to Lucy before. "He met you, Lucy, and saw a different kind of woman. He persuaded Imogen to agree to an annulment and married you. But don't forget, Imogen was bound to be in his mind and he would have been reminded of her when she told him she had cut her wrists – "

"On our honeymoon, don't forget," Lucy said bitterly.

"Yes, and he found out she was a liar, but needing his love. That would have quite a devastating effect on him."

Ernie took over the story again. "After this was

317

over, James did suggest taking you back to complete your honeymoon. A nice gesture."

Lucy had to admit it was, but then pointed out the result of the burning of the house.

"And a sick, desperate woman, was responsible. The awful thing was that James would have felt responsible," Ernie went on.

"The awful thing in my opinion was that James laid the blame at my door," Lucy insisted.

They talked until quite late, but although Lucy had a more reasonable outlook on the situation she was not yet reconciled that she should go back to James.

In bed that evening there were all sorts of fors and againsts, and the following morning she was really no further forward than she had been the night before. She did decide, however, that she would have to put James out of her mind if she was going to keep the shop.

It was not easy. At odd times during the day she would see him in her mind in Paris, smiling at her, teasing her; she was always relieved if a customer came in to distract her from her thoughts.

As the weeks went by and the weather became colder Grace began to talk about the Christmas trade and suggested looking in the warehouse for items that would make reasonable gifts.

Lucy said, "I was thinking about that this morning, thinking that some of the poorer children won't get gifts at all, and wondered if we could arrange a party. Get one of the men to be Santa Claus. I think that Mr Wainwright might be coaxed into playing the role."

"It's a nice idea, Lucy, but we are going away as

you know. I was hoping to persuade you to come with us."

"My mother wanted me to go to them and Mrs Trippet has asked me to go north. Actually, I don't feel I want to go away. It's not that I'm being a wet blanket, it's just this urge to do something for the children here. We had some awful Christmases when we were young and all my mother could manage was to give us an orange and an apple in our stockings, plus a shiny new penny. Lord knows how she managed to do that."

Grace grinned. "Now you're getting me interested. Ernie doesn't want to go away. What he wanted was to have all the family here."

"You musn't change your plans for my sake."

"It's for our sakes too. Leave it with me."

Two days later Grace arrived looking triumphant. "It's all arranged. The boys, their wives and children are spending Christmas Day with their wives' families and will come here on Boxing day. So where do we hold our lovely big party?"

"Oh, Grace, that's wonderful!" They laughed and hugged one another. And later began to plan.

Lucy was in her element. They needed a big hall. First she would ask Mr Wainwright if he would be Santa Claus.

At first he laughed at the idea but with some prompting from his wife he said, "Yeah, I'll do it. It'll get me out of going to me in-laws. Can only stand them for a couple of hours. The wife feels the same about my family. A good idea, eh?"

The trouble was in finding a church hall. They were all booked for Christmas Day, mostly to give the old folk meals.

Then Mr Wainwright had a suggestion. There was a

big hall at the end of the road. His uncle owned it. "He intended to do it up and rent it out, but he lost interest. I have some pals who'd put tiles on the roof. The hall would need a good scrub out too, but my missus has customers who would be willing to do that. Also she knows all the poverty-stricken families."

"It sounds great," Lucy said, "just the job."

And so this was the start of the arrangements for the Christmas party. Mr Wainwright got things under way, his wife started organising and before long the whole thing snowballed so that they had promises from people to contribute food, trestle tables and tablecloths, china and cutlery and one couple said they had a spare cooker to go in the kitchen. Children made paper decorations and Lucy and Grace were overwhelmed with gifts when they went to different people in their spare time asking for a contribution of toys. Shops and stores contributed and boxes of used toys and money came from wealthy families.

They had first seen the hall in a dilapidated state and wondered how it would all turn out. Later, they saw it with tiles on, floors scrubbed, walls distempered in a pale blue and later still, with the decorations up and with a huge Christmas tree.

Rules were laid down by Mrs Wainwright that those helping could not bring their own children. Hers were going to relatives for their tea. This at first caused a flurry of objections but she called a meeting at the hall and she explained that helpers, like herself, had several children, and as they had over twenty helpers they could be dishing out a free tea for an extra mass of people.

Laughter broke out and they all agreed she was right. No helper dropped out.

Mrs Wainwright also said she would be on the

door so that only children of poverty-stricken parents would be allowed in. She would see that everyone would have a ticket and that there could be no fraud. Every ticket would be stamped with a certain stamp.

Her husband said laughing, "Trust my wife to see that justice is done. But she's right, of course. We could have a lot of vagabonds, and much as we'd like to help, we can't give everyone a free meal."

When a woman asked how many children were expected and Mrs Wainwright said close to a hundred, there was a gasp and murmurs that they would not have enough food. She said, "There will be." Lucy was busy in the shop, but no matter how busy she had been she would go along to the hall after she had closed.

Deborah was staying in Paris for Christmas. Adin was going over to be with her. In her last letter she had said, *I love him. Always will. My three men friends have gone. I found out that all they wanted was my designs. But I still won't marry Adin until he agrees to my keeping on with my work. I'm hoping to persuade him to agree to this over Christmas. Will let you know what happens. Have a wonderful time at your children's party . . .*

A letter had come from Mrs Trippet to say that Joel's mother had died over a week ago. He had not wanted her to write and tell Lucy, not wishing to spoil her Christmas. She had also said that it really was a release for the poor woman, she was always so unhappy. Joel had been intending to stay with his aunt over the holidays but Mrs Trippet had suggested that they come and stay with her.

She concluded, *Hope to see you in the New Year . . .*

Dear Mrs Trippet, always wanting to help someone. And poor Joel who was now without his mother. She must write to him.

On Christmas Day over a hundred children arrived at the hall, with Mrs Wainwright confirming they were all from hard-up families. Where she had gone wrong, she said, was in not allowing for the fact that some families would send six and seven out of twelve and thirteen children. Then she added cheerfully, "We'll cope. We have enough food."

What astonished Lucy was the subdued attitudes of the children. Small children came in looking a little scared and clinging to the hand of an older child, and Grace reminded her that half of them would never have been to a party before.

They were shabbily dressed but all had been scrubbed clean. Some of the girls were in thin cotton dresses and a shawl wrapped round them. On every child attempts had been made to send the children as decent as they could. Mothers brought them and warned them in no uncertain terms what would happen if they misbehaved themselves. One young mother, who brought two little girls, confided to Lucy that the youngest might wet her knickers. She pushed a parcel in Lucy's hands. "I brought her a spare pair."

The party started at three o'clock and the helpers had been there since one. They needed to be. Some of the men went seeking some extra trestle tables and forms for the children to sit on.

Scarves had to have names pinned on to them and so did woollen hats and the boys' caps. But at last that was done and the children were all seated at the tables.

It had been arranged that a young church organist

would give a short talk to introduce the proceedings and he had been told to be firm about behaviour.

He was lovely. They all listened in silence and that was saying something from over a hundred children. He talked about the party, saying it had been arranged especially for them and they wanted all the children to enjoy it. They would have their tea then afterwards Father Christmas would come in and every child would receive a present. After that they would play games. The organist laughed; there were so many of them but he was sure they could manage something. The important thing was to make the party a success and this meant that everyone would have to behave nicely. If they didn't well . . . He chuckled. They would have to leave.

He paused. "And now, I shall let you all enjoy your tea."

There was a continuous service of helpers carrying in the plates of food and other people bringing round teapots, lemonade and milk.

The children began to talk to one another, mostly boys, and after a little while paper pellets started to be thrown.

The organist banged a gavel for silence then said in a firm voice, "Some boys are making a nuisance of themselves, throwing paper pellets. If this does not stop these boys will be removed without having anything to eat or getting a present. Now, do these boys want to leave now?"

There was silence. Not even a whisper or a nudge.

"Good, now you can all proceed with your tea."

"A good man for discipline," was the verdict.

Some of the smaller children needed help with their food, needing to have it cut up into smaller portions and other children watched their neighbour's plate to see if they had as much as the others, but all in all everything went well.

After the tables were cleared and moved into the back and the children were seated on forms around the hall, it was announced that Father Christmas would be coming in with the toys. There was the sound off stage of sleigh bells tinkling, a "Whoa!" and the next minute Mr Wainwright came in, looking perfect in his red costume and his beard and a bulging sack on his back.

There was a stirring among the children.

He was a big jolly man, who greeted them with, "Well, hello me hearties, and a merry Christmas to you all. I hope you'll allow my helpers to hand out your presents too."

Other sacks were brought in, each marked with "GIRLS" and "BOYS".

In the sacks for girls were dolls, teddy bears, books, games, ludo and snakes and ladders. In the boys' sacks were Meccano sets, books, paints, railway engines, cars and wagons and games.

Lucy was fascinated to see the children unwrap their presents and see the looks of joy on their faces. Girls hugged dolls and teddy bears and were watched by other children who had received something else, and as far as she could see the boys seemed satisfied with what they had. Mr Wainwright announced that if any child wanted to do a swop, they could go ahead. One or two children did, but the majority appeared to be satisfied.

There were many things Lucy remembered about that day, but what she thought she would always remember was a little girl about three years old handing back the doll as she was about to leave.

Lucy said, "Don't you like it?"

She looked up at her, her eyes swimming with tears. "Yeth, but me sister said I had to give it back."

Lucy bent down and handed the doll back. "No, my love," she said softly, "it's yours to keep, for ever and ever."

The child took it and hugged it, then a smile broke out and as a tear dropped she dashed it away. "Ta," she said and ran away to find her sister.

That night Lucy found herself longing for a child.

She was invited on Boxing Day to meet the Draycotts' relatives. Ernie came for her and he spoke highly about the party and said what a success it had been.

In the car Lucy said, "Do you know what it did for me, Ernie? It made me want a baby."

He beamed at her. "Oh, Lucy, that's splendid. You and James can get together again."

"It's not as simple as that. We can never be together while his mind is still with Imogen."

"I don't think it will be. I must try and get in touch with him."

"No, not yet, let the holidays end first. This might be just a flash in the pan. It was seeing all the little ones yesterday, seeing their surprise when they received their presents. They were so well behaved."

Ernie grinned. "Threatened with what would happen to them if they misbehaved!"

"But it was a genuine pleasure. Having food, playing games . . ."

"Well you can have more pleasure today playing with our grandchildren."

There was a houseful of people and a number of children. The youngest was a baby of five months and Lucy could not stay away from him. She kept asking to hold him and Grace watched her, a smile on her face.

It was the day after when Lucy became aware of her aloneness.

She had been invited back to Ernie and Grace's but they had to visit relatives, aunts and uncles and she refused, nicely, saying the shop would be open the next day and she had some work to do.

It was a holiday, they both protested, but Lucy was adamant.

Most of the morning was spent writing letters of thanks for presents received and the rest of the time she found herself going over many of the things that had happened in the last year. She relived both visits to Paris and it made Lucy wonder if she really understood James.

On the first visit to Paris he had rushed back home to be with Imogen, who was supposed to have cut her wrists . . . Later he suggested completing the honeymoon. How caring and loving he had been then. Unfortunately, that had been spoilt by coming back to have Imogen try to burn the shop and house down. A dreadful way for her to get revenge. Yet James had left her to be with Imogen.

James had put up a good argument and had been against Imogen's action, yet pleaded she was sick. Grace had told her that James had not responded to Imogen's fussing the day she had gone to watch the house. She might have accepted all this had James not accused her of being jealous of Imogen.

She was not jealous, she was furious that Imogen should merit such attention from her former husband. She should have been put into an institution for the insane, then the burning would not have taken place.

Then a voice inside her head said, Have you no pity for this sick woman?

Lucy got up and walked around the room. No, why should she? She had broken the thread of her marriage. It could have been a happy marriage had it not been for Imogen's mad action.

After a while she began to realise that she had made a mistake in wanting to be alone. There was too much time for thinking. It would be good when the shop opened tomorrow. Mr and Mrs Wainwright had told her to drop in and see them any time, but they had their families calling today.

She would go down to the shop and do some tidying up.

But it was impossible to work. She would not be busy the next day: she would do it then. She would have something to eat then go for a walk.

Lucy walked through the streets to come to a park, but looking in the windows of the front rooms of the houses she passed she saw families together, saw decorations and small Christmas trees in windows, some with tinsel wrapped around them and some with bright baubles and she could hear gramophones being played. One was playing, *If You Knew Susie Like I Knew Susie*, which brought memories of the night at the hall on the moors where she danced in the charleston competition. How exciting it had all been.

Who would have imagined she would have been walking alone in the streets of London on Boxing Day? Lucy straightened her shoulders and stepped out. It was her own fault. She had had plenty of invitations, all of which she had turned down.

The park was closed and she walked along into a more expensive neighbourhood and saw a repetition of families in front rooms, only the Christmas trees were larger and in the corners of the rooms and most were lit up with fairy lights. She felt kindly towards the people. Many had subscribed to the party.

A wind had sprung up and she retraced her steps and went back home; in the warm living room she had tea then settled down to a book. She felt a great deal better.

But after reading several pages and realising she had not taken in the gist of the story she put down the book and stared into the dancing flames of the fire.

She could see children round a Christmas tree . . . see people, dancing, couples . . .

A knock at the door startled her.

The street lamp outside the door showed her it was James.

"May I come in, Lucy?" he asked.

"Yes, of course." Her heart was pounding. Had Ernie or Grace been in touch with him?

He took off his hat and she held out a hand to take his coat.

"Sit down and I'll make a cup of tea, or would you prefer a drink? I have whisky – "

"Tea will be fine, thank you."

She wished she could stop trembling. She made the tea, poured a cup for each of them and sat down, ready for a talk.

James said he had heard about the party for the local children and wished he had known, he would have liked to have offered a subscription. Lucy said boldly, "You can still do it. Mothers would be pleased to have some extra money to feed their families."

"It shall be done." He paused then went on, "I've called full of humility, Lucy. I behaved badly the last

328

time I saw you. I felt so guilty about Imogen. I should have realised she was sick."

Lucy could not be nice to him. "You treated me badly, James. You made me your whipping boy."

"I deserved that." He sounded hurt. "I went to Silver Acres for Christmas and this morning I knew if it was possible, I had to see you."

"And I was sitting here, a lonely wife, just waiting for you? I don't need you, James." She spoke quietly. "I have no doubt that you suffered. But so did I. You simply abandoned me so you could go and suffer over Imogen. I was your wife, for God's sake. If you had stayed with me and asked me to go to Imogen's funeral I think I would have gone with you. It was the soulless way you walked out on me as if I meant nothing in your life."

"But I still loved you, Lucy. I mean it. I couldn't help it. It was the guilt I felt over Imogen. I should have understood her."

"And now that you are aware of how badly you treated me you come back and want me to live with you again."

He shook his head. "No, Lucy. I came to apologise and to ask you to forgive me for the way I behaved to you. I'm travelling to America tomorrow. I was offered a job some time ago and decided to take it."

"Oh, I see." She was taken aback. Here she was, preaching to him when deep down she wanted him back. She knew that now. Now it was too late.

James drained his cup and got up. "I've arranged for your money to be at the bank."

This time she refrained from refusing it.

"If you can bring yourself to write to me sometime and let me know how your business goes I would

329

be very pleased. Or if you need any extra money please let me know." But inside, Lucy felt bereft. How long would it be before she saw him again? But she wouldn't – couldn't – lower her pride to say she loved him.

"I'll drop you a few lines. Thanks, Lucy." He picked up his coat and shrugged himself into it. "I'm sorry that things have turned out this way, Lucy. One is always learning one's faults."

She wanted to say, "Don't go," but said instead, "I hope you do well in America."

"Thanks."

And then he was gone and Lucy sank into a chair and knew she deserved to be rejected.

That evening she was surprised to have a visit from James's Aunt Justine.

"This is a very much delayed visit, Lucy. I wanted to apologise to you for telling you about James's marriage to Imogen."

"It doesn't matter now."

"It does to me. He supports me and I was afraid that if he married you I might lose some of my money. I couldn't do anything about it when he married Imogen. Lucy, I'm so terribly sorry."

"It really doesn't matter now, honestly it doesn't."

"You're very kind, very kind indeed. I don't deserve it. I would have liked to have stayed for a while, but a friend brought me and she's waiting."

"Come again and see me."

"I will." Justine kissed Lucy and they parted.

Lucy sat for a long time, remembering how she had talked to James in a patronising way, treated him like a child. And she had wanted children, wanted James's children.

Chapter Twenty-Three

The next morning Lucy knew she would have to put James from her mind and get on with tidying the shop before they opened. They had been very busy on Christmas Eve and although most things had been put away, she had no idea if they were in the right places. Not that she expected to be busy today but the girls had said they would look in and see if there was any work to be done.

Before Christmas she had a letter from a hotel asking for some silk sheets and matching pillowcases. They could be started on and they could keep on making cushions. There was always someone wanting one.

Lucy had told the girls they need not come until ten o'clock but they were there at nine as usual and by then she had put everything in place.

Yes, they all said, they had enjoyed Christmas. They had gone to their grandparents' house and their Gran had cooked rabbits and made a Christmas pudding. It was delicious.

They all thanked her again, in a shy way, for the lovely velvet dresses she had bought them for Christmas and their parents thanked her for the parcel of groceries and money she had given them. "Ma cried," said Ada. "She said she had never had such a gift before. She'll be calling in to thank you herself sometime this morning." Ada was always the spokeswoman for the three of them, but the other two girls were beaming at the mention of the gifts.

Lucy did not have many customers that morning, but there seemed to be a continuous stream of mothers calling to thank her for arranging the party and to thank her for the food and money spent.

They were a godsend, said the majority, and it had given them their first real Christmas. They all said their children had never stopped talking about the party and were already looking forward to next Christmas.

Lucy smiled. "I'm glad it was enjoyed. So many people helped to make it a success."

When Grace came later she said, "So James has taken a job in America. Any suggestion of the two of you getting together?"

Lucy told her what had happened and added, "I regretted not being more agreeable." She paused. "I want a baby, Grace. Very badly." There was a tremor in her voice. "But I think he's finished with me."

"You've just told me he asked you to write to him."

"Yes, about how I get on with the shop."

"Really, Lucy, I could shake you. It's not too late to tell him you want a baby."

"No, no, I hadn't really thought it all out. There's the shop and I want to keep that on and . . . Oh, I don't know what I want to do. I must forget it for the time being."

Grace sighed. "You know something, Lucy, you are your own worst enemy. Wanting revenge. Yes, you blamed Imogen for that fault but you are just as bad."

"I know," Lucy wailed. "Why did I behave in such

332

a way? It's the things he accused me of earlier, not being understanding of Imogen. I was jealous, but I didn't want to admit it. I've been mean about my family, thinking that when they don't ask about me or ask about James that they're selfish. I forget that they are telling me about *their* lives. I don't deserve to be happy."

Grace took her in her arms. "Come on now, you've done a lot with your life. Think of the way you've worked. From getting all the things from Mrs Trippet. It was you who helped Deborah into getting ready to go to Paris. You organised the party. You're tired; James came at the wrong time."

"I don't know. He'll probably find someone else in America."

"He won't and you know he won't. Write to him, just little things about the shop. He has friends, but it's you he wants to keep in touch with."

"I will."

The weeks went by and Lucy settled down to dealing with the shop. She would wait to write to James after she had had her first letter from him.

Letters came from the family. One from Beth who said she was settling down nicely and was so looking forward to having the baby. Harold was so loving and she was trying hard to be a good wife and hoped to be a good mother. She added that her in-laws were so good to her. They had spent Christmas with them. She concluded that she hoped Lucy might manage a visit.

Lucy thought how good it would be to see them all. She would also like to see Mrs Trippet but she had been in bed for a week with influenza and Mr Davies was looking after the animals. She said how she would love to see Lucy, but not while she was in this state.

There was a lot of influenza about generally and the weather was bad. Lucy was not taking much in the shop, in spite of having sale prices on many of the goods.

She was, however, in a better state of mind. She had convinced herself that if she was to have James it would happen, without her worrying about it.

After hearing from Deborah that she had taken a shop and now employed six excellent seamstresses Lucy felt she was doing very well indeed.

The first letter to Lucy from James arrived a week later.

He said he had been waiting to get the feel of New York and its people. It was a busy place, totally different to London and he had found the people sociable. They had a different outlook on life; he still had not not been able to understood why.

There was terrible poverty, as there was in London. He felt he wanted to help, as Lucy had done with her Christmas party, but had been warned not to give anyone money or he would be hunted.

I feel I've been too blasé, he went on, *taking everything for granted. You told me once, Lucy, that I should start growing up. This I feel is what New York is doing to me. And yet, when I think about it, I have to ask myself if I'm doing anything different. I've been invited out a lot and I go because many of the people are involved in the firm.*

How is the shop doing? Hope business is good. I would be very pleased to have a few lines from you, Lucy. Will look forward to hearing all your news.

It was signed, *Yours sincerely, James.*

That evening she started a reply to him, telling him about all the mothers coming in to thank her for the party and saying how worthwhile it had all been. She

334

told him she could understand how he felt wanting to help the poor and said she also thought it interesting that he found the American people different to the British, but that she too was unable to explain it. Were the people more independent? She had heard that more American women were employed there in offices than in England and that having freedom would make the women less shy in company.

She mentioned how well Deborah was doing and about the family, then thought she had better stop there. It was long enough for her first letter to him. When she had to sign it she was puzzled about what to put. It seemed cold to sign it, "From your wife."

Eventually, it ended, "With good wishes, Lucy."

Lucy thought of keeping the letter for a while then decided to send it.

It was a month before she heard from him and by then she was so annoyed she decided he would have to wait longer for her reply. Then she began to read the letter and she brightened.

My dear Lucy,

How good of you to reply so quickly. I was feeling homesick when your letter came and how good I felt after reading it.

I felt I was there with you. You described everything so well. It lifted off the page. I wanted to reply right away but work kept me very busy. I had to join in some social gatherings and was so tired after getting back that I was in no mood for writing personal letters, especially one to you.

I thought if I could manage to get to England for a break you might even be able to spend a few days together. It won't be for some time, perhaps another few weeks but I would give you notice.

Lucy sat back with the letter pressed against her

chest. Perhaps they would get back together in time and . . . she left it at that.

She read on.

I'm staying with a family at the moment who have eight daughters and all want husbands. The girls are all lovely and full of fun. Their father dotes on them. They are all very sensible girls.

Lucy wondered if the word sensible was a dig at her.

The rest of the letter was about his social life.

It was still signed, *Yours sincerely, James*.

Lucy sat down that evening and penned a reply.

She said that it was nice to hear from him. She told him she had a busy social life too. She invented a very nice man, named John. She said he had taken her out to dinner several times. He was quiet, and an up-and-coming artist . . .

The rest of the letter was just generalities.

When this letter had gone she felt appalled at herself for making up stories. This had to stop. Why should she lie about having invitations to dinner? It was not necessary.

James's next letter was not about a lot of people this time, but about a place he had been to. A director of the firm had flown James in his plane to his country retreat for a long weekend. He was a quiet man, he said, and they spent most of the time fishing and walking, not saying very much to one another. It was heaven, just being oneself. He had told him he could go to his retreat anytime he wanted. James said he would certainly take him up on his offer.

Afterwards Lucy felt she wanted to cry. He was a loner, as she was, and both had talked about being entertained, not wanting the other to know the real situation of their loneliness. From now on she would be able to tell him about her own walks and how she had found pleasure in just feeding birds in the park and ducks. She told him about meeting mothers with children in the park and how she had become friendly with them all.

Their letters after this became totally different. Lucy would write about the weather, about a storm and how it would bring memories of the Yorkshire Dales to her, and remembering the first time that she and James had met. She added that she was a raw young girl then, with a lot to learn.

James spoke of his friend and how they would tramp the woods and study the birds, the plants, the trees. Franklin, he said, was a very knowledgeable man about nature but could be quiet other times.

There are many things I should like to talk to you about, Lucy, he wrote once, *but I shall wait until I come home*.

Lucy wanted this time to come quickly.

When Mrs Trippet asked Lucy when she was coming to see her again, she decided to have a long weekend up North at Easter time.

But before Easter came, James was swept into the shop on a stormy morning at the beginning of March. Lucy stood and stared at him. He took off his hat and grinned.

"Good morning, Mrs Dexter."

Had it been anyone else she had been so desperately waiting to see, Lucy would have run around the counter and hugged him.

Instead she said, "When did you arrive?"

"This morning, early."

When she had made coffee and sat down to it, Lucy wondered why she should feel so flat. She said, "I'm

337

sorry, James, you must be wondering what is wrong with me; I think it must be shock."

"Of course, I was just so impatient to see you. It's good to be back in England. I wish I was working here."

"Any chance that you might be?" she asked in a voice as though saying what a cold day it was.

At this point someone could be heard coming up the stairs. "It will probably be Grace," Lucy said. "She has a key."

When Grace saw James her smile was a mile wide. "James!" She flung her arms around her. "What a wonderful surprise, wait until Ernie knows you are here. How long are you here for?"

"Five days."

"Five? That's ridiculous. You must stay longer."

"I can't, but I shall be here again, soon."

"I must go. I just popped in to ask Lucy to dinner tonight. You will come too, of course."

"I'll be delighted to."

As hard as Lucy tried she was unable to make a real, emotional contact with James. Yet he talked easily about America and what a wonderful country it was. Then he got up abruptly. He must go home and get changed. He would be back at seven o'clock. Would that be all right?

Lucy told him yes, and wondered why she did not sound pleased. Perhaps things would be easier at the Draycotts.

She wore a dress that night that James had bought her in Paris.

"You look lovely, Lucy," he said, "that colour suits you."

It was a delicate blue with a lilac shading. It was long waisted, had two pockets under the yoke and down the front, and on the belt and around the narrow cuffs of the sleeves was a raised pattern, hand-stitched.

"It's a favourite with me," she said. "It's given me a lot of pleasure." But even after this, she still felt awkward.

She felt easier once they were with Ernie and Grace. James, at Ernie's prompting, talked about America, saying it was mercurial. Its air was electric, its pace of life fast. Yet there was a tranquillity about its tiny parks and squares of green, and there was also a culture in its magnificent museums and art galleries.

He spoke about the lovely brownstone houses which were three or four storeyed, scattered about the city and sought after by people with money.

Then in contrast he talked about the poor areas; and of the tenement buildings in areas like Harlem and Spanish Harlem, most of them the homes of countless Cubans and Puerto Ricans, which had had fire-escapes down the fronts of the buildings. An ugly sight, he thought.

Ernie and James talked about the people who had emigrated to America from all over the world and how many of them had come to find work and how many had died on the way.

The evening flew by and when Ernie said it had been a rewarding evening, Lucy and Grace agreed. But when Lucy and James were back again in the flat above the shop she had that awful flat feeling again.

James said gently, "What's wrong, Lucy?"

"I don't know, I really don't. I keep asking myself why? I wanted you to come home; I've been longing for you to be back."

"The important thing is, do you love me?"

"Y – yes."

"You're uncertain."

"No, I'm not. I do love you."

"Then can we start again, put all that unpleasantness behind us."

"Just tell me one thing, James, were you interested and I really mean interested in any of the women you met in America?"

"Of course," he teased. "Every one of them." Then he added soberly, "I swear that you are the only woman I have really and truly loved."

He put his arms around her. "I want you, Lucy, need you." She responded to the sensuality of his lips on hers and when he started to undress her Lucy began to undress him too, with frantic gestures. James drew a deep breath.

Lucy gave a little giggle as he locked the door then, taking him by the hand, she took him into the bedroom.

Once they were under the bedcovers the love-play began. Their passions rose to a quivering height but just when Lucy thought they would climax together all passions left her and it was James who enjoyed the fulfilment.

He rolled away from her and made no move to put an arm around her.

Lucy's heart began to pound. After a few moments he threw back the bedcovers and getting up began to dress.

"James?"

Without bothering to look at her her said, his voice cold, "Why can't you forget Imogen?"

"I have, I have never even give her a thought."

"It's either that or there's another man in your life. You were strange when I first came home."

"There's no man in my life but you, and that is the

340

truth." She drew herself up in the bed. "I didn't ask you what woman you were thinking about when you made love to me."

"Because all my thoughts were concentrated on you and you know it; but your thoughts were not wholly concentrated on me. Your so-called love session broke off at the wrong time."

"I couldn't help it. I don't know why it happened."

"Then think about it."

He picked up his coat and shrugged himself into it and was gone. She could hear him going down the stairs.

She lay back in the bed. What had happened? She had no idea. It had all happened so quickly.

Suddenly Lucy knew what had happened. James was right. For a split second a vision of Imogen had flashed before her eyes and she had wondered if James had ever made love to her.

Oh, God, it had ruined everything.

She could hear the wind howling and the rubbish being swept along the road with a swishing sound.

She wished she had gone after him but then knew how futile it would have been.

For the whole of the following day she was steeped in misery and when Grace came that evening it was to say that James had phoned them. He was returning to America, and that was it. He had then rung off.

When Lucy told Grace what had happened she said, "It's such a pity you can't put Imogen out of your thoughts."

"But I thought I had! It didn't come to me until afterwards."

Before Grace left she had convinced Lucy that

James would come back. He was upset, naturally, but he would get over it, she was sure he would.

A week later Lucy thought she might be pregnant. Her monthlies had not started. On the other hand there had been times before when she had been late.

Another week and she knew for certain that she was. She felt a difference in her breasts and she had started to be sick in the mornings. She decided she would not tell anyone. Not Grace, Mrs Trippet or any of the family.

Then her attitude changed. To bring up the child alone would be wrong. A baby needed a father and James wanted a child.

But then she thought, he had behaved badly. She would go on alone for the time being.

Lucy began to look into buying a pram. What would she have, a girl or a boy? Who would it take after? She hoped the baby would take after James.

After another four weeks she felt the need to talk about it to someone. But who? Grace, bless her, would tell everyone. She could tell Mrs Trippet, but if she came for a visit she would certainly broadcast it. No, Lucy was determined that she would keep it to herself, at least for the time being.

What a mess she had made of her life.

Chapter Twenty-Four

After a time Lucy's sickness stopped and she felt remarkably well. She hoped it would last.

She wrote regularly to Mrs Trippet and had to force herself not to tell her. It was her secret for the time being and she was rather excited about it.

Then when she had known for three months Mrs Trippet wrote and said, "Why don't you come for a long weekend? I'm dying to see you."

Lucy wrote back to say it would be lovely to come and see her. She had been careful in her letters not to talk about James, to let her think that all was well. No, Lucy was determined it would be her secret as long as possible.

Grace offered to come and look after the shop while Lucy was away and told her to stay as long as she liked. Ernie would be away for a while on business.

The first thing Mrs Trippet said when she met Lucy at the station was, "So, when is the baby due?"

Lucy was so taken aback she made no reply for a moment then she smiled. "I've been trying to keep it a secret."

Mrs Trippet beamed at her. "It's in your eyes, my darling girl. I want the world to know. But where is the baby's father?"

Lucy said she would tell her all about it when they

got home, adding, "Don't say anything if we meet anyone."

No sooner were they home than the story was told.

Mrs Trippet was shocked that James knew nothing about it.

"The baby is his child too. Why should he be denied the pleasure?"

"But he behaved badly."

"So did you. If anything you behaved the worst, holding a grudge against a girl who was dead and could do no harm."

"I admit I was jealous."

"We all have the Devil's touch on us at times and we suffer badly because of it."

Lucy looked up. "I haven't heard that expression before."

"Ah, but, my lovely girl, the Devil's boots don't creak." Then she added, "And now you will get writing to James."

Lucy teased her. "Can I drink my tea first, please, ma'am?"

Mrs Trippet got up and gave her a hug. "You can, but later this evening you will write to James." She held out a plate. "For now have a piece of cake." Mrs Trippet did not, however, forget about the letter.

But when it came to writing it, Lucy knew it would be wrong to write to James. She did not want to write to him unless he wanted to write to her and she begged Mrs Trippet to let her wait a little longer.

It took some persuasion for Mrs Trippet to agree but she gave in, saying, "Mind you, if he hasn't written in another two months then I shall write to him. He does have a right to know that you are carrying his baby."

That night Mrs Trippet told Lucy that Joel was sitting his first lot of exams. She also told her with a smile that he had become engaged.

"Oh, how lovely. I'm so pleased. Who is he engaged to?"

"You'll never guess." She paused a moment then beamed at her. "Polly."

"Polly?"

"Yes, Polly. After you all left she started to help out at the village school, and she progressed so fast she now teaches there. She even lives in the schoolhouse. "You just won't believe the change in her," declared Mrs Trippet. "She's a different person. She's been hearing all about Joel's work and she's so knowledgeable about vets. She speaks so well now, too. Cook is that proud of her. No, Polly hasn't changed in herself. She's still loveable and Joel said that he surprised himself and suddenly fell in love with her."

"I'm so glad," Lucy said softly.

"Now there's another thing," Mrs Trippet said suddenly. "I want to be godmother to your child. Is that possible?"

She looked so worried, Lucy laughed. "Of course you will. The baby will be brought here to be christened. That's a promise."

"But supposing James objects?"

"He loves you too," Lucy said softly. Mrs Trippet clasped Lucy's hands. "Oh, I hope it all goes well."

"I'm sure it will."

The next day when Polly came over Lucy gave her a hug.

"Congratulations. I'm so happy for you."

Polly had definitely changed, she was more sophisticated, but she still had her loveable quality. They chatted about Joel and Polly said earnestly, "I do hope I make a good wife."

"I know you will, Polly. I have proof of that. You are doing all you can to help Joel with his work and that is as it should be."

This had Lucy thinking about a lot of things. Had she been a good wife? There had been so many upsets and she had always been niggling on at James.

Walks on the moors with Mrs Trippet had given her another outlook on life and knew it was common sense that was taking over, common sense that came from Mrs Trippet. They talked a lot and laughed a lot and felt sure that all would be well.

Lucy felt only pity now for Imogen. The poor girl had never known her own mother and had lived with an aunt who had never wanted her. Lucy thought what her own life would have been like if she had never had a loving mother and brothers and sisters.

The morning Lucy was leaving Mrs Trippet said to Lucy, "Now, remember what I told you about James?"

"I will, I promise."

"I shall come for a few days when I'm godmother to the baby."

"You'll come for a few weeks, not a few days!"

When she was home, however, Lucy still waited to hear from James. And it was on the day when her baby quickened that James arrived.

Lucy was so excited at the movements that when he arrived, it was as though he was expected. She forgot he didn't know.

She took his hand and said, "Oh, I'm so glad you came. Feel the baby moving."

346

James, looking a little bewildered said, "Whose baby?"

"Ours of course." She put his hand on her stomach. "Can you feel it moving?"

His eyes widened with delight. "Yes, I can. You mean that this baby is ours?"

"Yes, it is." Her eyes were full of sheer happiness.

"Oh, my darling, I love you, want you; I want you both. Is it a girl or a boy? I . . . don't mind."

"I don't know. I wanted the surprise of knowing when it's born."

"Oh, there he is, kicking again. Isn't it wonderful? Lucy, do please forgive me for the way I've behaved. I behaved so badly towards you.

There followed talk about which one had been the worst and James said, "Does it matter? We are going to be parents. I still just can't believe it. For the past few weeks something was telling me I had to come home. Then five days ago I made up my mind to return. Thank heavens I did!"

He held her close and rocked her gently. "We've wasted so much time. I'll give up the job. There's only weeks to go before I have to give an answer as to whether I want to stay. With a child on the way how could they try and press me to remain in America?"

"I'm sure they'll let you go."

"We'll live at Silver Acres."

"Well, er, I – think I would rather live in London."

"What, when he will have the chance of all that open air!"

Lucy smiled. "Babies do live in London and grow up strong."

"Yes, I know but – "

"Listen, James. I may want to stay at Silver Acres

347

when the baby is born, but on the other hand I might also want to keep an interest in the shop. I'll employ a manageress, but I would like to spend a few hours a week there, keeping my hand in. I would take the baby with me when he's a few months old. Grace would drool over him. He . . ."

Lucy stopped and then she laughed. "We seem to have settled that this child will be a boy."

"I would like a son, but a little girl will be just as welcome.

"Yes, I'll agree to you keeping on the shop. I know that the baby will never suffer because of it."

James took Lucy in his arms and added softly, "What a fool I've been not to have come back to you before now."

"You're here, and there must be no regrets. I've been just as stupid."

She could feel the baby kicking and James said, "My goodness he must be strong."

Lucy smiled to herself, thinking she could have told him that little girls too kick strongly.

Then she thought, it was possible that they might have twins. There were twins in her family.

Now that would be lovely. She went into his arms . . .